W9-AUN-648

A DYING FALL
by Henry Wade

"A very entertaining piece of work."
—*New York Herald Tribune*

"This is one whose skill you can't appreciate fully until the last sentence." —*San Francisco Chronicle*

Also available in Perennial Library
by Henry Wade

THE HANGING CAPTAIN

HENRY WADE

A Dying Fall

"That strain again! It had a dying fall:"
Twelfth Night, Act I, Sc. 1.

PERENNIAL LIBRARY
Harper & Row, Publishers
New York, Cambridge, Philadelphia, San Francisco,
London, Mexico City, São Paulo, Sydney

A hardcover edition of this book was originally published by The Macmillan Company. It is here reprinted by arrangement.

A DYING FALL. Copyright 1955 by Henry Aubrey-Fletcher. All rights reserved. Printed in the United States of America. No part of this book may be used or reproduced in any manner whatsoever without written permission except in the case of brief quotations embodied in critical articles and reviews. For information address Harper & Row, Publishers, Inc., 10 East 53rd Street, New York, N.Y. 10022. Published simultaneously in Canada by Fitzhenry & Whiteside Limited, Toronto.

First PERENNIAL LIBRARY edition published 1981.

ISBN: 0-06-080543-9

83 84 85 10 9 8 7 6 5 4 3 2

CONTENTS

A DYING FALL

CHAPTER I

The Royal Cup

A FINE FEBRUARY drizzle was drifting across the course as the numbers went up for the 1952 Royal Cup. Disappointing, because the day had begun fine and this might spoil visibility, blurring one's race-glasses and even veiling the far side of the course.

Still, the business of the moment was in the paddock, and to this were trooping now the hundreds of members and their friends for whom the Shankesbury ' Royal ' was surpassed in importance and popularity only by the Grand National and the Cheltenham Gold Cup. Soldiers would perhaps have put their Grand Military next to the National, at any rate before the wars, but there were plenty of them here, among members, owners and riders, and even in the humbler enclosures and round the course itself.

Altogether this looked like being the best meeting since the war, and certainly there had been no greater crowd on Royal Cup day. The brightness of the early morning might have helped to this, but there was no doubt that a brighter and more hopeful spirit was in the air now that Winston was back in power again. Many people who had ' given it all up ', or were on the verge of doing so, now felt that life might be worth living, after all; who knew, perhaps ' Rab ' might make a bold plunge and knock a bob off income tax—if not this year, then surely next. Anyhow, there were people here today who had not been racing—not regularly, at any rate—for a long time.

Vouchers for the enclosure had been hard to come by, for those who had drifted out of touch or had left it to a

late decision. The unlucky ones were consoling themselves either in Tattersalls or round the course, not altogether sorry at saving the extra guineas, and sure of a
good view and lots of first-class sport. But in the paddock
now were the regulars, the faithful supporters of racing
under National Hunt rules, bent upon having a look at
the runners before deciding whether to stick to their fancy
or to ' have a little something on something else '—as a
saver.

The owners were beginning to dribble in twos and
threes into the parade ring, men and women, young and
old, rich and . . . not so rich as they hoped they looked—
the men mostly in bowler hats and wide-skirted overcoats
or macintoshes, the women in every variety of turn-out,
from well-worn tweeds to fur coat and high-heeled shoes;
only a handful of them, compared to the men, but numbers seemed to be increasing year by year. Noticeable
among them—in Persian lamb, too smart hat and too
small shoes—was Mrs. Waygold, owner of the favourite,
Ballnaceach; and round her were a little group of men
attracted by the glamour of expected success, by her by
no means negligible charms, or by her reputation for
riches and generosity. Mrs. Waygold's own attention,
however, was on her horse, which had just come into the
ring—a big, upstanding bay with powerful quarters and
flat, sloping shoulders that looked well up to the task of
carrying him and his rider at speed round the stiff three
and a half miles of this great race.

Many eyes were upon Ballnaceach, as he walked
sedately beside his stable-lad round the ring; he would
start at something like three to one—short odds in a
steeplechase with many runners of real quality—and he
was carrying a lot of public money. But there were other
well-backed horses, too, and among these was a beautifully
made grey mare, No. 15, Silver Eagle, owned by Captain

Charles Rathlyn, which was to be ridden today by Dan
Maston, one of the boldest and most successful jockeys
riding under N.H. Rules. This fact alone would have
attracted public money, but Silver Eagle had her own
good merits and had youth in her favour; she had not
yet won a big race, but was generally thought to have
been unlucky at Hurst Park earlier in the season.

Whatever public favour she had earned, however, the
mare was carrying today what to her owner seemed his
whole life. Charles Rathlyn, forty years old now, had
held a regular commission in the 1st/27th Lancers, which
had been 'converted' into armoured cars before 1939.
He was a born horseman, with a passion for race-riding,
and in the thirties had been left a useful little fortune by
an uncle, Pegram Rathlyn, who declared that Charles
was the only young Rathlyn who knew how to use money.
The young soldier had just begun to 'use' it, with good,
or at any rate pleasant, effect, when Hitler's invasion of
Poland put an end to all that.

Although no longer a horse-soldier, Charles had enjoyed
his armoured-car scraps with the Germans in that hectic
May of 1940, but his luck ended on the quay at Dunkirk,
where his leg had been smashed by a bomb. He got back
to England, but spent many months in hospital; the bone
would not set for a long time, and when it did the knee
was nearly stiff. There followed a spell of home service
at a cavalry training depot, but his C.O. did not like him,
and he spent the rest of the war switching from one dull
job to another, finishing up as a temporary major, second-
in-command of a prisoners-of-war camp.

Discharged unfit, with a small disability pension,
Charles found that he could no longer race. He could
ride, but his stiff knee made him clumsy and unbalanced;
he tried hunting, but he could not 'go' as he used to, and
that to a thruster by nature is misery. His income, too,

was greatly reduced by taxation; he had enough for comfort and one modest luxury, so he decided to concentrate on a small string of steeplechasers. He had no luck, however, and for three years had been going steadily downhill, almost to the point of selling his string and buying a farm. Then one lucky, or skilful, buy gave him fresh hope: Silver Eagle, bought as a three-year-old with no public reputation, suddenly developed into a first-rate chaser. Charles and his trainer, Fred Dartle, kept as quiet as possible about her—her failure at Hurst Park had helped them in that—so that she would start today, with a fine chance of winning, at a very fair price, and carrying, besides a good deal of ' cavalry ' money, the whole, or nearly the whole, of Charles Rathlyn's remaining capital. It was almost literally a case of ' victory or Wormwood Scrubs '. Which, as the saying goes, is where we came in.

Dan Maston needed no last-minute instructions. He had ridden Silver Eagle in every race she had run in Charles's colours, and knew exactly what she could do and how to get the best out of her. Charles gave the little man a leg up, patted his knee and said:

" You're carrying my last button, Dan."

Maston nodded, touched his cap, and then joined the string of horses making their way out on to the course— a way quiet or lively, according to their respective temperaments. The roar of the crowd rose to a new pitch as they appeared, but it made no impression on Charles's accustomed ears; he detached himself from Dartle and the other owners and made his way to the furthest, topmost corner of that section of the Members' stand which is reserved for owners. By nature Charles Rathlyn was a gregarious, sociable type, fond of good company and popular with his fellow men—with women too, except those who were disappointed to find that this eligible bachelor took less personal interest in them than in horses. But now he wanted to be alone—as alone as it was possible to be among thirty thousand people. Too much depended on this race; the strain, even for so hard-boiled a fighter as Charles Rathlyn, was terrific.

He was joined almost at once by his old brother officer and life-long friend, Gerald Fanthony, who had been feeling the book and executing one or two last-minute commissions. George had a half-interest in a moderate animal running in the last race, so he qualified for an owner's badge.

" She'll start at about sixes, I think, old man. Dropped a couple of points in the last half-hour; somebody knows something."

Charles nodded. Most of his money had gone on some time ago, and at much longer odds. He knew he would have been wiser to leave it at that, but when an unexpected dividend had been paid he had not been able to resist the temptation to invest that, too, on this desperate gamble.

" I got a couple of hundred on at eights. Best I could do. A bit for myself too. I'm backing her on your judgment, you know, old man. I don't know all that much about the mare myself. I was out of the country when she ran last at Hurst Park; what happened? Did she fall? "

Charles shook his head. " No; she was knocked into coming to the last but one—unbalanced; she couldn't get going again in time."

" Oh, that was it. Well, I hope you're right about her; she's carrying a lot of soldier money."

Again Charles nodded, but did not speak. His glasses were at his eyes now, bearing upon the bright patch of colour at the start. The rain had providentially stopped in the last few minutes, so that individual colours could be clearly distinguished. There was never any difficulty in picking out Mrs. Waygold's dazzling pale blue, white and gold—unless and until they became besmirched by mud. Charles's own sombre green and black—the nearest he could get to his Eton house-colours—were another matter, but Silver Eagle was the only grey in this race, and there should be no difficulty in following her.

The shouting had died down now and all eyes that could see were turned upon the wavering line of horses. The start of a long race under National Hunt rules is a very different thing from that of a six-furlong sprint on the flat, but nevertheless it is the starter's duty to see that each runner has a fair chance. Trained to the last minute for this race, some of the horses were almost literally on their toes—restless, quick-tempered, whisking round just as the line seemed steady, and in one regrettable case even lashing out and narrowly missing a jockey's leg. To Charles Rathlyn and others, owners and backers, for whom the result of the race was a serious matter, the delay seemed endless, but at last the tape flew up, the white flag fell and the twenty horses sprang forward as if released by a catapult.

The first fence at Shankesbury is a particularly awkward one as first fences go, having a marked drop; in the excitement of the start it is not every jockey who can get his horse collected and balanced in time to avoid a peck on landing, so that, with a large field almost in line, there is apt to be 'skittles' grief. Maston knew this well enough, and used his mare's exceptional turn of speed to get a length in front and avoid any chance of being knocked into. The big Ballnaceach—inevitably 'Ballycatch' to crowd and bookmakers—had no such speed, but he was a magnificent fencer, and it took more than a slight bump to upset him. As it happened, all but two got over safely, and before the second fence the field had spread out so that each rider could pick his place and take his own line. On the stand all eyes were now glued to glasses—all that had glasses. All, that is, except Gerald Fanthony. He was only pretending to look through his at the moment; he was watching his friend. The deep lines of anxiety on Charles Rathlyn's face told their story only too clearly; Gerald knew that this was a desperate matter, and he was thoroughly unhappy about it. Silver Eagle was an excellent mare, fast and stout-hearted, but her fencing was not immaculate, and her record of successes did not entitle her to carry a man's whole future. Gerald had heard that story of 'knocked into' before now, and he was never greatly impressed by it. It was the common excuse of the unsuccessful jockey, and though Dan Maston was anything but an excuse-maker, he might have wanted to ease his employer's disappointment. Still, the money was on now, and there was nothing to do but watch and pray—which Gerald was never ashamed of doing, even about a horse-race.

By the time he had reached this conclusion and really started to look through his glasses, the field had reached the far side of the course on the first time round. Three horses were out in front—Larkaway, the second favourite, Hunter's Holler, and a horse he could not identify. Five or six lengths behind came Silver Eagle, just clear of Ballnaceach, followed by a bunch of eight others; three or four were tailed off, and the rest had fallen. Ballnaceach was jumping beautifully, seeming to gain a length over every fence, and then running smoothly on with the long, effortless stride that took so little out of him, heavily weighted though he was. Silver Eagle was doing all right too—definitely 'there', though not in the same class as Ballnaceach as a classic fencer. As the two approached the formidable open ditch Gerald thought that Maston was pushing the mare a bit, perhaps trying to hurry the bay out of his stride.

"Ahh!" There was a gasp all round the course as

the grey brushed through the top of the big fence, sending
a cloud of gorse flying. She did not come down, but the
effort to recover balance took something out of her, and
Ballnaceach, jumping perfectly, was now a clear length
ahead as they approached the stand and beginning to
draw up on the leaders. Larkaway was still running on
strongly, but Hunter's Holler and the other leader—now
identified as Champerton—were beginning to tire; it was
now evident that, barring accidents, there were only three
horses in the race. Ballnaceach's jockey was still pushing
him up to the leaders.

"Too soon! He'll tire him!" Gerald heard his
friend mutter.

He did not speak himself; he thought that the race was
going exactly as Mrs. Waygold would wish it to go. The
Book evidently thought so too. Isolated cries reached the
top of the stand:

"Even money Ballycatch. I'll lay even money Ballycatch. Four to one bar one. Here, five to one bar one."

Charles did not speak again, but his face was flushed,
and behind his glasses his eyes were sparkling with excitement. He *knew* that Leddy was pressing the top-weight
too soon; it was exactly what he had hoped; Leddy was
afraid of Larkaway and had forgotten all about Silver
Eagle. But—barring that blunder at the open ditch—
the race was going exactly as he, Charles, had planned it
with his trainer and Dan Maston; the mare was still
fresh, and her lighter weight and superb turn of speed
would take her to the front after they turned for home
from the far side.

"Ahh!" Another gasp as Champerton toppled over.
Hunter's Holler was dropping back now; Ballnaceach
passed him; after the next fence Silver Eagle passed him
too. The bay was drawing up to Larkaway, and the
grey mare was within three lengths of the bay. Leddy

had not looked behind him; his eyes were concentrated
on Larkaway, when they were not on the fence ahead.

Four fences out Larkaway was beaten; Ballnaceach
passed him on landing and still strode resolutely on, but
he, too, was beginning to flag now and Leddy was riding
him. Suddenly the bookmakers and the crowd realised
what was happening.

" Here, three to one Silver Eagle; two to one Silver
Eagle; even money the field! "

There was hope in the cries; a victory for Ballnaceach
would be a blow for the Book. Silver Eagle, though well
backed, did not carry really big money and would hurt
nobody.

" Even money Silver Eagle! Even money! "

The mare was closing up fast now; between the last
two fences they raced side by side, both jockeys sitting still
and concentrating all their thoughts, their experience,
their skill on that last vital jump. Leddy knew that the
young mare would have the legs of Ballnaceach in the run
in; it was the jump that would give him his last chance.
Three strides out he pushed his horse hard, gaining half a
length as he came to his take-off, playing just the game
that Maston had tried to play at the open ditch. Maston
knew all about it now and did his utmost to steady Silver
Eagle, but the mare was young, inexperienced, her blood
was up; she jumped with Ballnaceach, jumped too big,
pecked on landing and was nearly down. A superb effort
by horse and rider kept them on their feet, but by the
time they were going again Ballnaceach was three lengths
clear.

The crowd was roaring now, roaring with excitement,
the backers of Ballnaceach roaring with joy. The sound
of it reached the ears of the two jockeys, each concentrating
the whole of his conscious being upon the last tremendous
struggle which would carry one or the other to victory.

For the first time in their joint racing careers Dan Maston took the whip to the mare. He was riding her now for all he was worth, and Silver Eagle responded with everything she had. Over that last gruelling uphill furlong she slowly began to overhaul Ballnaceach, crept up to his quarters . . . then, fifty yards from home, she faltered; Maston instantly dropped his hands, leaving Ballnaceach to sail past the post an easy winner by nearly two lengths.

. . . . .

On the top of the stand Charles Rathlyn slowly lowered his race-glasses. His face was deathly white, an expressionless mask. He stared straight in front of him across the course, seeing nothing, deaf to all sound. Only a tiny muscle twitching at the angle of his set jaw showed the intensity of his feelings.

By his side Gerald Fanthony stood, dumb and miserable. He knew that this must be a crushing blow for his friend; he did not quite believe in the exactness of the ' my last button ' statement—that was something commonly said, in one form or another, by men who had put more than they could afford on a horse. Still, he had little doubt that Charles was really hard hit.

Charles himself had no doubt at all. For a year or more he, with the help of his trainer, Fred Dartle, had played for this one stake, building up the mare—and the ' background ' too—for this race, the Shankesbury Royal Cup. Charles did not know whether Dartle had backed the mare himself; it was a question he never asked and one on which the trainer kept his own counsel; but Charles himself, little by little, starting as soon as the book opened and spreading little ' packets ' as widely and quietly as possible, had invested on Silver Eagle every penny that he could lay his hands on. It was only in the last few days that the mare's price had noticeably short-

ened; Charles had got most of his money on at really
generous odds, and he had stood to win a small fortune—
enough to keep him and his modest string going for a comfortable number of years ahead. Now all that was gone.
How, even, he was going to live, on little more than his
tiny disability pension, Charles had not attempted to
consider; all his mind was concentrated on the dreadful
thought that for him racing was over. He had faced the
loss of race-riding bravely enough; it was the price a
fighting soldier must be prepared to pay; but to feel that
he could never again even own a horse—and horses to
him were more precious than pearls or women—was a
deadly, shattering blow.

Gerald touched his friend on the elbow.

" Come and have a drink, old man," he said gruffly.

Charles nodded. Together they walked down to the
bar and had a couple of stiff whiskies. Charles was not a
heavy drinker and the spirit had an instant effect upon
him, restoring some sense of proportion.

" Come and have a look at the mare," he said. " I
ought to have come straight down and had a word with
Dan; he rode a grand race."

They found the mare being rugged up, Dartle watching
and lending an occasional hand, no expression on his
lean, tight-lipped face. Maston had already gone off to
change his jacket for another race.

" No luck, Fred," said Charles, as cheerfully as he could
manage. " No fault of yours; she was trained to the
minute."

" Thank you, sir. It was just a bit of bad luck, I think;
she was too game. I don't blame Maston."

" Oh, no; it was just one of those things."

For a time their attention was given to boxing the mare
—she was travelling by road. Then, when the heavy
ramp was up, Charles Rathlyn turned to his trainer.

" You must look out for a buyer, Fred—for her and the others."

For a moment the trainer's imperturbability was shaken; a look of real consternation appeared on his face.

" You don't mean it, sir? I . . . that's bad news indeed. But if it's necessary, wouldn't it be better to wait till she's won a nice race? She could hardly have run better than she did today, but buyers like a winner."

Charles shook his head.

" Better perhaps, but impossible. I'm clean broke. We'll go into details later, but you must take it as certain."

Dartle said no more, and presently Charles and Gerald strolled back to the paddock, where the horses for the next race were now parading. Suddenly they found themselves face to face with the victorious owner, flushed with success and perhaps just a glass too much champagne.

Kate Waygold gave Charles a brilliant smile, then quickly changed it to a look of sympathy.

" That was real bad luck for you, Captain Rathlyn. I'm sorry; I am indeed. If it hadn't been for that peck she had us beat. You deserved to win."

Charles had only met Mrs. Waygold on casual occasions. He appreciated her friendliness and told her so. She was passing on, when suddenly she stopped and looked at him shrewdly.

" Forgive me if I'm talking out of turn," she said. " Little birds tell me this may have hit you hard. If you want to sell Silver Eagle I'll pay your price for her. Think it over."

Charles gasped.

" I . . . I hardly . . ."

" No need to answer now," she broke in. " Anyway, come down to Tandrings for the week-end and we'll try to cheer you up. Bring Major Fanthony, if he'd like to come."

CHAPTER II

Tandrings

KATE WAYGOLD was the daughter of a turf accountant, Joseph Hillburn, now defunct. It is the common idea among the public, and particularly among those who back horses, that bookmakers are all very rich men. It is, of course, the fact that some of the bigger men do amass considerable wealth, but Jo Hillburn was not one of these; he had done well, had made his pile—but it had been a modest pile, and not enough to account for his handsome daughter's present affluence. It had been enough to enable him to send her to a good and even fairly fashionable school, where she had been taught to speak French with a Brighton accent, to mime and dance in the classic manner, and to ride—as well as some of the minor subjects of English, History, and Mathematics. Kate had enjoyed it all—except the riding. She was a big girl, rather clumsy in her movements, and not even the art of Genée, as administered weekly by Miss Lilla Lollarina—or some such name—could teach her to retain her balance gracefully on a moving horse.

Having left school, however, none of these accomplishments mattered very much; her beauty and gay spirits were enough in themselves to win the heart of a man who really was rich. Terence Waygold, a ' playboy ' in the modern expression, inheriting a large fortune from an American mother, had never needed to work, but spent his time and money amusing himself—owning a yacht, race-horses, and finally a beautiful young wife whom he could deck with pearls and precious stones and whom, to his own great surprise, he came to love with a complete devotion which lasted until he broke his neck out hunting the winter after his horse, Simon the Seventh, won the Gold Vase at Ascot.

That happened when Kate was in the early thirties and she, after a quick recovery from the shock, settled down to enjoy the astonishing wealth that her doting husband left to her, wealth that she enjoyed not only for the fun that it brought her but for the happiness that it could give to other people. For Kate Waygold was a generous woman, warm-hearted, equable, and at the same time shrewd enough not to be a prey to the sharks who flocked round her. With her husband's money she had inherited his stud and racing stable, even something of his genuine fondness for horses. She kept them on, and had a fair measure of success with them, though it was generally thought that her trainer, Carter Casling, was a bit too clever for her.

At the time of Ballnaceach's victory at Shankesbury, Kate Waygold was forty-six and was still a handsome woman, though, in the parlance of her racing friends, she was carrying a bit too much weight. She had had many offers of marriage, but had preferred to retain her freedom, though not averse from adventures of an impermanent nature. Gradually, as the years passed, these light affairs grew fewer and less attractive and the cold finger of loneliness was beginning to make itself felt. She could still have had her pick of husbands . . . of a kind, but they were not the kind that appealed to her. Terry Waygold, for all that he was technically a waster, had been a man, with a hard bone of courage and ruthlessness in his back; if she were to marry again, that was the type of man she wanted.

So, seeking for him, seeking but so far not finding, she kept open house at Tandrings, the lovely old Elizabethan house in Barryshire that Terry had bought just before he died. One of its attractions for Terry had been the fine

range of stables built by his predecessor and which he had
filled with good-quality hunters on which to follow that
excellent provincial pack, the Barrymore. Now Terry
was dead, but Kate kept on the horses as an added attrac-
tion to the men and women with whom she liked to fill
her hospitable house; it was among the men who loved
hunting that she hoped to find that type of courage and
recklessness that had attracted her so much in her husband.
She herself hunted occasionally, but she had never been
really at home in the saddle, and was obliged to confess
to herself that she lacked just those qualities that she
admired so much in others.

It was to Tandrings, then, that Charles Rathlyn and his
friend Gerald Fanthony came on that Friday evening in
February, following the Shankesbury Royal Cup; driving
down in Gerald's Lorte-Renton and arriving just in comfortable time for a whisky-and-soda and a bit of chit-chat
with hostess and fellow guests before going up to dress for
dinner.

Charles himself was still too shaken and worried about
his own precarious position to notice much about his
fellow guests; they were, in fact, of no great interest—
another racing man and two rather hard-faced women,
one married, the other not, and both following much the
same quest as their hostess. It was upon Kate Waygold
that Rathlyn's interest was centred—his interest and his
hope, almost his only hope. If she would pay him a really
good price—'your price' she had called it, in the flush
of her victory at Shankesbury—then there was still a
chance for him to rebuild some sort of position for himself,
though it must be a very modest one. To sell Silver Eagle
in the open market, with everyone knowing he was broke
and must sell, would inevitably mean something in the
nature of a knock-down price.

Knowing something about the quality of Tandrings

hospitality, Charles and Gerald Fanthony had both brought their hunting kit, hoping to be offered a mount. The meet, they had discovered, was at Eborn's Gorse, only a few miles away, and sure enough, horses were put at their disposal. Mrs. Waygold too was going, hoping to see something of Captain Rathlyn's performance across country, even though she knew that if hounds really ran she herself would soon be left behind.

Kate Waygold believed in hacking to the meet if it was within reasonable distance. It got her horse's back down and warmed her own blood before that chilly moment at the covert-side which, with the timid, is such a test of three-o'clock-in-the-morning courage. Today Charles Rathlyn made a point of riding beside her; his quick eye noted the clumsiness of her seat in the saddle, the nervousness with which she controlled her high-spirited horse, but nothing would have induced him to betray his knowledge.

" Will you pilot me, Mrs. Waygold? " he asked. " You know the country and I don't."

Kate Waygold laughed.

" You wouldn't see much of the hunt if you waited for me to pilot you," she said. " I'm no performer; I just like a ride and not too much jumping. Primrose will carry you at the top of the hunt, and there's no wire to worry about."

Rathlyn patted his mare's glossy neck.

" I'm sure she would, but I couldn't stay with her. You will have noticed that I've got a stiff knee; I'm no thruster now—balance gone and liable to fall off."

Kate Waygold felt a faint sense of disappointment. Still, she knew something about understatements, and hoped that this was one of them.

"Well, follow Kitten Dormer, then; she's fair to middling and knows the country."

Rathlyn had no wish to follow Miss Kitty Dormer, one
of the hard-faced guests, whom he had already noticed
eyeing him with appraisement. He wanted to please
Mrs. Waygold, and he sensed that she wanted him to be
a credit to her and to the lovely chestnut mare she had
provided for him, so when hounds ran he picked a line
for himself and was soon oblivious to everything but the
exhilaration of riding a perfect fencer over a good grass
country and fair, unwired fences. It was a sharp burst
of twenty minutes, and when hounds ran into their fox
at the far side of the first bit of heavy plough, Charles,
though not in the first flight, was not far behind.

He slipped off his mare, loosened the girth, and made
much of her. A thin-faced man, with a hooked nose and
dark moustache, riding a rather common-looking animal,
clipped trace-high, trotted up to him and followed suit.

"That's a good one you've got there," he said. "Am
I right in thinking she's from the Tandrings stables? I
have followed you at a respectful distance and admired the
performance."

Rathlyn smiled.

"Her performance," he said. "Yes, you're quite
right. Mrs. Waygold has kindly mounted me."

"I thought I recognised her—the mare. By the way,
my name's Netterly."

"Mine's Rathlyn."

"What, the owner of Silver Eagle?"

Charles nodded, feeling gloomily that this might be the
last time he could answer that question in the affirmative.

"A grand mare; it was wretched luck, that peck over
the last fence; I thought she was a certain winner."

"I hope she didn't lose you a packet."

Netterly smiled and shook his head.

"As a matter of fact I don't bet, but I like watching a
good race. Here's your hostess coming."

Charles Rathlyn looked over his shoulder and saw Kate Waygold approaching. He walked to meet her, nodding farewell to his new acquaintance. Kate was looking flushed and handsome, and Charles smiled at her cheerfully.

" Thank you for a grand ride, Mrs. Waygold," he said. " I hope you enjoyed that hunt."

" I should think I did. I followed you for two or three fields, but I couldn't keep it up. I didn't see much sign of falling off."

Charles laughed.

" That was Primrose; she caught me the other side. She really is a lovely performer, so smooth and sure. You should be riding her yourself."

Kate Waygold shook her head.

" I don't think she has ever carried a side-saddle, and in any case she's not up to my weight."

" Indeed she is. You ride no more than I do, Mrs. Waygold; twelve stone at the outside, I should guess. I wish we could change now, but it might be wiser to have her schooled to side-saddle."

Hounds were moving off to draw a fresh covert. Rathlyn rather laboriously clambered back into his own saddle.

" I ought to take her home. It isn't fair to tire someone else's horse."

" Oh no, do go on. I'm going on a bit longer myself."

So they followed hounds to covert, and when a fox went away, Rathlyn stayed with his hostess and piloted her on a very pleasant little hunt, not letting her scramble through the gaps made by other people but going his own line, picking easy places to jump and giving her plenty of time to catch up with him between fences. Plenty of confidence too; Kate Waygold enjoyed that little pottering hunt as she had never enjoyed a hunt before. They went home early, riding all the way and talking it all over as if it had been a six-mile point with the Pytchley. Charles was pleased with himself; he felt that he had sown some useful ground-bait. As for Kate Waygold, her eyes were sparkling as she lay and soaked in her hot mustard bath. She felt that she had found a man—and a man not entirely devoid of sympathy and understanding.

The other guests had enjoyed themselves too. Gerald Fanthony had had a smashing fall, and as his horse had not been hurt—a disaster with a loaned mount—he was at the top of his form, chaffing the ladies and drinking rather more Bollinger than was strictly good for him. Charles hoped that, on the crest of this cheerful wave, something might be said about Silver Eagle, but after a short and not very serious game of poker, Kate declared that she was sleepy and swept the ladies off to bed.

The following day, Sunday, produced a reaction. The men breakfasted alone, lolled about reading the papers, *Horse and Hound*, *Country Life*, and then strolled off to the stables to look at their horses and gossip with the grooms. The ladies appeared for lunch, but it was a quiet meal, and afterwards Mrs. Waygold took them round to the stables again, to examine the other horses, and then round the home farm—of all forms of Sunday exercise the most dreary, if you do not happen to be agriculturally minded.

Charles hardly had a word alone with Mrs. Waygold, and when she retired to her sitting-room after tea ' to write letters ', he felt that his fondly cherished hopes had flopped. When a rubber of bridge was started he was unlucky enough to cut out, so was sitting in an armchair, gloomily looking through the papers again, when a foot-man appeared and asked if it would be convenient for him to go and see Mrs. Waygold. He jumped up from his chair with alacrity—from the bridge-table Gerald cocked an encouraging eyebrow at him—and followed the foot-man down a long passage.

The room in which Mrs. Waygold was waiting for him had evidently been her husband's study or smoking-room. There was a man-size writing-table near the big window, on the walls were sporting prints, paintings of horses, and a group or two of soldiers. The only item that made it obviously not his room now was a large photograph on the writing-table of Terence Waygold himself—a handsome man, as Charles could see at a glance, clean-shaven and with the keen, far-seeing eyes of the race-rider.

Kate Waygold was standing by the fire. She was wearing a black cocktail frock of heavy silk that set off her fine figure to perfection. Though Charles Rathlyn did not realise it, she had spent the hour since tea re-doing her hair and attending to the lines—still only noticeable to the observant eye—round her handsome brown eyes. In the kindly light of shaded standard lamps and flickering fire it was difficult to believe that she was nearer fifty than forty; Charles Rathlyn, in fact, had no idea of it. Her appearance struck him very agreeably; although he himself was attractive to women, he had never taken them very seriously and had certainly never been in love; he had amused himself, but soldiering and racing had provided him with all the interest and excitement that he needed in life. Still, he did like a good-looking woman.

Mrs. Waygold pointed to a tray containing a decanter of sherry, two glasses and a dish of salted almonds.

" Have I dragged you from a rubber? "

Charles smiled his attractive smile.

" As a matter of fact, no; but I should have needed no dragging."

He filled her a glass of sherry and helped himself. She sipped hers for a moment or two and seemed rather at a loss for words. Then she sank on to a leather sofa and patted the seat beside her.

" Captain Rathlyn," she said, " I don't know how you

are situated, as they say, and perhaps I am talking quite
out of turn. Forgive me if I am. I wondered whether
you would consider becoming my racing manager."

Rathlyn's heart gave a bound. Nothing of this kind
had entered his head. His thoughts raced and he was
conscious—when he got them under control—of looking
extremely foolish.

" I . . . I . . . hardly . . . I had no idea . . ." he
stammered.

Mrs. Waygold checked him.

" Of course I don't expect an immediate answer," she
said, "—unless you want to turn it down flat. If you care
to hear, I will tell you something of what it would mean."

" Do please tell me. It sounds a wonderful idea."

Kate Waygold relaxed. She had not been at all sure
that she would not be turned down flat. She finished her
glass of sherry and held it out for more.

" I expect you know I have got horses under both Rules
—Jockey Club and National Hunt. As you know, Carter
Casling has my 'chasers at Ewcote; the others are with
Jack Herris at Lambourn; they are both within fifty
miles of here. I don't mind admitting that I don't really
know a lot about racing, though I am very fond of it. I
really kept them on so as to keep my husband's colours
flying. Jack Herris, I'm sure, is as straight as a die, but
I'm not too absolutely sure about Casling. This is absolutely confidential, of course—perhaps I ought not to have
said even that."

" That's quite all right, Mrs. Waygold," said Rathlyn
quietly. " I know this game. There's no need to say
any more—no need for either of us to. With all the
horses you've got, under both Rules, it probably would be
wise for you to have a manager. Question is: am I the
right man for you? I don't know a lot about the flat."

" It isn't really the flat that worries me—as I said. I

shouldn't so much mind dropping that, if necessary. It was steeplechasing that Terry really loved—and that's where I am not so happy. I feel sure that you know all about it, and I think you are just the man I want—if you care to take it on."

Mrs. Waygold was perfectly well aware that a prudent woman—a prudent owner of either sex—would have made a great many confidential enquiries before inviting a near-stranger to take on a post of so much responsibility, with so much money involved. But she had never been noted for prudence. She was impetuous, and enjoyed being impetuous. She had liked the way Charles Rathlyn took his beating at Shankesbury; she had liked the way he rode Primrose—maimed man as he was—across what seemed to her a pretty stiff country; and she had liked the way he had thanked her for the ride and then devoted the rest of the day to seeing that she enjoyed herself. He was not a moaner nor a boaster, and he clearly had more than the usual man's meagre share of unselfishness and thoughtfulness. So, without any enquiries worth speaking of—the idea had indeed flashed into her mind at Shankesbury and she had asked one or two casual questions of her friends—she invited him here and now to become her manager. Here and now he accepted.

CHAPTER III

Call me Kate

THE NEXT year, 1953, was on the whole a happy and successful one for Charles Rathlyn. By a stroke of great good fortune, a small house had recently come in to hand at the bottom of the park, and within a few weeks—thanks to the recent easing of the licensing restrictions—it had been sufficiently modernised and redecorated for him to move into it. He gave up the old-fashioned flat in St. James's with some regret, but he knew that without this wonderful windfall of a job he would in any case have had to quit it at short notice—quit it for some horrible bed-sitter in Battersea or a stuffy hotel in some provincial town.

Picking up the threads of his work kept him fully occupied. He paid one visit to Jack Herris at Lambourn and liked him. Herris was a man of few words and clear understanding. He did not question the appointment of a racing manager—that was entirely a matter for his employer—but he made perfectly clear to Rathlyn the line beyond which he would not welcome interference—a line, thought Charles, quite reasonably drawn.

Carter Casling was another matter. Charles knew him of old and had never much liked him, though he had had no business dealings with him. Casling was an able and successful trainer of steeplechasers, but he had the reputation of being rather 'fly', and the plain hostility with which he greeted Captain Rathlyn's appointment made the latter wonder whether there was not some good reason for his objection to supervision. Kate Waygold admitted that she had allowed the trainer to do almost as he liked, had paid, without question, the formidable bills which from time to time came to her, and was now patting

herself on the back at her cleverness in thinking up this
brilliant idea of a manager. Charles Rathlyn had laughed
at this.

"How do you know I am not just a bigger flea to bite
you?" he asked.

Mrs. Waygold shook her head.

"I call myself a pretty good judge of a man," she said.
"I trust you, and that's enough. I never quite trusted
Casling; I took him on when Terry died. I wouldn't
mind changing. What about your own trainer, Dartle?"

Rathlyn hesitated.

"Let's leave it to the end of the season. I don't really
know Casling now; I shall, I hope, by then."

Charles was not entirely sure that he wanted Fred
Dartle as Mrs. Waygold's trainer, much as he liked the
man. It might be wiser to cut right loose from his old
life and bring none of its shadows into the new one.

It had been arranged that Silver Eagle should remain
with Dartle for the present. Mrs. Waygold had bought
her for a fair price—not quite the fancy price that Charles
Rathlyn had had in his mind, but fair enough. He rather
admired Kate Waygold for the business-like way in which
she had dealt with this problem; she explained that the
offer of employment rather altered the position, and that
she would regard it as reasonable to settle the matter on
the lines of pure market value. She hoped he agreed with
her. He could hardly question that. The great thing
that mattered to him was that he would now be able to
keep his interest in racing and even some fairly direct
interest in the mare herself. He drove over to see Dartle,
explained the position to him, and settled on a plan for
the rest of the season.

There was not much left of the hunting season by the
time he was settled in his house. He had two more very
pleasant rides on Primrose, one alone and one in company

with his employer; then, as there were signs of an early
spring, he advised Mrs. Waygold to sell two of the less
satisfactory horses and to rough the rest off. When they
had had a good rest and settled into their summer coats
it would do them good to be hacked, if Mrs. Waygold
cared to ride.

As soon as he was settled into his house and had begun
almost daily discussions with Mrs. Waygold about her
racing interests, Charles Rathlyn began to learn a bit
more about the make-up of her establishment. The butler, Ludd, he had of course seen something of during his
first week-end visit; he had been conscious, too, of a
footman and of what seemed to him an almost pre-war
ration of maids of various categories. Now he realised
that there were three other people of greater importance
than the domestic staff. The first was Mrs. Waygold's
secretary, Philip Monner, a rather tall, thin man in the
late thirties, bespectacled and with a quiet, good manner.
Mrs. Waygold called him ' Philip ', and Charles learned
later that he was the son of a man, John Monner, who
had been for many years clerk to Jo Hillburn but who had
had a bad break and been sent to gaol for embezzlement.
The bookmaker had had a soft spot for his old clerk and
had had the son trained as a secretary and accountant—
roughly the job that he was doing now for Jo Hillburn's
daughter.

Then there was a young woman, called ' Isabel ' by
Mrs. Waygold and ' Miss Wey ' by the staff, whom Charles
had difficulty in placing; at first he thought she was Mrs.
Waygold's maid, but later judged her to be a sort of
confidante, or personal secretary. She was evidently about
thirty, and was good-looking, except that her mouth was
too thin and firm; a good figure, too, with dark hair
parted in the middle and brushed back to an almost
Victorian bun.

Finally, there was Mrs. Tass, the housekeeper, whom Charles did not meet in the flesh for months, though he soon realised that she was a power behind the throne. She had been Kate Hillburn's nanny, in the days when Jo and his wife were just burgeoning out into social ambitions and full-blown staff. She still ruled Kate—as far as Kate was willing to be ruled—and not even Isabel Wey was free from fear of her. When at last he did meet her, Charles saw her to be tiny in stature, with piercing blue eyes, a button of a nose, a warrantable moustache and a most determined jaw.

Why it was necessary for a young, able-bodied and capable woman to employ such a team of people to do her natural work for her Charles Rathlyn found it difficult to understand; but then Charles had not before come into such close contact with a very rich woman. One efficient young woman, trained to domestic science and secretarial duties, would have done the job very nicely, he, in his ignorance, thought. It did, indeed, occur to him that his own job as racing manager was somewhat redundant, but then he did not know what had been at the back of Mrs. Waygold's mind when she invited him to take it. In any case, he was not going to question it; he just wondered about the others.

The week-end parties, of course, took some organising, but these gradually seemed to tail off, and there was not a great deal of local entertaining. When they first came to Tandrings, Terry and Kate Waygold had been welcomed by all but the stuffiest of the ' county ' and very warmly welcomed by the hunt; not only was Terence Waygold a rich man, whose subscription would be a pillar of strength to the hunt's finances, but he was known to be a sportsman, a good man across country, and a generous host. His wife, too, was welcomed for her beauty and high spirits, so that Tandrings was always full of people

being entertained, and the Waygolds themselves were
invited to almost every house within a wide radius. But
after Terry's death things had changed. Kate had never
felt quite at her ease with these county people, and drifted
more and more into the racing set—a racing set of not
quite the highest category. Gradually the local entertaining dropped off and week-end parties of people from
London and other parts of the country took its place;
cheerful enough parties, but ' not quite the same thing ',
as Ludd once confided to Mrs. Tass—to be sent away with
a flea in his ear.

If Kate Waygold had really been a hunting woman this
falling off in her local popularity would not have happened. She subscribed generously and was always welcomed at the meet, at Hunt Balls and similar functions,
but she did not ' go ', so people who did, or liked to think
they did, lost interest in her. Kate had not seemed to
mind; she knew that it was not likely to be from among
these people that she would find the man she wanted to
marry—if she ever did find him. So she filled her house
with Terry's old racing friends and, later, her own racing
friends, and the county gradually dropped away.

Now, as spring came, and the new ' flat ' season opened,
she seemed happy enough with fewer guests; happy to
drive from one race meeting to another with her ' manager '—within reasonable distance that could be done, in
her Rolls-Bentley, in the day, but if it was necessary to
stay the night anywhere, there were always friends to be
stayed with or friends to stay with them at a hotel.
Everything was proper and above reproach; no serious
finger of scandal had ever been pointed at Kate Waygold
—even though, in fact, her widowhood had not been
entirely devoid of ' interlude '. Be good, but if you can't
be good, be careful; that was very sound advice, Kate
thought.

When they were not racing, or visiting the stables at Lambourn and Ewcote, Kate Waygold and Charles Rathlyn spent a good deal of time riding—riding in the park or over the considerable Tandrings estate. Charles had been quick to note how much Mrs. Waygold had enjoyed the two hunts she had had with him—enjoyed them because he had encouraged her to 'have a go' and yet had not asked too much of her. If only she could gain confidence and a little skill in the saddle she would enjoy it still more, and that would surely redound to his own advantage. For a time he tried to teach her to ride astride, believing that to be a much safer seat than side-saddle, but it is an art that should, by a woman, be learned young; Kate had neither the grip nor the natural balance required for the job, and he soon realised that she was frightened and gave up the attempt.

It was very pleasant riding about that lovely country-side in the spring and early summer. The horses which had been retained had been beautifully schooled and had perfect manners; they would stand quietly while gates were opened, stand, too, when their riders wanted to talk quietly to someone met by the way—a farmer, a labourer, a housewife on her way to the bus, the local bobby, the postman. Charles was good at this sort of friendly talk; people liked him and he seemed to like people. Kate Waygold felt more and more sure that she had at last found the man who could take Terry's place.

Gradually Charles began to realise what was happening. Free of the nagging anxiety of his dwindling income he was happy and able to enjoy life, even away from the excitement of a race-course. He enjoyed these rides, he liked being with Kate Waygold; she was a good-looking woman, she was 'fun', she was good company; her temperament was equable, and it was the rarest thing to hear her find fault with anyone—a very precious gift in a

woman. Slowly, too, it dawned on him that she liked
being with him, that she was not treating him just as an
employee, that she was even rather fond of him. In
public she called him ' Captain Rathlyn ', but in private,
especially on their rides, she had slipped into the habit
of using his Christian name, though she did not invite
him to call her ' Kate '.

Charles Rathlyn had heard one or two little stories
about Kate Waygold, in the days before he came to know
her. There was no malicious gossip, there were not many
people who even hinted at frailty—but there were a few.
There had been no sign of that with him. As her fondness
for him became clearer in his eyes he began to wonder
whether there was any more serious thought in her mind.

So the summer passed, cheerfully for them both, and
with growing hope and happiness for Kate Waygold. The
weather, indeed, was cold and gloomy, but the Corona-
tion spirit out-balanced that, and when the blue, white
and gold colours flashed past the post in one of the richest
races at Ascot there seemed no cloud on the horizon. By
the time of Goodwood, Kate Waygold—now called in
private Kate as she called him Charles—had made up
her mind.

CHAPTER IV

Marriage

THEY WERE married in the early autumn, and spent their honeymoon in the south of France. It meant missing the Leger, but as no Waygold horse was running that could be endured. They would be back soon after the serious opening of the N.H. season.

The marriage had come as little surprise to anyone but the principals. Most of their friends and neighbours had 'seen it coming', but had had the rare delicacy not to permit themselves any heavy-handed chaff on the subject. Gerald Fanthony, indeed, had not felt like chaff. The idea of Charles marrying a woman appreciably older than himself worried him; he had always expected that one of these days Charles would 'fall for a filly'—and Mrs. Waygold could hardly be classified as a filly. Gerry Fanthony scented danger; he was no philosopher, no deep thinker, but he was a man of the world, and he suspected that once the thoughts of a man, not hitherto woman-conscious, were turned in that direction they would stay there—but not necessarily on the same object. Kate Waygold was certainly attractive—now, but would she be in six or eight years' time? Then would come the danger, and Gerry feared for his friend.

Still, Charles was not an easy chap to talk to on personal matters, and this was not only personal but extremely delicate. Charles gave him no warning of what was about to happen—did he, indeed, know himself?—so that it was not until the engagement had been announced that Gerry Fanthony screwed up his courage and said his piece.

" I say, old man, this is a bit of a facer. You never told me you were contemplating matrimony."

Charles grinned rather sheepishly, but did not rise to that
fly. They were driving back from the station, where he
had been to collect his friend for a week-end visit.

" Have you really studied the form? I mean, are you
sure that marriage is the horse for your money? "

Gerry realised that he must not say anything about
' weight for age '.

" Looks like it. The money's on now, anyway."

" Yes, but . . . seriously; you've never thought of
marrying before. Are you really a marrying man?
Only fair to the woman . . . er, girl . . . to be sure of
that, what? "

Charles did not answer for a moment. His grey eyes
were fixed on the road ahead of him. Gerry wondered
uneasily whether he had given offence. Charles was not
an easy . . .

" I've thought about it a lot, Gerry. True enough,
I've never thought before about marrying, but I've had to
think about it now. You are my greatest friend, and I'll
tell you something I wouldn't tell another soul. I know
you won't either. Kate asked me to marry her; she
says she wants a husband and that I am the man she
wants. You'll realise that after that, if I said ' No ' I
should be out on my ear. Too damned embarrassing for
both of us. I'm in a job now that suits me down to the
ground. I should never get another like it; not a hope
in hell. And I'm broke—or have been—as you know.
I should be a fool to turn this down, even if I wanted to,
and I'm not sure that I do."

He took a cigarette, one-handed, from his case, lit it
from a gadget in the dashboard.

" I'm not in love, of course. I'm not the sort of chap
who falls in love—I don't know why. But I like Kate.
She's a good-looker. She's generous, easy to get on with;
in the seven months I've been her manager she's never

given me a cross word. That counts for something, you know, Gerry, especially when you set it against the reverse of the medal. Oh, yes; I've thought about it; I've made up my mind, and I'm quite happy about it."

Gerry saw the point of all that, but he also saw, or thought he saw, a little further. Dare he say any more? Easier not to, easier to let it go at that. But Charles was his best, his oldest friend; he didn't want him to make a muck of his life. Not for want of one word of caution.

" I see all that, old boy. As you say, she's a stunner, your Kate. But she's . . . what is it? . . . six or eight years older than you. Can you stay the course, old man? That's the question. It's a long race, you know—marriage; not just a six-furlong sprint."

Charles Rathlyn smiled and patted his friend on the knee.

" Bless you, you old Jeremiah; what d'you take me for—a philanderer of some kind? I'm not interested in girls. I believe I shall be very happy with a woman I like—as I do like Kate. I mean to make a go of it. I should be a cad if I didn't."

There was nothing more to be said. Only half con-vinced Gerry offered his congratulations to his friend and then, on arrival at Tandrings, more warmly to Kate Waygold. They had a very happy evening, the three of them, drinking their own healths and making plans for the future—including the wife they were going to find for Gerry.

It was true enough, what Charles Rathlyn had said. He was fond of Kate. He believed he could be happy with her, could make her happy. He had no interest in girls—no serious interest; never had had, apart from a bit of fun. He was a lucky man to have dropped into such a wonderful job, such an ideal life; a wife older than himself was a small price to pay for that luck.

There was just one fly in the ointment. One little nagging worry—about Kate. She did drink a bit too much. He had only come to realise that gradually. She was never tight—never made a fool of herself. It just was that she wasn't doing herself any good by it. As a racing man, an owner and one-time rider, Charles knew a good deal about fitness—fitness of horse and man. For a man—still more for a woman—drink worked the wrong way; it made for softness, flabbiness of tissue, weight—yes, the weight-for-age that Gerry had had in his mind, though the racing analogy was not really appropriate. If she went on as she was, Kate would be definitely fat in a few years' time; she would run to seed, physically and morally. That was what worried him. Could he check that tendency? Having no experience of managing women, he simply could not answer that question.

Anyhow, he had made up his mind before Gerry Fanthony expressed his own doubts, and soon afterwards —no point in waiting, at their age—they were married and were back at Tandrings, happily settled in as man and wife.

Kate at once made over to her new husband the study that had been Terence Waygold's and that she herself had used, with memories of him all round her, during her widowhood. Now she swept all that away—the photographs, the paintings of his horses, the leopard-skin rug in front of the fire. Cut the past right out—that was her cool decision, taken without slight to Terry's memory. The room was redecorated, a new carpet on the floor, new curtains, new covers on the chairs—except those which were leather. This was to be Charles's now. She herself moved back into what a former age had called the boudoir—a bright and cheerful room that neither she nor Terry had ever much cared for. She would care for it now. There was no need to change anything in her big,

lovely bedroom; they would be there together, and no
thought of anyone else would intrude upon them.

There were plenty of rooms in Tandrings. Not only
bedrooms but ' reception rooms '. It was just as well.
Dining-room, drawing-room, billiard-room—these were
needed for house-parties; a study for Charles, a sitting-
room for Kate. In addition, Philip Monner had a room
to work in, at his letters and accounts; he called it his
office, but it was furnished most comfortably and would
have been gladly welcomed as a study or smoking-room
by many a householder. Isabel Wey—Charles gathered
—had two rooms somewhere at the end of a wing on the
first floor; one as her bedroom, the other in which she
worked. Just what that work was was a bit of a mystery.
Apparently she did some of the finer ' make and mend '
for Mrs. Rathlyn, a little washing, ironing, pressing; but
she also seemed to attend to Kate's personal correspondence. She had a telephone up there and made appoint-
ments—' dates ', perhaps, before this happy marriage put
dates in inverted commas out of court. Charles was
rather intrigued by this young woman's position in the
household; it was, to say the least of it, unusual. And
she was a far from usual type herself, with her quiet good
looks, her assured manner, and her apparent lack of interest in anybody but herself.

Charles had wondered, too, as he had when he first
came to Tandrings, what Philip Monner found to do with
himself all day long. The estate was managed by a firm
in the county town, Barryfield. Monner did not touch
the racing side of his employer's interests; Isabel Wey
dealt with her personal correspondence and engagements.
What was left for Monner? He looked after Mrs. Rathlyn's financial affairs, certainly, and this apparently
included dealing her out cash when she needed it.
Charles had been rather shocked when he came to realise

what a casual arrangement this seemed to be. Mrs. Waygold—as she still was when he first began to take notice—would say: " Philip, I want twenty pounds ", or fifty or even a hundred, and Monner would retire to his office and return with the appropriate number of treasury notes. He must keep quite a supply of them, Charles thought.

Now that they were married, although he had no control over his wife's income or expenditure, Charles felt that some responsibility for her interests did rest on him. He broached the subject tentatively with her, and she just laughed at him and said that she trusted ' Philip ' absolutely; besides, how could anything go wrong? She gave him a receipt for all the cash she had, it was properly entered in the accounts and these were audited every year.

No doubt quite all right, but Charles thought he would just sound Monner himself on the subject. So one day, when the secretary had brought him some letters to sign, he approached it on a side wind.

" Can you cash me a cheque any time, Monner? " he asked. " I see you provide my wife with cash fairly regularly."

" Oh, yes, sir; I expect I generally can, if it's not too large a one."

Charles laughed.

" That's hardly likely. How do you manage it? She seems to ask for cash at any old time and for any amount. Do you have to keep a lot of bullion? "

The secretary's thin face, generally so expressionless, softened into a smile.

" It's not quite as unpredictable as all that, sir. Every month, or more often if necessary, Mrs. Rathlyn signs a cheque for a hundred or perhaps two hundred pounds, according to her likely requirements, taking any balance into account. I cash the cheque and keep the money in my safe; as she needs it she asks for it. I keep an account of course, and each month submit it to her for signature."

" Do you mean in detail? What it is wanted for or spent on? "

" Oh no, sir; I wouldn't know that. Just ' cash ' and the date and amount."

Charles would have liked to question this casual arrangement more closely, but he did not like to give the impression that he was doubting the man's honesty. Perhaps Monner noticed his hesitation, because he went on of his own accord.

" Mrs. Rathlyn keeps a copy of each month's account and I keep another. At the end of the year these are, of course, checked by the auditors with the bank statement. They are quite satisfied, except that they did suggest that it would be better if Mrs. Rathlyn signed for each amount received; we did that for a time . . ." he hesitated, and again the slow, pleasant smile lifted the corners of his mouth; ". . . I think Mrs. Rathlyn found it rather irksome. She said it was a bore, and the arrangement, so far as a receipt for each amount was concerned, petered out."

" Sounds all right to me. And you can let me have a pound or two now and then? Good. I don't know what my wife would have done without you all these years; you are quite invaluable to her. Only thing is . . . don't you get bored with this small-time work? I know you've got good technical qualifications—accountancy especially. Haven't you ever felt that you ought to be doing more important work? "

Charles thought that there was some slight stiffening of the secretary's manner.

" During the war, sir, I worked for the Ministry of Supply, and I believe they would have kept me on. But

Mrs. Waygold asked me to come back. I owe everything
to her and to her father, Mr. Hillburn. You may not
know, sir, that my father was sent to prison. We had no
money after that, and there would have been no chance of
my being trained for a profession if Mr. Hillburn had not
seen me through it all. When he died Mrs. Waygold—
Mrs. Rathlyn—took me on. I feel that it would be the
basest ingratitude if I didn't stay with her as long as I can
be of any help."

Charles smiled.

"It's refreshing to hear anyone take that attitude," he
said. "Still, if you ever feel you do want to move on to
something bigger, I am sure Mrs. Rathlyn would not
stand in your way."

It was refreshing. But did it ring true? Was it not,
perhaps, just laziness—the liking for a soft, presumably
well-paid job? Oh well, it was no business of his, thought
Charles, as he walked out to the stables and had a talk
with Ben Penny, the head groom, about the horses that
he and Mrs. Rathlyn would ride the following day.

As it happened, this was the last time that Charles and
his wife were to hunt together for some time. Kate had
developed some sort of pain in her back, which was
accentuated by the screw-wise action of riding side-saddle
—screw-wise, that is, for those who are not skilled horse-
women. The local doctor said 'rheumatism' and recommended treatment which did no good; a London specialist
diagnosed the fashionable 'slipped disc', gladly welcom-
ing another rich woman to his list of incurables. Kate,
however, was nobody's fool where doctors were concerned; she decided to give her back a rest, so far as riding
was concerned, and to have a course of massage and
electro-whatnot in Barryfield. But it meant that Charles
had to hunt alone.

He had persuaded Kate to take on Primrose for herself

and had sent the mare, before the hunting season started, to be schooled to side-saddle—with complete success. He himself rode either Robin, a well-mannered brown horse, a good fencer but rather slow, or Dashalong, one of his own steeplechasers now touched in the wind and retired to the hunting stables. Of the two he greatly preferred Dashalong, a big-hearted bay who lived up to his name. His disadvantage was that, being accustomed to brush fences, he was not too sure of himself with timber; the Barrymore is a rather ' hairy ' country, with many a fence that was unjumpable save over some post-and-rail gap, often under a tree. Not quite what a steeplechaser is accustomed to. Still, he was definitely a more exhilarating ride than the safe-and-sure Robin.

Charles and Kate seldom took out second horses. They did not like long days: Kate because of her weight (and clumsiness) and latterly her back; Charles because his stiff knee, unbalancing him as it inevitably did, made riding and jumping a much more exhausting business than it is to an able-bodied man. That was one reason why they had reduced the number of their horses to four. Now, with Kate not hunting, it would be a job to keep those four adequately exercised; road-riding by grooms was not really enough when horses were corned up. Charles looked about for someone who might like an occasional hunt on one or other of them. Especially on Primrose; only a good one must ride her, and if possible it should be side-saddle, so as to keep her accustomed to it.

There was one girl who came into his mind at once in this connection. Her name was Anne Faery, and she was the daughter of a Captain Faery who was a horse-dealer in a fair way of business. She was a slim, pleasant-looking girl, but it was her riding that had caught Charles's eye. She had the quiet, assured seat and the light hands of a first-class performer; she rode her father's horses to show them to customers and had the priceless quality—from the dealer's angle—of being able to make even a flashy, chancy six-year-old look a safe, well-mannered hunter. Normally she rode astride, but Charles had seen her ride side-saddle, and she appeared to be the very person for Primrose—till Kate was ready to ride again. It would have to be a business arrangement, of course; if she rode Primrose she would be no use to her father that day.

That was how it worked out. Captain Faery said that he would spare her one day a week, at so-much a day; that would still leave her free to ride his young hunters three other days a week, if needed. Charles Rathlyn thought she must be a pretty tough young woman to do four days a week, week in, week out, all through the hunting season. She didn't look it. But then girls, he had begun to suspect, were like that—much tougher physically, mentally and perhaps even morally—than they looked.

Gradually he got into the way of riding much of the time with Anne Faery, allowing her sometimes to pilot him over country that he did not know well. He found that it was all he could do to keep her in sight if hounds really ran. It did not occur to him that she sometimes eased her horse in order that she should remain in sight. He liked her. She was a nice girl, quiet, modest, no nonsense. On the days when she rode Primrose they hacked home together, and that is always a pleasant end to a day's hunting. It was perhaps as well that Charles Rathlyn was, as he had declared, ' not interested in girls '.

CHAPTER V

'An Awful Thing'

MR. JORROCKS was accustomed to tell his admiring
audiences that ' a fall is an awful thing '. As a generalisa-
tion that was, perhaps, an overstatement, but it is a fact that
a hunting fall can be most unpleasant and have lasting
consequences not anticipated at the time of the incident.

On a Wednesday in January, when Anne Faery was
riding Primrose and Charles Dashalong, there had been
no scent in the morning and no hunt worthy of the name.
Primrose was a bit above herself and they were anxious
that she should have a good gallop, so they stayed on
into the afternoon, and were rewarded—as they thought—
when hounds pushed a fox out of a small spinney and went
away to a great cry. The day had warmed and scent
was suddenly good, so that the pace was a fast one and
Primrose got her gallop. This time Anne let her go, and
Charles found that even Dashalong had difficulty in
keeping up with her. Fortunately the going was not
heavy, so his touched wind did not greatly worry him; the
timber was what caused the trouble. As long as he was
close up to Primrose he followed her gallantly over post
and rail, as well as laid fence, but a moment came when
she was out of sight, and there before them was a hairy
bullfinch with just one gap filled by a really big bit of
solid timber over which Primrose, with her light-weight
rider, must have gone. Charles hesitated, and his
hesitation probably conveyed itself to his horse; he put
him at it, and Dashalong, too, checked in his stride, rose
half-heartedly and crashed into the top rail. It broke,
but only just, and the horse turned slowly over and came
down on its rider, pinning him to the ground.

The heaviness of the fall knocked the wind out of both horse and man; fortunately, perhaps, because Dashalong did not roll, but when he had recovered his breath, rose carefully to his feet and stood looking down at his prostrate rider. Charles continued to lie still; he was not 'out', but his senses were whirling and he was only conscious of a severe pain that he had not located. Presently he was aware of a hand on his shoulder and, opening his eyes saw, mistily at first, a small face under a velvet cap. It was Anne Faery.

"Are you hurt, Captain Rathlyn?"

A stab of pain shot through Charles and he located it now as in his damaged knee. He closed his eyes again and found himself thinking that there had been a note of anxiety in the girl's voice. Opening them again he saw her face clearly and there was the same expression— anxiety. He could not remember that anyone had looked at him like that before; it was rather heart-warming. Of course, anybody hurt would probably make her—or any other girl—look like that. Still, it was . . .

Charles pulled himself together and began to raise himself. Immediately a hand pressed him firmly back and a man's voice said:

"Lie quite still."

The voice was vaguely familiar, and when the speaker moved round into his field of vision, Charles saw that it was the man with whom he had talked at the end of that first hunt that he had had with the Barrymore. What was the name? Hatterly? Netterly?

"I'm quite all right," Charles said. "The old boy just chose to lie on my groggy knee; probably torn a ligament. I can manage quite all right."

"Half a minute."

Netterly knelt down beside him, ran his hands expertly down his ribs, over his collar-bones, down his spine, down each leg. Gently he moved the left leg, and another stab of pain shot through the knee. Charles drew in his breath sharply.

"Felt that all right; good. Wiggle your toes? That's fine. I don't think there's much damage, but you had a very heavy fall, and that's a shock. I told someone to telephone for an ambulance as soon as I saw the fall; it will be here quite soon. Just lie still."

There was an authoritative note in Netterly's voice and, anyhow, Charles was not loath to lie still for a bit. He did feel rather groggy. Something—a thick, dark coat—was tucked round him. The good Samaritan, in shirt-sleeves now, rose to his feet.

"I'll just trot down to Raddlett's farm and borrow a jacket. The ambulance will come there, and I'll pilot him. I'll take your horse, too, Rathlyn, and put him in the stable till you can send for him."

"Is he all right?" asked Charles, ashamed that he had not thought to ask before.

"Perfectly. Cut shin; I've put some iodine on it. It won't mark him."

Efficient devil, thought Charles, not very gratefully. For a moment he thought he was alone. Then Anne Faery stood beside him.

"I was just tying up Primrose. She has been standing like a lamb, talking to Dashalong. But when he went off she naturally wanted to go with him."

She sat down on the grass beside Charles.

"I say, don't do that. The grass is soaking."

The girl laughed.

"I'm accustomed to getting wet."

"But you must go on; you'll lose the hunt. It was terribly good of you to come back, Anne, but I'm really quite all right."

It was the first time he had called her by her Christian name, but she did not seem to notice.

"I heard the crash of that timber; it was terrific. When you did not appear I guessed what had happened and came back. You looked rather bad."

Anne's face was still a bit white, but the anxiety had cleared from it. She talked quietly, largely to keep him quiet; it was soothing, pleasant—he began to feel sleepy. Presently there was the sound of footsteps—his ear, close to the ground, picked them up even on the soft going—and Netterly reappeared, accompanied by a man in blue, carrying a stretcher over his shoulder. Expertly they shifted Charles on to it, carried him slowly across the fields, slid him into the light ambulance. He was tucked up in blankets and a hot-water bottle put between his knees. Anne climbed in too and sat down on a seat close to him; the back was shut.

"He hasn't brought an orderly, so I'm coming along too —just in case."

"You really shouldn't bother. I ought to have thanked that chap. Who is he?"

"Colonel Netterly? Oh, he's the . . . what is it? . . . Chief Constable. I don't really know him, but I think that's right."

"Oh. No wonder he's efficient. Good of him to bother, though. I say, Anne, are you all right? It's awfully cold in here."

Anne leaned forward and touched his hands, which were outside the blanket. They were icy cold, and she thought he looked rather blue round the mouth. Shock, of course. There ought to have been another hot-water bottle. She left her warm hands on his and gradually the chill left them and he seemed to doze off.

.   .   .   .   .

Colonel Netterly had completed his efficient job by ringing up Tandrings and telling Mrs. Rathlyn what had happened, advising her to get the doctor to look over her husband, though there was probably not much wrong. When the ambulance reached Tandrings she was waiting for them, evidently in a good deal of a fuss; Charles thought that she was looking flushed and somehow rather old. She had met Anne Faery once or twice before when she hacked Primrose back, had been quite nice to her and given her tea, without disclosing any particular interest. Now she did not notice her at all.

Charles was carried upstairs, still on the stretcher, and Kate helped Ludd to undress him. No; no bath, darling; not till the doctor has been, anyhow. Charles hated being fussed over; no woman had ever done such a thing to him before; he had been nursed, of course, in hospital after he was wounded, but not *fussed* over. Still feeling muzzy, it was not till he was settled in his bed that he could properly collect his thoughts. There were the horses to be got back. And Anne . . .

"I say, Kate, what about Anne—Anne Faery, I mean?"

"What about her, dear?"

"Well, she's here, isn't she? She looked after me."

"I thought it was Colonel Netterly who did that. It was he who rang up."

"Oh yes, he did, but so did Anne Faery—look after me, I mean. She came back in the ambulance with me; didn't you see her? She must be got home. And the horses; they are at Raddlett's farm, near Cheddicote. They'll have to . . ."

"Now don't bother about all that, darling. I will see to it. You must try to . . . ah, there's Dr. Jennerel; I can hear his voice."

It was not till half an hour later, after the doctor had reported no bones broken and only minor injury to the knee, that Kate Rathlyn went off to ' ' see to ' Anne Faery. She did not find her. It had not taken Anne

long to realise that she was not wanted and, her first
interest being the horses, she had gone out to the stables
and had a talk with Penny. The head groom had at once
arranged for a car to take her and a groom to Raddlett's
farm, from which the groom would ride and lead the
horses home while Miss Faery was taken on to her home.
Ben Penny even saw to it that she had a cup of tea and a
piece of cake before she went.

                    .   .   .   .

Dr. Jennerel had ordained that Charles should stay in
bed, have a good dinner and later take something to make
him sleep. Kate knew that Isabel Wey had some Dormonal tablets, as she suffered from insomnia. The
doctor had pricked up his ears at that, declared that Miss
Wey was not his patient but that Dormonal would do
provided that not more than two—repeat two—were
taken.

Charles disliked the idea, but did as he was told, and by
ten o'clock was in a deep sleep. When he woke he felt
heavy and his knee was throbbing. The room was in
darkness but yet not quite dark; he realised that the door
was open and a faint light was coming through it. He
put out his hand and found that Kate was not beside him.

The luminous hands of his watch showed that it was
half-past two. He began to doze, woke again with a
start and saw that ten minutes had passed. Kate was still
not there. Where on earth could she be? Then a
sound outside caught his ear—a footstep; she was coming
back, wherever she had been. But she did not come into
the room, and again a footstep, perhaps on a loose board,
sounded as far away as before. Charles began to feel
worried; he slipped out of bed and hobbled painfully
to the door. What he saw made his heart miss a beat.

The main staircase at Tandrings rises from the hall in a
noble sweep and reaches a landing and a gallery which

runs round three sides of the 'well' so formed. On to this gallery the doors of bedrooms open, while passages run from it to the wings. A low balustrade, of beautifully worked iron with oaken handrail, guards—rather inadequately—this gallery, and lest any stranger should blunder over it in the dark a light is always left burning in the hall below. By this light Charles now saw that his wife, in her nightgown only, was walking quietly up and down the gallery, her fingers just touching the handrail and re-seeking it each time she turned.

Something about her appearance frightened Charles; she was staring straight in front of her, her face expressionless; when he moved forward out of the doorway, though she was coming towards him at the time, she did not look at him. With a shock he realised that she was asleep.

Charles did not know what to do. He had heard, or read, that it was dangerous to wake a sleep-walker. And yet . . . he had always thought that balustrade dangerously low; if she leant over it she might fall straight down on to the stone flags of the hall below. He shuddered at the thought. Should he go and meet her, guide her back to bed? Call to her? He might startle her, cause her to fall. Should he . . .?

With a gasp of relief he saw her turn the corner of the gallery and walk towards the door of their room. He stole back into it and she followed him in, shutting the door quietly behind her. It was quite dark in the room now and he could only tell of her movement by the sound; he heard the bed creak under her weight and crept into it himself, lay there quietly, listening to her untroubled breathing. Presently he slipped out of bed again, locked the door, and put the key under his pillow.

In the morning he was awakened by his wife shaking him.

"Charles! Did you lock the door? Have you got the key? Alice can't get in."

Ashamed of himself for over-sleeping, Charles produced the key, muttering: "Tell you later". Kate unlocked the door and got back into bed, while the young housemaid brought in the tea, drew back the curtains and, after what seemed an age of fiddling about the room, withdrew.

"Well, what on earth?" Kate was staring at him.

Charles would have liked to have a talk with Dr. Jennerel first, but he knew it was no good beating about the bush.

"My dear, I think you were walking in your sleep last night."

Kate's face cleared.

"Oh, that," she said; "I've done that all my life—or so I'm told. Not much since I grew up—which was lucky, because it's apt to lead to misunderstanding," she added with a laugh. "What did I do?"

"You walked up and down that gallery outside there."

Kate stared at him.

"What on earth did I do that for?"

"I don't know, dear; but it scared the life out of me."

Kate's eyes softened.

"Did it, darling? Bless you; that's sweet of you."

She put her bare arms round his neck and drew him down to her. It was not unpleasant, but rather over-powering. A tea-cup slid on to the floor and smashed.

"Oh dear," exclaimed Kate; "I suppose it is rather late in the morning for love's young dream. And I've never asked about you; how did you sleep? Did I wake you? How is your knee?"

CHAPTER VI

Gerry was Right

CHARLES COULD not take that sleep-walking as lightly as Kate appeared to. He questioned her closely about it, and gathered that while she had done it fairly often when she was quite young, it had not been of a serious nature and she had generally woken up of her own accord. She had apparently grown out of it, because she could only remember the same thing happening once or twice after—quite soon after—she was married.

" Must be something about matrimony that makes me walk o' nights," she added with a rather girlish giggle.

Charles ignored this.

" Who else knows about this? "

" Oh, no one except Nannie Tass."

" Mrs. Tass? Your housekeeper? "

" Yes; she was my Nannie, you know."

" But Dr. Jennerel; doesn't he know? "

" Oh no; there has never been any need to tell him. It's not an illness, you know; just a sort of trick."

Charles was not so sure of that. He was silent for a time, then asked:

" Does nobody else in your present household know? Are you sure? Isabel Wey, for instance? "

Kate looked at him sharply.

" Certainly not. Why should she? Why do you ask about her? "

Charles hesitated.

" Kate, what exactly is Isabel? I can't make out if she's a maid or a secretary or what."

Kate laughed.

" I suppose it is rather a vague arrangement," she said.

" She was my maid for five or six years. Somehow I never could get into the way of calling a maid—a lady's-maid—by her surname, which is the proper thing to do. Something in it really, I expect, because the relationship is rather close . . . rather intimate; one is liable, perhaps, to get on too familiar terms. Perhaps that was what happened with me and Isabel; I got very fond of her, and I got into the way of letting her do all sorts of things for me, till she gradually became what she is now—more of a secretary, really. The rest of the staff don't like it, of course; Philip, in particular, hates it. He thinks he ought to be my personal as well as my business secretary, but I should never like that. I trust him, but he's terribly strait-laced; I should always feel that he was disapproving of me. . . ."

Kate checked herself and looked at Charles.

" Not now, darling, of course; nothing he could disapprove of now that I'm a respectable married woman again."

They laughed, and the subject was changed, but Charles was not quite easy in his mind. There was something odd about that girl; was it a sort of slyness? She was quiet and, as far as he had seen, respectful, but she sometimes had a look in her eye that was . . . what was it? mocking? knowing? Charles wondered whether she could possibly have some sort of hold over Kate. It couldn't be anything bad—not anything like blackmail—because Kate quite evidently liked her. Anyhow, it was no business of his. But now that she was married to him no one was going to blackmail Kate, whatever she might have done.

Kate absolutely forbade him to talk to Dr. Jennerel about her sleep-walking; she said that he was an old gossip and that she did not trust him not to tell other people and she might be laughed at. She agreed to his asking Mrs. Tass about it, because ' Nannie ' would not talk. So Charles hobbled off to the housekeeper's room one morning and found that formidable old lady sitting straight up at a table, checking lists of some kind. Not really old, perhaps; Charles thought about sixty-five; but remarkably like the pictures of Queen Victoria in the later years of her reign. After polite enquiries into Mrs. Tass's health, which met with little response, Charles plunged into the object of his visit. He was worried about Mrs. Rathlyn's sleep-walking and would like to know anything Mrs. Tass could tell him about it.

The housekeeper showed some signs of being human.

" Dear, dear," she said; " is she doing that again? I didn't know nothing about it."

Charles told her what had happened on the night of his accident.

" I expect your being hurt upset her, Captain Rathlyn. She used to walk a bit when she was quite young; never came to any harm. We all thought she'd grown out of it. Then it happened once or twice again after she was married to Mr. Waygold. Some sort of excitement I made it out to be that caused it. She wouldn't go to a doctor about it, and it never did her any harm that I could see. I don't think you've any cause to worry about it, sir."

Charles hesitated; curiosity urged him to poke his nose into that other problem.

"Would anyone else know about it, do you suppose, Mrs. Tass? In this household, I mean? Miss Wey, perhaps? " (What ought he to call the damn girl, talking to the housekeeper. Miss Wey? Isabel?)

Mrs. Tass sniffed.

" I don't see why she should know anything, sir. Not without Mrs. Rathlyn told her. She's said nothing to me."

The housekeeper's manner was frigid now. Charles decided to draw off his hounds from this cold scent. In any case, there seemed to be nothing more that he could do about the matter, and as time passed it ceased to worry him.

The damage to Charles's knee had not proved serious and he was soon about again, but Dr. Jennerel had advised him not to ride for a month or so—certainly not to hunt. That was disappointing, in a way—a way which Charles was careful not to examine very closely. He and Kate had driven over to see the Faerys on the Sunday following his fall, to thank Anne for her help and—on the part of Kate—to apologise for neglecting her on that occasion.

The visit fell rather flat. Anne was her usual quiet self and made nothing of the help or the neglect. It was the first time Charles had seen her not in riding-kit and he realised how attractive she looked in a skirt—which is not always the case with women who look so well in a saddle. Charles did not see much of her, Captain Faery monopolising him and inevitably taking him round the stables to admire the horses, of whom he hoped that Captain and Mrs. Rathlyn might buy one or two. Charles did just manage to snatch one moment alone with Anne, to thank her warmly and to tell her how much he was going to miss their hunts together. His heart, for some reason, beat a little faster when he saw the girl's brown eyes light up with pleasure, but Kate was calling to him from the car, so he had to go.

Soon after this it occurred to Kate that it would do them both good to have a glimpse of sunshine and some fun in the south of France—at Cap St. Baise, where they had spent their honeymoon. The currency restrictions, of course, were impossible, ridiculous, but Kate had friends there who would make everything easy—for a fortnight, at any rate. They could manage that and still be back in time for the Royal Cup, in which Silver Eagle was to run again; Ballnaceach was being reserved for the National.

It was lovely at St. Baise. The sun shone warmly, there were amusing people to talk to, plenty to drink, delicious food, cards, roulette; money proved to be no problem. They even danced, though Charles's stiff and still slightly painful knee made that amusement no great joy for him; Kate loved dancing, but she was no light weight and was no better balanced on her feet than in a saddle.

Kate enjoyed every moment of it. She was deeply in love with her husband, in love with being in love again at forty-six, no—forty-seven now. She wrapped him in her warm affection and saw to it that he was never dull, never alone. She had been touched by the anxiety and sympathy he had shown to her over that sleep-walking; she felt that he must really love her—as he assured her that he did. She decided to be perfectly frank with him about the future. After all, she was a few years older than him, and it was only fair to him that he should know what he might expect if she were to predecease him.

She told him that it appeared to her right that the bulk of her late husband's money should remain in, or rather return to, his family. Most of it would go to Terry's brother, George Waygold, as residuary legatee; he was not really much of a chap, but he was a Waygold. She hoped Charles would understand what she felt about that. But Charles himself would have her horses, both hunters and racehorses, and some capital.

" Not much, Charlie dear, but you will be comfortable and you will be able to keep my colours flying."

Charles winced. He hated diminutives—Charlie, Katie, Annie; they set his teeth on edge. But he was grateful for Kate's consideration, for her generosity. As for

what might come to him if he survived her, that hardly
need be thought about now; there is no reason to worry
about death when one is still in the forties.

What did worry him was that his early, nagging fears
looked like being realised. Kate was drinking more;
not, he thought, because she was unhappy or needed
stimulant, but from habit, perhaps inherited habit. And
out here, in the brittle gaiety of this, to him, unnatural
life, she was matching the gaiety—and that largely meant
the alcohol consumption—of those about her. She did
not become maudlin or tiresome, but even in these two
short weeks she had deteriorated: she looked an older
woman, her skin had lost its softness, her eyes their clear-
ness; her temper, too, was shorter than he had ever known
it. None of this impaired her affection for him; indeed
she tended to overwhelm him with love, and there were
uncomfortable moments when he found himself shrinking
from her embraces. Her flushed face, the taint of gin
in her breath, repelled him; try as he would, he could
not always feel for her now the love that she asked for.

Charles Rathlyn found himself thinking more and more
often of the happy days he had spent hunting in the early
part of the winter; the open-air life, the exhilaration of a
good gallop, of fences cleanly jumped. He thought of the
girl who had hunted with him, so young and slim, so
simple and unaffected. There would swim into his vision
that small face, rather white, with anxiety in the brown
eyes looking down at him as he lay, shaken and hurt, by
the broken rails. With bitter doubt Charles began to
wonder whether his old friend Gerry Fanthony had not
been right.

But the fortnight ended, and with infinite relief Charles
found himself back in the cold, damp atmosphere of
hunting England. He decided that he must pull himself
together, pull the marriage together—and that meant

doing something about Kate and her drinking. The
result was their first quarrel. Charles had tried to
approach the matter with delicacy and tact, but those
feeble flowers wilted before the anger of a shocked and
offended woman. Nobody had ever before suggested to
Kate that she should mind or mend her ways; it had never
occurred to her that she was drinking too much; that
such a thing should now be said to her by . . .

They made up their quarrel. Kate even admitted that
there might be something, not much, in what Charles had
said. Secretly, she had a good look at herself in the glass,
and was shocked and frightened by what she saw there.
Was she getting *old*? Might she even be in danger of
losing Charles's love? Not being a very clever woman,
she reacted by loading him still further with her affection.
But their relations were never quite the same again;
there was no longer complete trust.

Charles's knee was now quite all right again—as right
as it ever would be. He could not resist the temptation
to have another hunt or two before the season ended, if
only for the sake of Dashalong and Robin. Primrose had
continued to get her hunt a week, ridden by Anne Faery.
He rang up Anne and told her that he was coming too next
Wednesday; the pleasure in her voice as she replied
warmed his heart.

When he told Kate that he was going to hunt again she
was not at all pleased. Surely, she said, it was silly to
risk damaging himself again so late in the season; why
not wait till next season, when she hoped to accompany
him? He spoke about Dashalong and Robin, not
mentioning Anne. On the Tuesday night she suddenly
asked about Primrose, and he was obliged to tell her that,
as arranged a long time ago, the mare was hunted every
Wednesday by Anne Faery; yes, presumably she would be
going tomorrow. The meet was some way off and Penny

was boxing the horses over; he would either himself go in the horse-box or follow in the small car.

Kate said no more, but Charles noticed her expression freeze up, her mouth set in a sullen line. When morning came he dressed early, went out to the stables and settled with Ben the details of where the box would meet him; he had decided to go himself by car. Then he went in to breakfast, and was just finishing his porridge when the door opened and Kate came in. To his astonishment, she was in her hunting habit and stock, a thin yellow cardigan over her silk shirt. She looked extremely handsome. But Charles was not thinking of her looks; as he stared his thoughts raced.

" My dear! Are you . . . are you coming? "

She flashed him a brilliant smile.

" Looks like it, darling. Are you pleased? "

He took a quick pull at himself.

" Of course I am; I'm delighted. But . . . you haven't ridden for so long; ought you to start with a hunt? "

" Oh, I shan't stay out long. I shall be sure that you don't stay too long either."

" Well, that's grand. I'd better just ring through and warn Anne Faery that she won't be wanted."

By some unlucky chance the Faery telephone was out of order that morning, so Charles had to drive his wife to the meet knowing that Anne would be there, expecting a hunt on Primrose. Although it was a business arrangement, he felt that she might be disappointed. Sure enough, near the cross-roads a mile from the meet, where several horse-boxes, including that from Tandrings, were waiting, there was the little Morris with Anne sitting by herself at the driving-wheel. Charles drove his car well past it, stopped near the horse-box and walked back towards the Morris. Anne did not notice him until he came up and bent down to the window; he saw her face light up with welcome, but he checked her as she opened the door.

" Anne, I'm so sorry—don't get out. It's off, our hunt together. My wife is going to ride Primrose."

" Oh ! "

The smile faded from her face.

" Oh, I am sorry. But, of course, that's splendid—that Mrs. Rathlyn is going to hunt again."

Charles felt his own disappointment deepen; deepen to something like misery.

" Anne, I am so disappointed."

She did not answer, but bent her head to pick up a glove. He saw a glint of tears, and in a flash he knew what had happened; to his mingled consternation and joy he realised that he was in love. He longed to take the girl in his arms and tell her so, but it was impossible for him to do that—wrong, in any case, and especially impossible here, in public, with her sitting in a car and him outside it. He slipped his arm through the window, put his hand on hers and squeezed it gently. Then he turned away and walked back towards the horse-box. As he went, he heard the self-starter of her car and then the car moving off, the sound dwindling into the distance.

Kate was already in the saddle when he got back; she moved off without waiting for him, and he did not catch up with her till they were approaching the meet. Then she smiled brightly at him and broke into a chatter of one-sided conversation, presently greeting others at the meet with quite unusual gaiety. Charles did not want to talk; his mind was in a whirl—as well it might be, for a man of forty-one who has suddenly realised himself, for the first time, to be in love.

Hounds drew blank at the first covert and there was a long hack to the next—a big wood which took a long time

to draw. Charles had remained punctiliously beside his
wife throughout, and now she suddenly turned to him and
said:

" Oh, Charles, this is such a bore and my back's
hurting. Let's go home."

He looked at her in astonishment.

" But . . . the horses have had no sort of exercise.
Primrose is all right, of course; she's been hunted
regularly and she's got manners. But old Dashalong is
mad fresh."

It was true enough. The big bay horse had been on his
toes ever since Charles mounted him. Now, suddenly,
there was a long blast on the horn and the field was
instantly in motion. Dashalong sprang away with the
rest and Charles could not check him; he could only fling
a ' Come along ' over his shoulder. He managed to pick
an easy place at the first fence, but he could not slow his
horse; when at last he was able to do so and looked round,
Kate and Primrose were nowhere to be seen. He waited,
with Dashalong fighting for his head; then one of the tail-
enders lumbering past called out to him: " Looking for
your wife? She's gone back on to the road. She's all
right."

With a shrug of the shoulders Charles Rathlyn let
Dashalong have his head and they galloped on after the
receding hunt. When it was over—a point of two or three
miles—he rode slowly back to where they left the box.
It was there, with Primrose already inside; their car, with
Kate, was gone. He did not question the groom but,
boxing up, himself drove the heavy vehicle home. He
knew that he must apologise for going on alone, and he
wanted to get it done before going up to have his bath.
Ludd told him that Mrs. Rathlyn was in her sitting-room.

Kate had already changed into a cocktail frock, much
smarter than she usually wore on such occasions. She was

heavily made up, and even across the room Charles was conscious of a heady, exotic scent. She was on the sofa, with her feet up, but when he came in she swung them to the floor and walked across to the fire.

" I'm so sorry, dear . . ." he began.

She swung round on him, her eyes blazing with anger.

"What the hell do you mean leaving me alone like that? I know what sort of a game you have been playing; I saw you with that little ——"

Charles stood aghast, as his wife poured out a stream of abuse and accusation against him, against Anne, using language that he had never heard her use before—dating back, perhaps subconsciously, to the early original Jo Hillburn. At first he tried to check her, but for a full minute she went on, screaming at him, fury in her voice and eyes. Then suddenly she stopped with a gasp.

"Oh darling, don't look at me like that! Oh, what have I been saying? Oh, forgive me, darling." She flung her arms round his neck. " Oh, love me, Charlie, love me! I've got no one in the world but you."

Charles put his arms round her and gently patted her shoulder, but the expression on his face, as he looked past her, was hard and grim.

CHAPTER VII

Mediterranean Autumn

NOTHING SEEMED to go right for them now. Silver
Eagle fell at the third fence in the Royal Cup, and in the
National Ballnaceach was knocked over by a loose horse
at the ' Chair ', second time round, with only one in front
of him. That would have been all in the game if they had
been in reasonably good spirits, but Kate was moody and
irritable and Charles was not helping her. He had seen
nothing of Anne since that last hunt, except for a few
minutes in front of a thousand eyes at Shankesbury,
when they could speak to each other only as casual friends.
For all he knew, that might be all she really thought of
him; the ' glint of tears ' might have been pure imagination on his part—or a cold in her head. That thought did
nothing to cheer him.

Then came another blow; Jack Herris, Kate's trainer,
suddenly died, within a few days of the opening of the flat-
race season. Neither Kate nor Charles liked what they
knew of the man who was taking over the establishment,
and Charles had to go to Newmarket to interview a
couple of trainers whom they had in mind, then to
London for business with Weatherbys, with a bank, a
solicitor—and he might as well see the osteopath who had
done a good deal for his knee in the past. It would mean
two, if not three nights in London; Kate was not coming,
as she was out of sorts.

On the way through London Charles suddenly had an
idea. He had the Faerys' telephone number in his diary
and, ringing up, he was lucky enough to get through to
Anne.

" Anne, this is Charles Rathlyn. Look, I've got to be

in London for a few days—I'm there now. Would you care to come up and do a show. I know you've got an aunt in Chelsea or somewhere."

He heard a little gasp of surprise; there was a moment's pause and then:

"Oh, yes; yes, I'd like to, Captain Rathlyn. I've got to come up and get some summer clothes, anyhow. We've about finished roughing off."

They fixed it up and Charles rang off, his heart feeling ridiculously light and with scarcely a twinge upon his conscience. After all, there was an aunt in Chelsea.

When the evening came he collected her from Cheyne Row, took her to a 'musical' and then to the Berkeley, where they had supper and danced. Dancing with feather-weight Anne was a very different business from the tugging round that he had had to do at Cap St. Baise. In her semi-evening dress she looked lovely, thought poor Charles, who had hardly thought of her looks before. They were happy together, said nothing to one another that might not have been said before a thousand ears, and when he deposited her on her aunt's doorstep at a not unreasonable hour she thanked him as any girl would thank a man older than herself who has given her a pleasant evening. He held her hand, perhaps, just two seconds longer than was necessary, and when she turned away to unlock the door he felt such a wave of longing surge over him that it was all he could do not to spring forward and take her in his arms. A moment later, with a final wave of the hand, she disappeared and the door was gently closed.

As he walked away, lonely and miserable, he cursed himself for his folly in linking himself to a woman he did not love. Nothing but misery could be ahead now— misery for himself, misery—he feared—for Kate. He had been prepared—for the sake of the security and comfort she gave him—to face the ordinary wear and tear of a loveless married life; had been prepared to give her all that he had to give—friendship, affection perhaps, all the protection that a man can give a woman; to do his utmost not to let her know that he did not really love her at all. But that was when he had only himself to think of, when he was completely heart-whole, when he was 'not interested in girls'. Now he had fallen deeply in love with a girl who seemed to him exactly to fulfil all that a man could hope for in a wife—a girl genuine, simple, capable, sweet in nature and appearance; he even dared to believe that she might—if he had been free to court her—have come to care for him, to give him the lifelong happiness that such a love can give.

And this he had thrown away for . . . security! . . . comfort! God help him, what a mockery! And how rightly was he now to be punished for his selfishness. Anne! Anne!—her name rang with his footsteps on the deserted pavements. He pulled himself up with a start. What nonsense he was talking—thinking; if he had not married Kate he would never even have met Anne; there would have been no Primrose for her to ride, Dashalong would have been sold along with the rest of his steeplechasers. He might, of course, have met her racing; she had told him that she went to any meeting within reach if she could get the day off. And she had been at Shankesbury and seen Silver Eagle's fatal stumble at the last fence; had even wanted—though of course would never have dared—to tell him how she sympathised with his disappointment. She had known him by sight, then, had felt some interest in him, however impersonal; that might have . . .

So Charles's thoughts flogged on, as he strode down the King's Road and eventually picked up a homing taxi to take him to his club. He spent a restless night, and on the morrow returned to Tandrings, to tell Kate what he had arranged about her horses and to try and counterfeit pleasure in being with her again. He tried his best, but from now on his impersonation of a happy married man did not ring true. Kate sensed it soon enough, and her unhappiness drove her to accentuate everything that he most disliked—her cloying affection, her drinking, her bursts of suspicion and jealousy. Quickly the breach widened, till everyone in the household must have been aware of it; even the normally unimaginative Gerry, down for a week-end before Ascot, saw that something was badly wrong, but had not the heart to question his friend.

Two good wins at Ascot did something to raise everybody's spirits. Seeing no more of Anne, Charles wondered momentarily whether it would be possible to forget her. For a few days he would flog himself into that belief, then the longing for her would close down on him again and the effort to be pleasant with Kate, to laugh off her accusations, to accept her embraces, almost drove him to distraction.

The weeks passed, Goodwood came and went, the anniversary of their wedding day approached (could it really be only a year?). Kate had talked again of the South of France. She had not attempted to ride again during the summer and he had not encouraged her to. She even thought of selling her race-horses. Why should they not make a complete break? While they were young enough, why not travel, see the world, perhaps stay for a year in New Zealand . . . ?

Listening, Charles felt the blood congeal in his veins. He knew it was exactly what was needed, the one thing that might break his infatuation for Anne, save his marriage with Kate . . . he could not face it. Winter was coming; the hunting season would be on them in a month or two—cub-hunting was here now. Even though he was sure that Kate would not again agree to Anne riding Primrose, Anne would be out, riding her father's horses. He would see her every time he hunted himself; Kate could not stop him doing that, however much she might try. No, by God, she couldn't. . . .

. . . . .

One day late in September Kate told him that her brother-in-law, George Waygold, was coming for the week-end. This, Charles knew, was the brother-in-law, her only one, to whom Kate was willing back the bulk of her late husband's estate. He felt some curiosity to see the man. Kate's description of him was frank and uncomplimentary.

"George is just a wet," she said. "He's never done a thing worth doing in his life—not even get married and raise a family. The old man—their father—had such a poor opinion of him that he left everything to Terry and asked him just to keep George out of the workhouse. Terry was very generous to him in his lifetime, and though he left most of his money to me, he did leave George enough to keep him in reasonable comfort. He hoped that George might some day marry and settle down."

Charles saw tears well into Kate's still handsome eyes; they did that all too easily these days. She dabbed them with a handkerchief.

"Poor Terry; he did so want to have a family himself, to carry on the name. He was proud of the Waygolds, even though all the money came from his mother. Somehow, we didn't have one—I don't know whose fault it was. And then he was killed. And now there's only George. So you see . . . we must get him married somehow, Charles; find a nice girl for him. With the money he'll have some girl will take him—if we let it be known that he'll have money. He's not bad-looking."

He was not bad-looking. Indeed, Charles thought that he was not at all unlike the handsome Terry Waygold whose face he had seen looking at him out of a large silver frame in the study before he married Kate. Before he married Kate! Oh God, how that thought tugged at Charles's heart now.

Good-looking, like his brother; but though the jaw was prominent, the mouth was weak, the fair hair was thinning, though he was little over fifty, the blue eyes were shifty and tended to fall before a steady gaze. He came on the Friday evening—it was 24th September, to be exact— and after a day walking up partridges on the Saturday retired with Kate to her sitting-room after tea. While they were dressing for dinner—Kate liked Charles to leave the connecting door to his dressing-room open so that they could gossip—she told him that it was the usual story.

"Poor old George is in trouble again. He will play poker; fancies himself at it, and of course he's just a pigeon. They rook him. You've only got to look at him to see that. Now he's given out a lot of I.O.U.s and I shall have to pay them off—can't let the name of Waygold stink at—— whatever the club is that he plays at. But Charles, dear, there's something good coming out of it, I believe. One of these friends he plays with—a very rich man, he says—has got a yacht, and he's arranging a Mediterranean cruise this autumn—all over the Mediterranean, just strolling about, he calls it; perhaps going even further than that if they feel like it. George believes he could get us invited. We might have to pay some of the expenses; that would be only reasonable, as we don't know the man. It's just exactly what I've always wanted to do—and now especially, just as we've been talking about it. If I pay George's debts . . ."

Charles had only listened with half an ear at first, but

soon his fingers dropped from the tie that he was tying and
he stood in front of the mirror, staring at his own white,
set face.

     .   .   .   .   .

Isabel Wey was sleeping badly that night—Sunday
night, the 26th September, a date she was not likely to
forget. She often slept badly and, as Kate Rathlyn had
told Dr. Jennerel, she had a bottle of Dormonal tablets,
prescribed for her by her landlady's doctor when she was
on holiday, which usually did the trick. But Isabel was a
girl—a woman; she was over thirty now—of considerable
strength of character. She knew perfectly well that
sleeping tablets of the hypnotic group could become
dangerous enemies if treated as too dear a friend. She
used them only rarely, as a last resort; normally, if she
lay awake or woke in the night, she could get to sleep in
time—it needed time—by reading, by making herself a
hot drink, by re-filling her hot-water bottle, sometimes
even by taking a hot bath. She was *not* going to make
herself a slave to any drug.

This Sunday night she woke at three o'clock, and after
ten restless minutes switched on her light, reached out for
her book . . . then with an ejaculation of annoyance
remembered that she had finished it before turning out her
light. There was another she was interested in—Hartley's
latest—down in Philip Monner's office, in which, by one
of the odd arrangements in this unusual household, she
had her supper in company with him and sat afterwards
if she felt inclined. With a shrug of annoyance she rolled
out of bed, put on dressing-gown and slippers and went
out into the passage. The shortest way for her was down
the back stairs, but . . . Isabel did not often use the front
stairs and it sometimes amused her to do so—pandered to
her imagination— when it could be done with no one to
criticise her. No one would see her, criticise her, at three

o'clock in the morning; there would be no need to switch on lights—that light in the hall was always burning. She walked along the passage from her room, seeing the dim light ahead; came out on to the gallery above the hall. Suddenly she noticed that the door of Mrs. Rathlyn's bedroom was open. She checked, drawing back; then some instinct made her steal forward and look over the balustrade.

What she saw made her heart bound; she shrank back, then stole forward again and peeped cautiously down into the hall. A man was kneeling there, almost below her but not quite, a man in pyjamas; it was Captain Rathlyn. He was bending over something on the floor—a heap of something—of clothes? Isabel knew quite well what it was; it was the body of his wife.

CHAPTER VIII

Rather Surprising

CHARLES RATHLYN withdrew his hand from his wife's heart, stood up and, after a moment's hesitation, walked to the telephone which stood on a table near one of the big windows. Presently Isabel Wey, crouching on the landing, could hear his voice, curt but calm.

"That you, doctor? This is Charles Rathlyn. Could you come over to Tandrings at once, please? My wife has had a fall and she is very seriously hurt; I think her neck is broken, or her back. Yes, I am afraid so. Thank you very much. No, I won't try to move her till you come."

He rang off, picked up a photograph frame that was on the table and, going back to his wife, held the glass before her lips. Looking at it, he shook his head. Then he stood looking down at her for a moment. She lay on her back, her head and neck at an awkward angle: her eyes were open, but there was no sign of life in them. Then he walked across to the fireplace and pressed the bell, in a series of long bursts; it rang in the pantry and Ludd, a bachelor, slept in a snug little room next door. Looking down at him, Isabel could not see his face clearly; it was white but expressionless. After what seemed an age but was probably little more than a minute, Ludd appeared, in trousers and dressing-gown. He looked at Captain Rathlyn, who said quietly:

"Ludd, I'm sorry to say that your mistress has had a very serious accident."

He walked back to where his wife lay, and Ludd gasped in horror as he saw the still body on the floor.

"Oh, sir! Is she . . . should we try and carry her up to her bed, sir?"

Charles shook his head.

" If she is alive it might do her serious harm to move her, inexpertly. Help me put these rugs round her— very gently. I have sent for Dr. Jennerel. He may want some help."

" Shall I call Mr. George, sir? "

" Good God, no. Go and wake Miss Wey and tell her to get dressed. If the doctor wants her we will send for her. Then bring me my dressing-gown and slippers."

Isabel slid back from the balustrade, behind which she had been crouching; silently she sped back down the passage, slipped into bed and turned out the light. She lay there in darkness, her heart pounding; then presently Ludd's measured footsteps and a knock on her door.

" Miss Wey! Miss Wey!! Are you awake? "

Isabel lay still. The door opened a crack.

" Miss Wey! Oh, Miss Wey, the Captain says will you please get dressed and be ready to come down if wanted? Mrs. Rathlyn has had an accident and the doctor is coming."

Isabel switched on her reading lamp, nodded to Ludd, who closed the door and padded off down the passage. Shivering with excitement, Isabel slid out of bed and began to dress.

Down in the hall Charles Rathlyn was standing by the empty fireplace, his hands deep in the pockets of his dressing-gown. He wanted desperately to smoke a cigarette, to drink a strong whisky and soda, but he refrained. Presently there was the sound of a car outside and Charles opened the front door, admitting Dr. Jennerel. The tubby little man, usually so cheerful, had drawn a mask of solemnity over his face. He walked across to the body of Kate Rathlyn and, kneeling down, made his examination. When he had finished he joined Charles, who was now sitting on the club fender, in front of the empty fireplace. He sat down, too, and put his hand on Charles's shoulder.

" I think I needn't tell you that she is gone," he said gently. " Tell me about it."

Charles continued to stare at the floor in front of him, the stone floor, covered here by a Persian rug.

" You didn't know about her sleep-walking, did you? "

" Sleep-walking? Mrs. Wayg . . . Mrs. Rathlyn? "

Charles nodded. He told of what had happened on the night of his hunting accident eight months ago, of what his wife had told him, and Mrs. Tass.

" Didn't know a thing about it. And that happened again tonight? "

" Yes. I woke up and found her gone, and when I went out on to the landing she was leaning over the balustrade. I don't know whether she heard me, or whether she woke up, but she suddenly seemed to slip and toppled over."

Charles Rathlyn shuddered.

" The sound of the fall was awful. I shall never forget it."

Dr. Jennerel patted the shoulder on which his hand rested.

" You should have told me—about her sleep-walking, I mean. I might have been able to help her."

" She wouldn't let me. She said . . . she didn't want what she called a fuss. I let her persuade me."

" Yes. Well, there it is. They don't often hurt themselves, but sometimes it happens—like this."

He stood up, paced once or twice across the hall, then sat down again.

" You know, Rathlyn, that there will have to be an inquest; that's inevitable. It would have been easier if I had known about the sleep-walking. I shall have to ring up the police. I think it will be better if I get straight on

to Colonel Netterly—the Chief Constable—now. He will **have** to know at once, and you don't want that fat fool Sergeant Danding blundering round with his silly questions. Do you think . . ."

The door from the back regions opened and Ludd, fully dressed, came in, bearing a tray of steaming hot coffee and biscuits.

" Bless the man; just what I was going to ask for," said Jennerel. "And when you've drunk yours, Rathlyn, get upstairs and dress. There'll be no more sleep for you tonight, I'm afraid."

They drank their coffee, and when Charles had gone upstairs to dress, Dr. Jennerel went through into the study, where he knew there was another telephone, and had a talk with the Chief Constable. The two men knew each other well, and it was not necessary to say much; Colonel Netterly said that he would be along in half an hour and ' bring somebody with him '. Jennerel had made no attempt to move the body of Mrs. Rathlyn from where it lay, and Charles had not suggested it.

. . . .

Colonel John Netterly was one of the last of the old-fashioned type of Chief Constable; a regular soldier— an ex-gunner—who had had a spell of police experience in India and had been selected by the Barryshire Standing Joint Committee as their Chief Constable directly after the close of the Second World War. He was now fifty-three years old, had a quiet manner, and was generally liked and respected in the county. As Charles Rathlyn had noticed when he first met him out hunting, he was middle-sized, thin, and had a hooked nose and dark moustache. He had his own ideas about police-work and had done a good deal to bring the Barryshire force up to date since he joined it, including the development of a C.I.D. branch of its own.

When he arrived at Tandrings that Monday morning in late September he left his two companions in the car and was at once admitted by Ludd, who had been on the lookout for him. Charles Rathlyn had remained up in his dressing-room, but presently came down and joined Colonel Netterly and Dr. Jennerel in the study. The Chief Constable offered his sincere condolences and explained why it was necessary for the police to appear in the matter.

"There has to be a formal enquiry when any sudden, accidental death takes place. The Coroner, of course, holds the enquiry, but the police have to provide him with whatever evidence he considers necessary. We shall do our best to make it as little distressing as possible for you, Rathlyn, but I am sure that, as an old soldier, you will know the sort of thing that has to be done."

Charles nodded.

"Of course; I understand that perfectly," he said. "I don't know how much the doctor has told you already —I am quite ready to go over it again."

"He has just given me an outline, but may I now call in the two senior officers I brought over with me? It is their job really, not mine. I thought it better to cut out the earlier stages—the local constable, sergeant and so on."

He went out and returned with the two police officers, one in uniform and one in plain clothes.

"This is Superintendent Binnerton," he said, indicating the uniformed man, "and this Superintendent Hant. If I may, I will leave them here now and return later in the morning. Binnerton will want a word with you, doctor; no doubt Captain Rathlyn won't mind if he takes you first, and then you can get away. You've got your car, of course? Is there some room my officers can use, Rathlyn? I don't want to monopolise your study."

So the solemn business of routine questioning went on —in Charles's study because that, after all, caused least inconvenience to the household and had a telephone. Superintendent Binnerton did the questioning, and if it turned out that ' routine ' was all that was necessary, the case would remain in his capable and experienced hands. He was the Superintendent in charge of the Division in which Tandrings lay. The man in plain clothes was, in fact, Detective-Superintendent Hant, head of the C.I.D. of Barryshire, working directly under the Chief Constable. Colonel Netterly had not mentioned that word ' detective ' when introducing him; it had an ugly, ominous ring which he wanted to spare the bereaved man if it proved reasonably possible to spare him. But Hant should be there, using his ears—and his very observant pair of eyes.

Dr. Jennerel told Superintendent Binnerton that Mrs. Rathlyn's neck was certainly broken and that that was presumably the cause of death. There was also a fracture of the skull. Neither man thought it necessary to enlarge on that answer at the moment; Binnerton knew well that the experienced doctor would make quite sure that the fall and the broken neck were not just a cover for some other form of death; he would also look for marks which might indicate violence before the fall. The police have an uncomfortable habit of not taking things at their face value; Dr. Jennerel knew all about that.

" This sleep-walking, doctor; I understand you mentioned something about that to the Chief on the phone."

" I did. You mustn't take what I say as evidence. Captain Rathlyn told me this morning that he had found his wife walking in her sleep some months ago—in January, I think; it was the night after he had a bad fall out hunting. He thinks she must have been doing the same thing tonight."

" You think that possible, doctor?   That she fell while sleep-walking, I mean."

Jennerel hesitated.

" It's possible, certainly," he said.   " I suppose one must say that that is probably what happened.   On the other hand, it does rather surprise me; people who walk in their sleep are generally very sure-footed, well-balanced —their physical balance is good, I mean.   I should have expected her to walk along a passage, up or down stairs, without stumbling."

" I haven't had a chance to look round, sir.   Is Mrs. Rathlyn's bedroom far from the top of the stairs? "

" No; her room opens directly on to the gallery near the top of the stairs."

" Then she might have walked straight out of her room on to the gallery and knocked into the balustrade and fallen straight over? "

" From the position of her room, yes.   That could well have happened."

" But you are surprised that it did? "

That question came from Detective-Superintendent Hant, who had clearly had some difficulty in keeping his mouth shut so long.   Dr. Jennerel looked at him.

" I wouldn't go so far as to say 'surprised'," he answered quietly.   " If she was walking in her sleep, in such familiar surroundings, I should have expected her to turn to right or left when she came out of her room and either go along the passage or down the stairs."

Hant relapsed into silence and the big, grizzled Binnerton took up the story.

" This previous sleep-walking in January; you were told about this at the time, I suppose? "

" No," said Dr. Jennerel curtly.

Both policemen stiffened slightly, as a pointer stiffens when it becomes aware of the presence of game.

" No, doctor? "

" Not a thing. Never heard a word about it, either then, or previously."

" Isn't that . . . rather surprising? "

Jennerel hesitated.

" Again, I don't know that I can go as far as that. I did show some surprise to Captain Rathlyn when he told me about it tonight, but he said his wife had refused to let him tell me at the time—didn't want what she called a fuss." The doctor gave a rather angry snort, as if fuss was a word that should not have been applied to himself. " Perhaps natural," he added more graciously.

" Anyone else know about it, sir? "

" Can't say, I'm sure. Only heard about it myself an hour or so ago."

Binnerton glanced at his colleague, who shook his head.

" Won't keep you any longer, sir. We'll send the body along to the hospital mortuary at once."

Dr. Jennerel rose to his feet and shook himself as if glad that the questioning was over. Then he said:

" You're not going to . . . you won't have to do a lot of photographing and all that business? "

Superintendent Binnerton shook his head.

" There would be no justification for that, sir," he said.

Nevertheless, when the doctor had gone, and before the body of poor Mrs. Rathlyn had been carried away on a stretcher, Superintendent Hant knelt down beside it and made a few discreet chalk marks on the stone floor to indicate its general position. Then he looked straight upwards and sniffed.

" Mighty odd fall," he muttered.

CHAPTER IX

Cause of Death

AS SOON as the body had been moved from the hall the two police officers returned to the study and word was sent by Ludd, asking if Captain Rathlyn could make it convenient to come there.

When he appeared, now shaved and fully dressed, Superintendent Binnerton offered his own condolences and once more apologised for the necessity of these enquiries.

Neither of the police officers had met Captain Rathlyn before this melancholy occasion, and Superintendent Binnerton, at any rate, liked what he saw of him now. Charles Rathlyn was at this time nearly forty-two years old; his dark hair was slightly tinged with grey and his face was weather-beaten and lined, but the complexion was clean and his grey eyes steady and clear. At the moment he was, naturally, looking haggard, but at times he showed an attractive smile. Superintendent Hant, who was to see more of him, came to realise that he could look hard if circumstances were difficult for him.

Gently led by the kindly Binnerton, Charles repeated the story he had already told Dr. Jennerel—how he had awakened to find his wife gone, how he had seen her leaning over the landing balustrade, how, at the moment of his appearance—perhaps because he had startled her—she had overbalanced and fallen to the stone floor of the hall. She had not moved or spoken after he reached her, and he felt sure that she had died instantly. He told again of the previous sleep-walking episode in January, and of how he had begged her to consult Dr. Jennerel; of how she had refused to do so or let him do so; of how she had told him that Mrs. Tass knew about her early tendency and of how Mrs. Tass had confirmed this. He believed that no one else knew anything about it. Superintendent Binnerton did not cross-question or press him at all.

" Would you and Mrs. Rathlyn have been alone in the house last night, sir? " he asked. " Apart, that is, from the staff? "

" Yes—oh no, there was Mr. George Waygold. Good Lord! I had forgotten all about him. I must . . ."

He looked at his watch and found that the time was still long before George Waygold's normal hour of rising.

" I must go and tell him as soon as you've done with me. Shouldn't like him to hear of it from the servants."

" A relation of the late Mr. Waygold, sir? "

" Yes ; his younger brother. A bit of a . . . oh, well, that's neither here nor there. I believe he is the only surviving member of the Waygold family. Mr. and Mrs. Waygold—my wife—when they had no children of their own were anxious that George should marry and do something about it, but he never has. Perhaps he will now— more likely to find someone to marry him."

Superintendent Hant's sharp ears detected a note of bitterness in the voice, faint though it was.

" Is Mr. George Waygold the heir to the estate now, sir? " he asked.

Charles Rathlyn looked at him directly for the first time.

" Yes, I understand that is so," he said.

Hant thought that he would venture just one step further.

" Does that mean that Mr. George Waygold would be the sole legatee? "

He saw the expression fade out of Captain Rathlyn's face, leaving it a wooden mask. He was to recognise that sign in days to come.

" I couldn't possibly answer that, Superintendent. I have not seen my wife's will. She told me that she intended to leave the horses to me, including her race-horses, and some money so that I could keep her colours flying. That was her expression. But that is all I know."

Hant pressed the point no further, and soon afterwards Superintendent Binnerton released Charles so that he might go and break the news to his guest. The uniformed officer looked enquiringly at his colleague, but all Hant said was :

" That will'll bear looking into."

Ludd was next questioned, but was unable to throw any light on the tragedy. He had heard nothing until awakened by the ringing bell and he had no previous knowledge of any sleep-walking. As to that, he thought that either Mrs. Tass or Miss Wey might be able to help.

" And who would Miss Wey be? " asked Binnerton.

Ludd gave a most unbutler-like sniff.

" Madame's personal secretary she likes to call herself. Was lady's-maid." With difficulty he restrained himself from further comment.

" Anybody else we ought to know about, Ludd? I mean, who might be able to throw any light on this unfortunate accident."

" I don't think so, Superintendent, unless it would be Mr. Monner. He's Mrs. Way . . . Mrs. Rathlyn's business secretary and accountant."

That seemed to be all, but as Ludd was leaving the room to summon Mrs. Tass, Hant said to him casually :

" Was it quite sudden, Captain Rathlyn finding his wife's body? I mean, did he have to rush down in his pyjamas, or had he gone to look for her in his dressing-gown, slippers and so on? "

The butler was not a man very quick in the uptake; he answered this quite simply, without bothering about its significance.

" Oh, he was just in his pyjamas—bare feet, too. He must have run straight down, poor gentleman, when he heard her fall."

Did he hear her fall? That was not quite what he had said himself. He had said that he 'found her gone' and had then seen her leaning over the balustrade. If, knowing her sleep-walking propensity, he had been going to look for her, would he not have slipped on his dressing-gown and bedroom slippers? Well, perhaps not. Alternatively, the bare feet might have been intended to impress witnesses with the surprise and shock of his discovery. Hant tucked those considerations away in a pigeon-hole of his capacious brain.

Mrs. Tass was clearly not well pleased at being summoned by two policemen; she would have expected them to wait upon her; it only showed that some people did not know what was proper. She was, naturally, greatly distressed at the death of her mistress, whom she had served faithfully for so many years. But she had complete control of herself and her emotions, telling the police officers exactly what she had previously told Captain Rathlyn. She knew nothing of the circumstances of this night.

It was, in fact, night no longer, and the morning sun was shining brightly in at the study window when Isabel Wey came into the room. Superintendent Hant, respectable married man as he was, had some difficulty in suppressing a whistle when he saw the newcomer. Though he did not know it, Isabel was in fact looking quite a new woman; her figure was always trim and attractive to the eye, but now there was colour in her normally pale cheek and a spark in the eyes that were wont to be dull. Her mouth too—usually, by reason of its thinness, her worst feature—had an upward tilt at the corners. She gave the impression of a woman who was enjoying herself.

Binnerton, older and less impressionable than his colleague, motioned her courteously to a chair.

" A sad day for you, I'm afraid, Miss Wey," he said. " I understand that you stood in a sort of confidential capacity to the late Mrs. Rathlyn."

" I was her personal secretary."

" Exactly. You would know a good deal about her affairs. Any cause of worry, that you know of? "

" Worry? "

Isabel's dark eyebrows rose in what she believed to be the correct curve of surprise.

" I will be frank with you, Miss Wey. We know, of course, that there is a history of sleep-walking—you know of that, by the way? "

A slow smile tilted the corner of Isabel's mouth.

" Oh, that! Well, yes; I suppose I do, though I'm not supposed to. I did once see Mrs. Waygold—as she was then—walking down a passage in the middle of the night. I . . . well, I thought . . . you know. I didn't say anything, of course; but she must have known I had seen her, because she told me she had been walking in her sleep. Told me not to say anything to anyone."

Again that Giaconda smile. But it was lost upon the police officers, who merely thought that this was a delicate way of hinting at a visit to ' the smallest room '. They could not know that there was no need for Mrs. Waygold to walk down a passage for that purpose.

" I asked you that, Miss Wey, because of course we have to clear up all possible explanations. I mean, I asked you about worries for that reason. We have to be quite sure that Mrs. Rathlyn did not take her own life."

For a moment Isabel Wey appeared to be taken aback. She quickly recovered herself.

" Oh no; I know of nothing that would make her do such a thing," she said firmly.

" No money worries? No, I suppose not. No personal worries? Got on well with her husband? "

" Oh yes. They have only been married a year, you know."

Binnerton nodded.

" I had hardly realised it was so short a time," he said. " Naturally one would expect them to be quite happy together."

He paused for a moment and then asked sharply:

" And they were? "

" Were? Were what? "

" Happy together."

" Yes, certainly—so far as I know."

" And you would know, eh—in your confidential position? "

Again that very faint smile.

" I expect I should . . . have an idea."

" Then you would yourself reject the idea of suicide? "

" I certainly would."

" Or anything else? Murder, for instance? "

It was Hant speaking, abruptly—a method he had been taught to believe was often effective with a ' cagey ' witness. Isabel Wey looked quickly towards him. There was no smile on her face now; indeed, a little of the colour seemed to have left it. She answered quietly and firmly:

" That seems to me impossible."

They did not keep her any longer, but the suspicious Hant tucked away in one of his pigeon-holes the notion that she might be concealing something.

Philip Monner was formally questioned, without any

fresh evidence or idea emerging, except the name of Mrs.
Rathlyn's solicitor, and then an invitation was sent to the
presumed heir, the surviving Waygold.

George entered the room looking rather shaky and
bearing with him a spirituous aroma not normally
associated with breakfast. The early September sunlight
was in his eyes, which watered slightly and did not inspire
confidence. He nodded to the uniformed Superintendent
and sat down in an armchair, taking a cigarette from a
packet of ten and lighting it with a hand that trembled
slightly. Binnerton said his condolence piece and asked
if Mr. Waygold had heard or seen anything of the tragic
happenings of the night.

"Not a thing. Slept like a top—head spinning a bit,
you know." George gave a feeble grin, presumably in
support of a time-honoured jest.

"The first you knew of it was . . . when?"

George Waygold glanced at his watch.

"Some damned early hour. Charles came and told me
—woke me up, to be exact. Shock—hell of a shock it was."

"Have you ever heard that your sister-in-law was in
the habit of sleep-walking?"

George stared.

"Sleep-walking? What . . . really sleep-walking,
d'you mean? Or just having a bit of fun?"

"I mean really sleep-walking, Mr. Waygold," said
Superintendent Binnerton, who was not sure what the
chap meant but didn't like what he took it to mean.

"Never a word. Mind you, I haven't seen much of her
in recent years—not since poor old Terry—my brother—
died. Doubt if he'd have told me either—not the sort of
thing you'd want to tell people about your wife."

Binnerton thought he would get no further on this line.
He sounded Mr. Waygold cautiously about his ' expectations ' and at once realised that he had touched a nerve.

Here was something in which the surviving Waygold really was interested; he denied knowing anything or having any idea as to whether he might expect to benefit by his sister-in-law's will. He did know that his brother had left her the whole of his estate absolutely—not just a life interest. He said nothing about the object of his visit to Tandrings.

That completed the immediate police enquiry, and as they drove back to headquarters in Barryfield they reviewed what they had learned and exchanged their impressions of the several witnesses. Binnerton had formed a definitely favourable opinion of Charles Rathlyn and believed that he had been telling the truth in all he said. He regarded Miss Wey as a sly hussy but doubted if she knew anything more than she had told. George Waygold struck him as a poor fish, quite incapable of any action requiring initiative or courage.

On the latter point Hant agreed and also, in the main, about Isabel Wey, though he reserved judgment about her ' whole truthfulness '. He, too, had liked the look of Charles Rathlyn, but he thought him a man quite capable of decisive and possibly unscrupulous action; he had a very definite note about the dead-pan expression of his face when asked a difficult question.

" I'd like to put that gentleman through a really tight bit of questioning—on the spot," he said. " Get him to show me just exactly where he stood and she stood and how she fell. But that would be showing our hand; I take it we'll need authority from the Chief to go that far."

Binnerton nodded.

" I see no harm in your going and having a word with the lady's solicitor. May tell you something, may not. No harm, as I say, in trying. Can't do much more till we get the P.M. report from Dr. Jennerel."

The *post-mortem* examination had, in fact, been carried out by Dr. Lane-Fallick, the chief police surgeon. Dr. Jennerel had, of course, been present, and both doctors came together to see the Chief Constable late in the afternoon.

The immediate cause of death had been a fracture of the spinal cord in the upper vertebrae of the neck, but there was also a severe fracture of the skull with laceration of the brain, which would have been in itself sufficient to cause death. There was heavy bruising on the right arm and leg, but no sign of any other recent injury, no bruising to suggest a blow to cause unconsciousness, no poison or narcotic in the stomach. In fact, nothing to suggest that the death had been other than accidental.

The Chief Constable asked one question:

" Could the fractured skull possibly have been caused by a terrific whack on the side of the head with some heavy, blunt instrument? "

Dr. Lane-Fallick smiled.

" Could have, perhaps, but she must have hit that stone floor a ' terrific whack '; whoever hit her one with a blunt instrument would have to be pretty clever to guess which side of her would hit the floor. It wouldn't have done, you know, to have a smashed skull on *both* sides of the head."

CHAPTER X

A Lot of Money

DETECTIVE-SUPERINTENDENT WILLIS HANT
was a man of striking but not entirely prepossessing
appearance. He was short, square and strong, with
heavy black eyebrows, hooked nose and rather full lips;
he was clean-shaven—but that had to be done twice a
day if he were to retain his smart appearance. It may
have been the hooked nose that first won him the favourable consideration of the Chief Constable, who was
similarly equipped. Colonel Netterly had promoted him
to his present important post about a year previously; he
had done so hopefully, because of the man's excellent
brain and admirable record in the County's C.I.D., but
also with a slight feeling of doubt—which still persisted.
Superintendent Hant was sure of himself—perhaps a little
too sure, a little too off-hand with his superiors and his
peers. He was generally right, but he needed to be right
if he were to get away with that manner.

At the time of Mrs. Charles Rathlyn's death Hant was
forty-five years old—eight years younger than the
Divisional Superintendent with whom he was now
working. Binnerton was a mild, good-natured man, not
easily ruffled, who respected his colleague's brain and
overlooked his occasionally off-hand manner. He felt
no jealousy, and his advice to Hant that he should go and
interview Mr. Hume Lorriner, Mrs. Rathlyn's solicitor,
had been given with a genuine intention to be helpful.
Hant seized on it, with little acknowledgment, and
promptly put it into effect.

Mr. Lorriner was a young man, somewhere in the mid-
thirties, ambitious, anxious to stand well with the police

—and indeed with all men and women who might bring grist to his professional mill. He listened to Superintendent Hant's enquiry, gave it careful consideration, and decided that his duty to his client did not in this instance compel him to withhold information from the police. He was not prepared to hand Mrs. Rathlyn's will to Superintendent Hant for inspection, but he would give him an outline of the main provisions.

An annuity of three hundred pounds a year, free of tax, was accorded to ' my life-long friend ' Amelia Victoria Tass; one hundred a year, similarly tax free, to Ben Penny, groom; a legacy of five hundred pounds each, free of duty, to Philip Monner and Isabel Wey. ' To my dear husband, Charles Rathlyn ', was left a legacy of eighty thousand pounds, free of duty, ' together with my race-horses, including steeplechasers, and other horses '; the residue of the estate to George Waygold. Mrs. Rathlyn also expressed the hope that if her executors found it necessary to sell Tandrings in order to raise additional capital with which to pay the legacies they would not do so for at least one year, in order that her husband might have ample time in which to make his future plans.

Mr. Lorriner told Hant that he had tried to explain to his client the practical difficulties involved in that final ' hope ', but that she had insisted on its being included in the will. This was not a point that had any particular interest for the detective. What did interest him—in fact made his eyes goggle—was the size of the gross estate if legacies and annuities on that scale were to be paid free of duty.

" Does that leave much for Mr. George Waygold, sir? " he asked.

Hume Lorriner smiled.

" You've grasped the point," he said. " Not nearly as much as the residuary legatee will probably expect at first hearing. Still, it is, even now, a very large estate, and I expect there might be something like a hundred thousand pounds coming to Mr. Waygold when all is cleared up. That is a guess, of course, and you must not count on it. It is also strictly confidential."

Superintendent Hant nodded. He promised himself that he would do one or two calculations when he got home—he was fond of mathematical problems. At a mere shot he estimated that the gross estate on which duty would have to be paid must be somewhere in the nature of six or seven hundred thousand pounds. The particular point that interested him now was, of course, the size of duty-free legacy to Captain Charles Rathlyn. What was it that the Captain had said about his expectations? ' The horses and some money to keep her colours flying '; that was a bit of an understatement, to put it mildly. Had he not known? Or had Captain Rathlyn been deliberately misleading him, in order to minimise a possible motive for murder? Hant's heart had quickened its beat as he thought of all the implications of what Mr. Lorriner had just told him. But here was the solicitor with another bit of information.

" I don't know whether you know, Superintendent, that I was out at Tandrings this morning."

Hant shook his head. Why should that interest him? Naturally the solicitor would have many duties to attend to over such a tragic event.

" I went there," continued Mr. Lorriner, " not because of Mrs. Rathlyn's death, which I did not hear about till my arrival—and a pretty grim shock it was—but because she wrote and asked me to come."

Had the solicitor something up his sleeve? He seemed to be hinting at something of significance.

" A long-standing engagement, sir? "

" She wrote yesterday—Sunday afternoon post—asking

me to come at eleven o'clock this morning. She said she
wanted to discuss her will."

Yes; significant enough, this sudden and imperious
demand for attendance—especially on such a subject.
The solicitor knew no more, but clearly he was intrigued; Hant wondered whether it was this that had
made him so willing to divulge information. As the
detective walked back to headquarters he pondered over
what he had learnt and decided that the Chief Constable
must be gingered into turning on the heat.

As it happened, Colonel Netterly had already had a
preliminary talk with the Coroner. Mr. Purde was an
elderly Barryfield solicitor, a man of wide experience and
strong will, with a well-defined sense of the importance of
his venerable office. He was a perfectly reasonable man,
but he was not going to be dictated to by any policeman.
For this reason, in any tricky or important case the Chief
Constable liked to have a canter over the course himself,
before letting loose the rather less tactful detective-
superintendent in this field of tender corns. That, at any
rate, in his own slightly mixed metaphor, was how he
described it to himself.

Netterly then had already explained to Mr. Purde that
even though the autopsy might reveal nothing suggestive,
it would be necessary for the police to make a number of
enquiries before they could feel satisfied that death had
indeed been accidental; suicide was an obviously possible
alternative, and even murder could not be ruled out at the
moment. If there were any suspicions under the latter
head he would rather not disclose his hand too soon.

Mr. Purde nodded, stroking his well-shaven chin.

" I see your point," he said; " I shall very likely decide
to sit without a jury and will just take formal evidence and
then adjourn for a fortnight. That suit you? "

Netterly thanked him, and knowing that a solicitor's

time was precious—to say nothing of his own—took his
leave without further ado. Purde liked the Chief Constable; he was always courteous and was undoubtedly
a shrewder man than his aristocratic appearance and
manner might lead one to assume. If Hant, with his
brusque manner, had come on this errand, it is unlikely
that Mr. Purde would have been quite so promptly open
to suggestion.

It was soon after the Chief Constable's return to headquarters that Detective Superintendent Hant also arrived
there and promptly asked for an interview. Netterly
called him into his office and also sent for Superintendent
Binnerton from the police-station next door; although the
work on this case—if it was a case—would now fall mostly
to the detective, Netterly always saw to it that the
Divisional Superintendent concerned was kept fully in
the picture.

The two older officers listened carefully to what Hant
had to tell them. The detective was rather disappointed
that no particular excitement was noticeable on his chief's
face when he gave details of the large sums of money which
Captain Rathlyn and various others were to inherit.

" That's very interesting, Mr. Hant," said Colonel
Netterly. " I'm rather surprised that Mr. Lorriner told
you all that so promptly. Congratulations."

" I think there may have been a reason for that, sir,"
said Hant modestly, and went on to tell of Mrs. Rathlyn's
summons to her solicitor. This certainly did appear to
ring a bell.

" We must try and find out something more about that,
Hant. Captain Rathlyn may know something about it,
or the secretary."

" The man or the woman, sir? " Hant explained—as
far as he understood it—the dual secretarial position of
Philip Monner and Isabel Wey.

" The man, surely. Anyway, try him first—unless you
get all you want from Captain Rathlyn."

" I'd like to turn the heat on there a bit, sir, if you'll
allow me."

" On Captain Rathlyn? Why, exactly? "

Hant's stubborn look stole over his face; he could sense
opposition from the Chief Constable. ' Gent doesn't eat
gent ' was one of the rather tiresome bees he had in his
bonnet.

" A.1 opportunity, sir; obvious motive—as I've just
discovered."

" Yes; but why suspect murder? " asked Colonel
Netterly quietly. " I agree that we must clear up all
possible alternatives, as I have just explained to the
Coroner, but surely accident is much the most likely
answer."

Superintendent Hant's black brows drew together.

" There's a lot more I'd like to know about before I'd
be satisfied to accept that," he said doggedly. Colonel
Netterly knew the expression on the stubborn face; it
always made him feel doubtful of his own judgment in
appointing the man to a post of such responsibility,
requiring so much discretion and balance.

Perhaps fortunately, it was at this moment that the two
doctors arrived with their report on the *post-mortem* examination. Interesting as it was, it certainly contained no
support for the theory of murder, though it in no way ruled
it out. It did, however, have the effect of slightly de-
flating Superintendent Hant, and he remained silent after
the doctors had left. Characteristically, Netterly at once
began to feel more sympathetic towards him; he was the
last man to discourage keenness and initiative.

" I suggest you go over to Tandrings tomorrow," he
said, " and see if you can find out anything more about
Mrs. Rathlyn's letter to Mr. Lorriner. Somebody—

most probably Captain Rathlyn—may well know why she suddenly took it into her head to want him at such short notice. Then—if we still feel we ought to look further—we will wait till the inquest has been adjourned, and that will give us a better excuse for asking more pertinent questions."

So Hant went to Tandrings next morning and, finding that Captain Rathlyn was over at Ewcote, asked to be allowed a word with Mr. Monner. The secretary, silent and rather solemn in manner, took Hant to his own office and offered him a cigarette, which the detective declined. Monner sat down at his desk, after waving Hant to a chair beside it. He waited for the detective to speak.

"There is just one point the Chief Constable wanted me to find out about, if possible, Mr. Monner. You were Mrs. Rathlyn's secretary, and it seems likely that you may be able to help. It appears that Mrs. Rathlyn sent a letter to her solicitor, Mr. Lorriner, asking him to come and see her yesterday morning; the letter was dated Sunday. Would you have written that for her, Mr. Monner?"

"Was it typewritten?"

Hant was conscious of a blunder; he should have found that out from the solicitor. He had to admit that he did not know.

"I only asked so that I could tell you whether it might have been written by Miss Wey. I did not do it, and Mrs. Rathlyn does not . . . did not use a typewriter. If it was a confidential letter it would in any case have been written by Miss Wey, if not by Mrs. Rathlyn. Miss Wey did all Mrs. Rathlyn's confidential work."

Hant was aware of a coldness in Monner's voice; he sensed that there was no love lost between the two secretaries, but that did not appear to be a matter that he need concern himself about.

" You don't perhaps know, then, what it was that Mrs. Rathlyn wanted to see her solicitor about? It appeared to be a rather urgent summons."

Hant knew what it was about, but this seemed the only approach to more delicate questioning.

" I don't know anything about it, Superintendent. Hadn't you better ask Miss Wey, if you want to know? "

Hant agreed and asked how he might best get hold of her.

" I'll ask her to come down here; you can have this room to yourselves."

A few minutes later Miss Wey appeared. Hant still thought her an attractive young person, but her mouth certainly did appear rather thin and hard. She sank into an armchair and, as Monner had done, waited for the detective to speak. Hant repeated his tentative approach, but Miss Wey shook her head.

" I didn't write it, or hear anything about it. Didn't Mr. Lorriner know what she wanted to see him about? "

Hant left that unanswered.

" I think you told us yesterday morning, Miss Wey, that you stood in some sort of confidential capacity to Mrs. Rathlyn."

Isabel smiled slightly.

" That was how your . . . what was he? . . . super-intendent? . . . described it. All I said was that I was her personal secretary."

" But you did know a good deal about her affairs? "

" Perhaps I did. I didn't know about this."

" This might be rather important, Miss Wey. As Mr. Binnerton told you, we have to take all possibilities into account. I won't beat about the bush; what I want to ask you is whether you know of any reason why Mrs. Rathlyn might have wanted to alter her will? "

" Was that what she wanted to see Lorriner about? " asked the girl sharply.

It would not be right to disclose what the solicitor had told him in confidence.

" It's just a guess of mine—sort of thing people do send for their solicitors in a hurry for. Do you know of any reason? "

Isabel Wey looked at him thoughtfully. She seemed to be hesitating, but she shook her head and declared that she knew nothing about it. At that moment there was the sound of a car outside and then a voice, apparently in the hall.

" That's Captain Rathlyn; you had better ask him."

So presently Hant found himself back in the study, facing a tired-looking but apparently quite friendly Charles. After the usual offer and refusal of drink or smoke, Hant got to work.

" The Coroner will require rather more information upon one point we touched on yesterday, sir—your wife's testamentary intentions. You told us yesterday that Mr. George Waygold was the heir to the estate but that you yourself were to receive a legacy. Do you . . .? "

Charles Rathlyn interrupted him.

" I told you that I understood that; I don't know it for a fact. My wife told me so about six months ago; she may have changed her mind, for all I know."

" Have you any reason to suppose she did? " asked Hant sharply.

" None whatever."

" Did you know that Mrs. Rathlyn had sent for her solicitor to come here yesterday? Wrote on Sunday."

Charles showed no great interest in this. He smiled.

" Ladies with money often do want to see their solicitors and generally expect them to come pretty quick. I didn't know she had sent for him or what it was about."

" She had said nothing to you to suggest that she intended to change her will? "

Charles looked steadily at the detective.

" What is all this about, Superintendent? " he asked.

Hant realised that he had been pressing too hard.

" I'm sorry, sir," he said apologetically. " I get a bit worked up about nothing at times. This is a perfectly routine enquiry, for the information of the Coroner. Am I to take it that you know nothing? "

Charles smiled.

" Keep this to yourself if you can, Mr. Hant," he said. " My wife did tell me that her brother-in-law had come to try and get some money out of her. He's got some gambling debts—I've had them myself before now. She might have wanted to see Lorriner about that."

It appeared a reasonable explanation—to anyone who did not know that Mrs. Rathlyn had mentioned her will. Alternatively, this man might be trying to point the finger of suspicion at another man.

" Have you any idea how much Mr. Waygold would inherit? "

" Not the very foggiest. Not by several rows of noughts. It's a big estate, but the death duties will be crippling."

" And you yourself, Captain Rathlyn? "

Once again Hant saw all expression fade from the soldier's face. Dead-pan once more.

" I have no idea."

" But would it be likely to be a large sum? "

" It depends what you . . . and all that. I have been a poor man for some time now. Five thousand pounds would be a large sum to me; it would be chicken-feed to my wife."

" I'm sorry to press you, sir. Of course, I know nothing, but would such a sum as fifty thousand pounds be the sort of thing? "

" It might be. How can I say? "

" It wouldn't surprise you? "

" It's a lot of money.   But, Superintendent, I told you that my wife wanted me to keep her horses in training. How much do you think it costs to keep a string of twenty at Lambourn, as well as half a dozen chasers? All that lot, of course, would be out of the question, but even half of them?   And what would be my net income on fifty thousand capital?—say about twelve hundred pounds. Even if I could earn the whole of my own living—and I don't know how—it's going to be no easy job."

CHAPTER XI

Plans for the Future

THERE WAS a good deal more that Hant would have
liked to ask Captain Rathlyn, but the Chief Constable
had told him to wait until after the inquest. He had been
rather impressed by what the Captain had said about the
cost of keeping horses in training; he had not thought of
that. Of course, the actual sum was larger than the fifty
thousand he had quoted, but even so . . . say he managed to get a ' better than four ' per cent return, that
meant a gross income of, say, three thousand five hundred;
that, again, would attract surtax as well as income tax,
and it was doubtful if the net income would be more than
eighteen hundred. Of course, there was no guarantee
that he would keep those horses in training; it had only
been a wish, he gathered, not a condition. But surely a
man living in comfort in this grand house, with a rich wife
plus all those horses, was in a much better position than
he would be as a widower with eighteen hundred a year.

That, no doubt, was too simple a way to look at it.
Rathlyn might need the capital and need it quick. He
had confessed to having had gambling debts in the past;
he might have them now—though that confession would
hardly have been volunteered by a man who had just
committed murder to raise the money for their payment!
But there were other uses for capital. And other reasons
for getting rid of a wife. Oh, well, there was a lot to be
found out yet, and meantime . . . the inquest.

Kate had not mixed much with her neighbours or taken
interest in local affairs—Women's Institute and so on—
so not many people had been much interested in her—
except the shop-keepers, who valued her custom. Her

death had not, therefore, caused much popular excitement, so no great disappointment was felt when Mr. Purde, after taking only formal evidence, adjourned his enquiry for a fortnight. He gave his certificate for burial, so the funeral was arranged for Thursday, in the little, untidy churchyard a stone's throw from the Tandrings stables.

Charles Rathlyn had hoped that possibly Anne might be there, but she was not—any more than she had been at the inquest. Perhaps it was natural that she should not; Kate had not really known Anne, or taken any interest in her, so the girl might feel that she was pushing herself forward if she appeared on either occasion. She had written to him—a very sweet but quite impersonal note of sympathy. Charles treasured it, but he could not persuade himself that it showed the smallest sign of anything warmer than sympathy.

When the funeral was over the few mourners returned to the house and refreshed themselves on the generous fare provided by Mrs. Tass. They then departed and Charles and George Waygold were left alone—save for Mr. Lorriner. There was no old-fashioned reading of the will, but the solicitor took each legatee aside and gave him an outline of what was to be expected. He was careful to pipe down very thoroughly the residue which George Waygold might look for, but he undertook to provide at once a sufficient sum to clear George of his ' debts of honour '. Having done this, Lorriner saw such of the minor characters as he could find—Philip Monner, Isabel Wey, Ludd—but Mrs. Tass was too distressed to receive him, and Ben Penny was occupied with the vet and a sick horse.

Charles took himself off to his study and sat down to think out his position. The eighty thousand pounds was a much larger sum than he had expected, in spite of what he had said about the cost of keeping horses in training, but having done the same sums as Hant, he realised that his future would not be free from care. He would do his best—register Kate's colours in his own name and keep a handful of 'chasers, if nothing more; he was not deeply interested in the flat. He might even train them himself; that would be fun, especially if . . . ah yes, everything turned on that . . . if Anne would have him life would be wonderful and nothing should stand in the way of their happiness. He believed she cared for him, but she was a shy, honest girl and had given him no sign that could make him feel sure; he had been a married man then, so naturally a girl of her sort would give no sign. But he was a widower now and things might be different—not yet, of course, but before too long. His thoughts flickered between hope and despondency; it was a gamble; the whole thing was a gamble; life was a gamble—and he had been a gambler all his life.

Charles's own solicitor was in London, so the following day, Friday, Charles went up to see him and to discuss his own plans. He had already met the executors of his wife's will—Mr. Lorriner and a representative of her bank's trustee department; they had told him that while it would naturally take a considerable time to settle the affairs of so large an estate, it was not likely that they would be able to avoid selling Tandrings and obviously the time to do that would be the beginning of the following summer. Charles felt that he would probably have six months in which to form his future plans and look round for a new and more modest home . . . and possibly for a job. His solicitor advised him to seek that job in the one sphere in which he had some expert knowledge—horse-racing; the manager of the former Mrs. Waygold's racing interests would surely be able to find similar employment, even though on a smaller scale.

Charles was not so sure; it was only by a few very rich or very busy people that racing managers were needed. As for becoming a trainer, of course he knew a good deal about the game, but he would have to get a licence, and that might not be easy. It was a profession, moreover, that carried a good deal of risk; one depended entirely upon confidence, and that was not something that could be built up in a few months. Still, with capital, he could afford to hold on.

In the meantime there were some stiffish fences to be crossed; he was under no delusion about that. The courteous questions of Colonel Netterly and Superintendent Binnerton had not blinded him to the fact that they were clearly going to satisfy themselves about the circumstances of Kate's death. Even if there was no directly suspicious circumstance it was obvious that such a fall would have to be explained, that every possible alternative must be sifted. People might not even take their own lives—and suicide here was an obvious possibility—without the coroner having to know all about the whys and wherefores. And this other man, whom Charles had now discovered to be the head of the county's detective service, was clearly a Nosey Parker of the first water; even within a few hours of his bereavement Hant had not hesitated to question him about his ' expectations '. His second visit had carried him even further down that particular trail. Charles thought that he had damped the fellow's ardour a little bit by his answers, but he was not sure that he had seen the last of him.

On Saturday morning, the day after his visit to London, Charles was sitting in his study, pondering these things in his heart, when Philip Monner came in and asked if he might speak to him on a private matter.

" Of course, Philip; sit down; have a cigarette."

Charles noticed that the secretary's hand was trembling

slightly as he lit his cigarette.   Chap's nervous, he thought;
what's it about?

" I am not quite sure how I stand, sir.   I have never
experienced . . .   never lost my employer by death before.
Am I in your employ now, sir?   Or Mr. Waygold's?
Just for the moment, I mean;   until I have been given
notice and so on."

Somehow, that point had not occurred to Charles.

" Oh, mine, surely;   I don't think Mr. Waygold suc-
ceeds to any human chattels.   What are you thinking of
doing? "

Philip Monner looked still more uneasy;   he fidgeted in
his chair.

" That's really just what I wanted to ask you about, sir.
Is there any chance of your retaining me in your employment? "

" Oh, my dear chap, surely you must do better for yourself now.   I understood your loyalty in sticking to my
wife's service—I appreciated that, as I know she did.
But that's over now;   you must get out into the big world
and make a real career for yourself.   In any case, of
course, I shall not be in a position to employ a secretary,
even if I wanted to.   Even with the generous provision
that I understand my wife has made for me I shall be a
comparatively poor man."

" Mrs. Rathlyn has been very generous to me too, sir—
in her will, I mean."

Charles wondered whether there was a slight note of
coldness in the voice.   Five hundred pounds down was
not, of course, a very large lump of capital with which
to step out into the big world.   Ought he, perhaps, to
supplement it?   But why should he?   Philip Monner was
nothing to him, and surely was well trained enough to
earn an excellent living.

" You will have no difficulty, I am sure, in finding just

what you want in the way of a job. But don't hurry over it. I shall probably be here for the next six months, and you can stay with me—in my employment, I mean—as long as you like till I go. Give you time to pick and choose."

"That is very good of you, sir; very good indeed."

Charles hoped the man would go now; he had made the position quite clear; there was nothing more to discuss. But Philip Monner sat on.

"I don't think you quite understand the difficulty of my position, sir—about finding employment," he said. "I told you that my father was sent to prison—for fraud. In fact, he died in prison. That sort of thing tells against an accountant, where unimpeachable honesty is required."

Charles stared at him.

"You're not telling me that the fact of your father having done time would tell against you? Oh, come off it, man; it might have in Charles Dickens's day, but not now."

"I assure you that it would, sir," said Monner quietly.

Incredulous as he was, Charles was half persuaded by the man's sincerity. He obviously did fear that he might have difficulty in getting work. Then a thought flashed into Charles's head; could it be that Monner had a black mark somewhere in his own past—a blot in his copy-book —or, more likely, his account-book? It was an uncomfortable thought, but Charles was not going to worry about it; he had told the secretary what he was prepared to do, and he would do no more.

Realising this, Monner rose to go; Charles's heart softened when he saw the anxious look on the thin, sensitive face; probably this was a man who worried himself without cause.

"Cheer up, Philip," he said. "We'll get you a job. Oh, by the way, what about Miss Wey? I suppose for the moment she is in my service too." He laughed. "Well, no one will expect me to keep two secretaries. I can make my own personal dates."

Charles spoke in jest, but he noticed that Philip Monner's face had hardened; Charles realised—as Hant had noticed before him—there was no love lost between these two. Oh well, plain jealousy would account for that, so far at any rate as the man was concerned. How uncomfortable, though, it must have been for them, having their meals together. He wondered that his wife had not realised this.

Better settle this up at once; no time like the present. He told Monner to ask Miss Wey to come and see him. Charles had always felt slightly intrigued about Isabel Wey. She was a girl—a woman; he supposed she must be best part of thirty—of considerable personality. Just how she had come into such closely confidential relations with Kate Charles hardly knew, but he guessed that it might have been loneliness on his wife's part—loneliness after her husband died and before he himself came into her life. Isabel was certainly attractive to look at; she had a lovely figure, her eyes were large and well lashed and her dark hair, parted in the middle, had a slight natural wave.

Charles looked at her now, as she came into the room, and again was conscious of her attractiveness. He had thought her sullen, her mouth hard and thin; it was not so now; indeed, she looked rather demure as she stood quietly half-way between the door and his desk. Charles felt slightly uncomfortable; he did not quite know how to carry off this interview.

"Sit down a minute, Isabel. We have hardly had a chance to talk since this dreadful thing happened. You will be wanting to get off to another post, of course, and I want you to feel quite free to do that when you like.

Of course, you are entitled to proper notice; what would it be—a month? "

" I don't think there was ever anything said about that, Captain Rathlyn. I was paid monthly."

Charles realised that he had no idea what she was paid. Philip Monner would know.

" Well, that at least. I have just been telling Mr. Monner that as long as I am here—probably six months— he can stay till he has found just what he wants. But naturally you will not want or need to stay long. You will have no difficulty at all about finding a new post."

" Is Mr. Monner leaving? "

" Oh yes, of course. He must get something much more interesting. In any case, I should have no need for an accountant; I'm going to be a poor man again."

Charles saw a smile flicker into the dark eyes.

" If Mr. Monner is leaving will you not need someone else to be your secretary? I am not trained as he is, but I have picked up a lot by experience."

" Do you mean . . . that you would like to stay with me? "

Charles was suddenly conscious of a little flutter of excitement. Quickly he crushed it down. What on earth was he thinking about?

" That's very nice of you, Isabel; but I'm not going to need a secretary."

Isabel rose to her feet.

" Very well, then, Captain Rathlyn; I will begin to look around. It will certainly be a help if I may have a little time. I have no home to go to."

Again Charles's heart softened, as it had with Philip. He did not like to think of the girl being homeless, with no one to help and advise her. She must have come to look upon Kate as a friend, perhaps almost as a mother.

" There is no hurry at all. As I say, any time in

the next six months. But you are going to be awfully bored."

Again that flicker of a smile.

" I don't think I shall be that, Captain Rathlyn," Isabel said, and left the room.

Well, that was those two matters settled—or practically settled. What about old Ben Penny? He would probably want to retire now. A hundred a year—Charles had heard of that legacy—was not much, but he must have saved a tidy bit, and there was the O.A.P. Ben would be all right. He would probably want to stay till the place was sold. Might as well have a last season's hunting, Charles thought. Primrose and Dashalong; he would keep them and sell the rest now. Ben would manage them with one boy. And perhaps a third horse; better keep one for Gerry, if he wanted a hunt. At the back of his mind Charles hid the hope that it would be Anne Faery who rode Primrose, at least occasionally, this season—and perhaps for many seasons more.

CHAPTER XII

All Clear

DETECTIVE-SUPERINTENDENT HANT thought that a decent interval of about two days should be allowed after the funeral before renewing his enquiries about the accident. It was on Saturday morning, therefore, shortly before mid-day, that he arrived at Tandrings, accompanied by a young detective-sergeant with a camera. He met Captain Rathlyn just on his way out to the stables, having completed his talks with the two secretaries. Hant apologised for troubling him again.

"Just one or two matters I shall have to clear up for the Coroner, sir; a photograph or two—you won't mind, I'm sure. I've brought Sergeant Knott along."

"Of course, take what you like. You won't want me, I suppose?"

"Not if you would just show me first the exact positions, sir." Hant explained that he wanted to see just where Mrs. Rathlyn had been standing when she fell, where Captain Rathlyn himself had been, and so on. Charles turned abruptly back into the house and led the way upstairs. Standing in the door of the bedroom occupied by himself and his wife he said:

"This was where I was when I saw her. I checked at once, so as not to startle her, but at that moment, as I told you, she seemed to overbalance—she was leaning over the balustrade when I saw her—and fell straight down."

"And she was standing . . . just where, sir?"

Charles walked a few feet along the gallery and put his hand on the rail of the balustrade.

"About here, as far as I can judge."

Hant looked down into the hall. He could not see

from here the small chalk marks which he had made on the floor, indicating the position of the body. He had told Ludd to see that those marks were not removed but, to double assurance, he had also made two small marks with indelible pencil, which would not be easily removed.

" I want you to be as sure of this as you possibly can be, sir. I will stand here; will you just go back to the doorway and look again? "

Charles went back to the doorway, looked at the leaning figure, and nodded.

" That's about it, I think."

" There was no chance of your covering that distance and checking her before she fell? "

" I was standing still, not wanting to startle her. It was a complete surprise to me—her falling. I suppose I was rather rooted to the ground—by the surprise, I mean —but even if I had jumped straight forward I don't think I could possibly have reached her in time. I . . . I have always understood it is dangerous to startle a sleep-walker."

" You are sure she was asleep, sir? " asked Hant quietly.

Charles stared at him.

" What are you getting at? " he asked.

" Only that the Coroner is bound to take all possibilities into account. He is sure to ask you something like that sir."

Charles Rathlyn's face was drawn, his mouth set in a hard line. He looked at the detective without further question.

" That's all right, sir. If I may just take these photographs and take a measurement or two—height from the ground and so on. I needn't trouble you to wait."

Charles hesitated, then turned on his heel, walked downstairs and out at the front door. The two detectives followed him down, and when they were alone Hant pointed to the chalk marks—faint by now; the two little purple dots were clearly visible.

" Stand here, Knott, and if anyone comes look as if you were taking notes."

Hant himself went upstairs again. It was a cold, blustery day outside and he was wearing a rather heavy overcoat, which he had not removed. The pockets seemed to be bulging with papers and gloves; in fact they contained two good-sized bags full of sand, and the weight on his shoulders was considerable. From one pocket he now drew a coiled fishing-line with a weight on one end; standing where Mrs. Rathlyn had stood he slowly lowered the weight until it touched the floor, then tied a knot in the line by the handrail.

" That'll give us height of fall, when we measure it," he said.

But it was not the height that interested him. What he saw was that Knott was standing some three feet further out in the hall than the point where the weight was touching the floor.

Looking quickly round to make sure that there was no one about, he took off his overcoat, folded it roughly and then gave it a sharp push outwards. The heavy coat fell as a body would fall—not fluttering about—and hit the floor quite close to the marks, rather to one side but just as far out. Fortunately the bags had not burst, and Hant, hurrying down, picked up the coat and laid it on a chair. The detective's eyes were glistening, but he made no comment.

Knott went through the business of taking some photographs, then the two police officers left the house and returned to Barryfield.

During the week-end that followed Superintendent Hant thought very carefully over the case, so far as he had been able to take it. He had formed a strong impression that Captain Rathlyn had murdered his wife, had deliberately pushed her over that balustrade, either when she was sleep-walking or under some other circumstances. How he could do that if she were awake and conscious without her struggling and screaming, it was difficult to see; some more medical evidence was needed on those points. But he believed that Rathlyn had done it. Motive, with that inheritance, was obvious—well, not perhaps that, in view of the considerations to which he had already applied his mind—but good enough for a jury. Opportunity was unquestionable. All that was needed was proof.

All that was needed! And how far away that was. Just that one point—the position of the body, too far out into the hall for a straight drop. Well, he must take it to the Chief and get his instructions.

Early on Monday morning, therefore, he asked for an interview, and hearing what Hant wanted, Colonel Netterly summoned a full conference—himself, his Assistant Chief Constable, Mr. Janson, Superintendent Binnerton and Superintendent Wite, the chief clerk. They listened in silence while the detective described what he had seen and heard and gave his general impressions. When he had finished, Colonel Netterly looked at Binnerton.

" Any views, Mr. Binnerton? "

" I know very little about the case, sir, apart from what we learned last Monday and what Mr. Hant has told me. I'd agree that there's a possibility of murder, just as there is of suicide. If she *threw* herself over she might well land further out in the hall than a plumb drop. I think we should need a lot more before we asked the Coroner to consider either murder or suicide."

" You, Mr. Janson? "

The Assistant Chief Constable had not been very long

in Barryshire; he had had wide experience in the Metropolitan Police, both in the uniformed force and in the
C.I.D.; he was being very very careful not to throw his
weight about too soon—not until he had got to know his
Chief Constable and his Chief Constable had got to know
him.

"I think it is too early to judge, sir," he said quietly.
"I agree with Mr. Binnerton that there is at the moment
no case to justify our going for a murder finding at the
inquest, but I am sure that Mr. Hant is quite right not to
be satisfied to take things at their face value. I wouldn't
lay too much stress on the position of the body; if the
woman, feeling herself falling, gave a violent kick with
her legs she might well land quite a distance out in the
hall—from a height of thirty-five feet, wasn't it?"

"That's right, sir," said Hant. "I quite see that point.
But we can't get away from opportunity and motive."

Janson smiled.

"I don't think the money motive is a good one; he's
much less well off now than he was. Have you looked for
an alternative?"

Hant hesitated.

"Well, sir, of course one looks round for the obvious
alternative—a woman. I happened to hear only yesterday that Captain Rathlyn had been seeing a good deal
of one young lady out hunting last season—a Miss
Faery."

Colonel Netterly sat up with a jerk.

"Oh, come," he said, "don't let's build theories on
anything so flimsy as that. Miss Faery was schooling one
of Mrs. Rathlyn's horses and she gave him a helping hand
when he had a nasty fall. So did I, for the matter of that.
No, no; we've got no case at present, and unless something fresh turns up before the thirteenth I think we had
better offer no fresh evidence to the Coroner. But that

doesn't mean closing the case; we will just keep our eyes and ears open. I can see that Mr. Hant is still smelling a rat, and he isn't often wrong, though at the moment my personal opinion is that this is a straight accident."

So it was decided, and the days drew on to the date of the adjourned inquest, with nothing fresh coming to light which Hant could put forward as supporting his suspicions.

Charles Rathlyn had asked his own London solicitor, Mr. Warwick Harty, to watch the case on his behalf. Mr. Harty had done more than that. He at once saw that a vital point was confirmation of the sleep-walking explanation. There was his client's own story, of course, and Mrs. Tass's evidence was invaluable, but someone more completely independent would be even more convincing. Mrs. Tass's memory of early days proved, under questioning to be unreliable, but she did remember the name of ' old Doctor Torrance ' who had looked after the Hillburn family in the days of long ago. Old Doctor Torrance would be dead now, but one of Harty's clerks, reconnoitring the town where the Hillburns had lived, discovered that the practice had been bought by a Doctor Lacey, and Doctor Lacey, himself now old, had hunted through forgotten case-books and discovered confirmation there which could not be challenged.

Even so, when Mr. Purde, still sitting without a jury, announced his finding it was to the effect that death had been due to a broken neck, the result of a fall, and that there was no evidence to show what had caused the fall.

Walking away from the room in which the enquiry had been held, Charles said:

" Does that mean a finding of accidental death? "

" Well, not quite," said Mr. Harty. " An open verdict. It would have been so much better if Dr. Jennerel had known about the recent sleep-walking. Mrs. Tass and Dr. Torrance's case-book were all very well, but they refer to very old history—which someone might use as cover."

Charles looked thoughtfully at his solicitor.

" That, of course, points to me. Are you seriously suggesting that I killed my wife? "

" Oh, good God, no. I am merely suggesting what might be the explanation of the open verdict."

.   .   .   .

On the whole, in spite of the ambiguous character of the ' open verdict ', Charles Rathlyn felt a sense of real relief that the adjourned inquest was over. He had not been able to conceal from himself that the police had been uncomfortably persistent in their questioning, and he found it hard to believe that photographing and measuring were really necessary ingredients of a purely routine enquiry. Still, it was over now—all clear; the Chief Constable had said a friendly word to him as they left the building, he had got rid of his own solicitor and could settle down to a whole-hearted planning of his own future.

What really worried and depressed him now was that there was still no sign from Anne; just that one kind but quite impersonal letter of sympathy. Answering it, he had said just that little more than was really necessary— enough to show her that her sympathy meant something real to him. He had left a loophole for a return letter from her—and no return letter had come. It was all quite reasonable, of course, taking their respective positions into account—especially the fact that he had only recently lost his wife; it was quite reasonable, quite proper, and he was unreasonably and deeply disappointed.

Well, time would show whether all his hopes and plans had been in vain. In any case, he was not going to give up hope now; if necessary, he would fight all the harder to win her. Now that the funeral and the inquest were over he could properly start to go out in the world again. Cub-hunting would give him his best chance; it was, to

him, not a pleasure but a duty that a member of the hunt
owed to his Master—helping him to kill off some of the
surplus cubs, because a plethora of foxes was almost as
bad for sport as a dearth. Anne, he knew, had the same
sense of duty, and she had the further one of schooling
her father's young horses, particularly in the difficult
lesson of standing still. Yes, he would meet Anne cub-
hunting, and then, in less than a month, the season itself
would open and they would be able to hunt together as
often as she would allow him to join her. Charles's heart
swelled with happiness at the thought and then, as is the
way with the hearts of men in love, sank into his boots at
the further thought that Anne probably would not want
to hunt with him at all.

He was churning these thoughts over in his mind as he
sat in his study late on that Wednesday night in mid-
October, when the door opened quietly and Isabel Wey
walked in. Charles stared at her in astonishment; never
before had she come to see him in his study at this time of
day, but it was not just that—it was her appearance. She
was dressed quietly enough in black, but somehow it did
not look like the dress of a secretary, even off duty;
Charles had no understanding of women's clothes, but he
could be conscious of effect. This dress was of a soft
material, moulded to the lines of her figure; although it
was a 'high' dress the neck was cut in a low V that
revealed the graceful line of the girl's throat and even a
little of her breast; it was, though Charles did not know
it, a very expensive cocktail dress, made by a first-class
London dressmaker.

But Charles's eyes went quickly from her dress to her
face, and it was here that astonishment struck him. Not
only was the thin, sullen mouth no longer in evidence;
even the touch of demureness that he had noticed when
they discussed whether she should stay with him had

gone. In its place, in the whole expression of her face, there was mischief—in the sparkle of her eyes, in the lifting corners of her mouth, the very colour of her lips.

" Can I come in and have a talk? " she asked.

Charles rose hesitatingly from his chair, too much taken aback to answer. Walking to the big leather sofa, Isabel sat down, patted the seat beside her. Still almost mesmerised by astonishment, Charles weakly did as she suggested.

" Happy about the verdict? "

A queer sensation of discomfort, uneasiness, passed through Charles.

" I . . . I'm glad the inquest is over," he said.

Isabel smiled.

" I'm sure you are ; so am I. Now we can talk."

" Talk? What about? "

" Well, not 'cabbages and kings'. Shall we say : Why you killed your wife? Or how you killed your wife? "

Charles felt the blood drain from his heart, leaving him icy cold. He tried to rise, to express his furious indignation, but just for a moment he could neither move nor speak.

" It all worked out very neatly, didn't it? "

Charles was himself again now.

" You must be quite mad. Why are you talking this nonsense? "

He rose quickly to his feet.

" Please go now and leave the house tomorrow. You shall be paid."

Isabel Wey remained seated. She gave a little laugh— quite a pleasant laugh.

" How well you do it," she said, "—the righteous indignation. Of course, you can't know ; I saw the whole thing."

" Saw what? "

" I saw you push your wife over the balustrade."

" That's a damnable lie! I did nothing of the kind."

" Oh, but you did; I saw you. I had woken up and was coming to get a book. I know I had no business there, but I *was* there. Bad luck for you, Captain Rathlyn. I saw the whole thing."

Charles's face was grim now, his mouth set in a hard line.

" Then why didn't you tell the police what you . . . pretend to have seen? "

" That wouldn't have done anyone any good; you— or me."

" I suppose this is some sort of blackmail. You are simply inventing the whole thing—on what you have heard."

Isabel gently shook her head.

" I can easily prove to you that I was there. Do you remember what you said to Dr. Jennerel when you rang him up? You said your wife had had a bad fall and was very seriously hurt—that you thought her neck was broken, or her back. You said: ' Yes, I am afraid so ', and that you would not try to move her till he came."

Charles remembered his words too well to have any doubt that she had heard him.

" You may well have heard that. You were probably awakened by the fall and came along in time to hear that and now you are trying to build up some infernal lie. Tell the police what you heard."

Isabel Wey leaned back and raised her arms, clasping the hands behind her head. The action displayed her figure to perfection.

" I might tell them . . . if I don't get what I want," she said softly.

" They wouldn't believe you now—any lie you told."

" I rather think they would. You see, I know the answer to the other question—*why* you killed your wife. Do you remember the last time Mrs. Rathlyn went out hunting and came home alone? When you got back she let fly at you, and told you that she knew all about your making love to Anne Faery; she screamed at you—anybody might have heard it but it happened to be me. I don't think anyone else knows about Anne, but I'm sure the police would like to."

Charles turned slowly away and, walking across to the fireplace, looked down into the dying flames. Blackmail! What might not the police believe—any story that bolstered their suspicions? That talk of his with Jennerel; the doctor would remember that; it sounded like confirmation of what this woman said. And Anne; she would be dragged into the horrible business, her name bandied about, smeared . . . somehow he must save her from that—at almost any price.

"What is it you want?" he asked in a low voice. "It is all a lie. I did not kill my wife, and you know it. But you can make hell for Miss Faery, as well as for me; I can see that. What do you want?"

Isabel rose from the sofa and walked across to him. Against his will he turned towards her. She smiled up at him.

"Oh, not very much. Just a little pin-money. And not to go away from here . . . just yet. And . . ."

She came closer, raised her bare arms and slipped them round his neck.

"And be a little nice to me."

She looked very beautiful, her dark eyes gazing into his, her red lips a little parted. The perfume she was wearing flicked his senses. Slowly, as if hypnotised, Charles put his arms round her and kissed her.

CHAPTER XIII

Still Interested

CHARLES RATHLYN sat alone in his study, staring at the dying fire. From time to time he dropped his head into his hands, pressed them against his eyes, as if trying to blot out some nightmare scene, to expunge some hideous folly. Why had he done that? Why? Why? He should have thrown the woman out neck and crop, handed her over to the police, charged her with attempted blackmail. Why had he been so weak, so madly foolish, so vile, so treacherous to Anne? Had he wanted to give himself time to think, to fob her off, while he could make a plan? Something of that kind, perhaps; but Charles could not hide from himself that there had been something more—some horrible fascination, even some longing for a woman's caress in his misery and loneliness. Even the caress of a vile harpy, such as this Isabel Wey must be.

But what an act of folly—to show weakness even for a moment. It could only strengthen her, multiply her demands. And how could he face Anne now—after such an act of treachery? Of course, it had not been . . . anything like he felt for Anne. Not love—not in any way. Hardly even lust. It had been—some horrid fascination. And for the moment it would buy time to think. Without proper thought he could not drag Anne into the slough of mud and horror that was sucking at his feet. There was danger in this—real danger. Such a story, with so much circumstantial confirmation, might fortify the suspicions that so obviously had been in that detective's mind, if not in those of the Chief Constable and the uniformed Superintendent. How could he be sure that his word, his story of what had happened, would be accepted now? And the ' motive ', which Isabel Wey's story about Kate and Anne would provide; that alone would mean danger. Hant had obviously been after a money motive—those questions about his legacy—but here was something fresh, something much more plausible, less easily refuted.

But would they believe her? Would they believe a woman who had kept all this up her sleeve while the police enquiries were going on and only produced it in an obvious attempt to blackmail—as he, Charles, would claim? But might she not say that she had been silent because of her horror at the idea of giving evidence that would lead a man to the gallows—her own kind employer—some sentimental tosh of that kind? She might even declare that he was her lover and that she could not bring herself to betray him—until she realised that he was indeed deserting her for Anne Faery. Filth upon filth, flung not only upon him but upon Anne.

His word against hers. That was what that story of the fall would be. Which would the police believe? Especially with that fatal suggestion of motive. And what had all those investigations of Superintendent Hant's been about? That measuring and photographing? Those marks upon the floor, obviously where Kate's body had been found? Charles had seen them the next day. Did they mean anything significant to the police? What did they mean?

So Charles Rathlyn's thoughts flung themselves from side to side, till he was dazed and giddy. Almost staggering, he dragged himself to bed, but not for a long time to sleep. Only when the veiled October sun was rising did Charles at last drop into unconsciousness, his tired brain worn out, unable to function any more. And as he slept at last, a few miles away Anne Faery was sitting alone on her young horse outside a covert, automatically

tap-tapping the saddle with her riding-whip to keep the
cubs from breaking. But her thoughts were not on what
she was doing; she was thinking of the man whose own
thoughts had been revolving about her: of Charles Rathlyn, who had been kind to her, friendly, hospitable,
honourable—as not all men, in her experience, were
honourable—and for whom she was only too well aware
that she had come to feel a warmth that was more than
gratitude, more than friendship; a married man who
was no longer married and who she believed, with all
her modesty, felt for her some of the dear affection that
she had for him and who was no longer hopelessly beyond
her reach.

.   .   .   .   .

The season opened, but Charles Rathlyn was not at
the opening meet of the Barrymore, nor at any of the
meets that followed in the weeks ahead. Ashamed and
miserable, he could not bring himself to meet Anne Faery
now. Until he knew better where he stood, until he could
clear his mind of the shock—the shock of Isabel Wey's
threat, of his own weakness in submitting to it—until he
could make some sort of plan that might lead him back
to security and a decent life, he dared not risk meeting
the girl who was so closely, so innocently involved in his
dreadful dilemma. He did not trust himself to conceal
his feelings if he met her, especially in the dear and close
association of the hunting-field as it had been in the previous season. The only way was to keep away.

It was difficult to meet the reproach in Ben Penny's
eye. The old groom could not understand why, now that
his late mistress was decently buried, 'the Captain'
should not start hunting again, a sport that he so genuinely
loved. Here were the horses eating their heads off.
They were exercised, of course, and the Captain took his
share in that, but with high-mettled horses road work is

no substitute for hunting. Captain Rathlyn said that he did not feel like it just yet; well, presumably people knew their own minds best, but what waste it was.

To Charles's surprise, Philip Monner seemed to be making little effort to find fresh and more responsible employment. He assured Charles that he was 'looking about him', that he had written about one or two posts which appeared suitable, that he had given Captain Rathlyn's name as a reference, but no letter came to Charles asking for his opinion of the ability and trustworthiness of the secretary and accountant; it seemed that there was no 'situation vacant' into which he might suitably be installed. Naturally enough, the man looked depressed, his lean face looked thinner and paler than usual, his dark eyes more deeply sunk; never what might be called 'a little ray of sunlight' in the house, he was now just one more shadow in a gloomy scene.

Not that Isabel Wey was gloomy. To the rest of the household she appeared as she had always done, silent, reserved, not a good mixer, but quietly efficient in her work—which was little enough now; Mrs. Tass, who pondered these things in her heart but did not discuss them with others, wondered what on earth the girl was staying on for, but she had learnt that Isabel had a sharp and acid tongue and she did not provoke its use by questioning her. Only with Charles Rathlyn was Isabel her real self, and he kept his knowledge of her deep in his own heart; she was discreet, but she was playing her game, and Charles hardly dared to ask himself what the fullness of it might not be.

So the weeks slipped by and the long job of settling up the deceased lady's affairs and her estate proceeded on its well-ordered course. The executors came from time to time, but seldom troubled Charles. One of them, Mr. Lorriner, had taken charge of all Mrs. Rathlyn's papers and was methodically examining them—not a particularly difficult matter, thanks to the efficiency of her two secretaries, one of them a trained accountant. They told Charles that Tandrings must be sold and that they would be glad if he could ' make his own plans ' by March at the latest. ' Get out ' was what they meant, Charles was only too bitterly aware. Well, he would have to get out—but how? And where to? How could he plan with this millstone of danger and blackmail hanging round his neck?

Drearily he began to look about for somewhere else to live. He knew that he would be wiser to go right away, to cut loose, even perhaps to leave the country, but—apart from the risk that Isabel might put her threat into effect—he could not bring himself to go away from Anne, from his chance of some day seeing her again, of being able to start afresh, even if it was only on the lines of quiet friendship that they had followed during Kate's lifetime. While that clear little flame of honest love remained alight Charles could not bring himself to fly away from it.

Once he had, with the help of his solicitor, been closely into the question of his financial position, as it would be when Kate's legacy was paid to him. Charles realised that it would be quite impossible for him, on the income that it would bring, to keep more than a handful of race-horses in training. It would be absurd to keep one or two steeplechasers and one or two for the flat; better to concentrate on keeping Kate's colours flying under one set of rules and abandon the other. It was National Hunt that she had really enjoyed—steeplechasing—and that was his own true love. He decided to sell the string that had been in Jack Herris's charge at Lambourn and were now at Newmarket under their new trainer, Light. Orders to that effect could be sent in writing, though naturally he would go down to Newmarket and discuss procedure with John Light in person.

Having taken that decision, Charles thought that he would try to shake himself free from his worries for a day by going over to Ewcote to discuss with Carter Casling plans for the National Hunt season which had just opened. The thrill of steeplechasing was still in Charles's blood, and the sight now of Silver Eagle, Ballnaceach and the others did for a few hours drive his horrible dilemma into the background of his mind. As has been said before, neither Kate nor Charles had ever quite liked Casling, and they had contemplated transferring their 'chasers to another trainer, but the death of Jack Herris and the necessity of finding another man to take that string had caused them to leave the 'chasers for the time being with Casling. The latter's hostility to Charles's appointment as racing manager had died down after the latter's marriage to Mrs. Waygold, and he had appeared genuinely sympathetic when the tragedy of her death occurred, so that relations between the two men were now amicable.

Charles had gone over in the early morning and had watched a training gallop, had watched, too, Silver Eagle being schooled over jumps and particularly over the type of open ditch that had put her down at Shankesbury in last season's Royal Cup. The fall had shaken her confidence, and Casling was taking an infinity of pains to restore it to her; an open-ditch jump of quite moderate proportions had first been constructed, and when the mare had assured herself that there really was nothing in the obstacle at all and was jumping it with ease and even enjoyment, the jump was slightly enlarged . . . and so on and so on, until now it was not much less formidable than the open ditch which she would encounter at her first engagement in the following month. Charles was impressed with the patience and thoroughness of the trainer; he began to feel that his own lack of confidence in the man might have been misplaced, and that feeling made him more friendly than he would normally have been. When their business talk was over he accepted an invitation from the trainer to lunch with him, and had the pleasure of meeting a buxom and attractive Mrs. Casling, who expressed the warmest sympathy with him in his loss.

When Charles was getting into his car to leave, Casling asked if he could get in with him and be given a lift to the village, but they had not gone far and were in a quiet stretch of road when the trainer asked him to stop and pull in to the side. Charles did so, wondering what it was about.

" Just wanted a word with you, Captain, where there's no chance of anyone hearing. I may be butting in where not wanted, but somehow I feel you ought to know this. There was a fellow came to see me the other day—a police officer he turned out to be, a detective of some sort —some name like Harris or Hankey."

Charles's heart had given a bound at the word ' police ', but he remained silent, merely lighting a cigarette to distract attention from any sign there might be on his face.

" Came to ask questions about you, it seemed, and about the running of Silver Eagle. Of course, he didn't get anything out of me. I didn't refuse to answer questions, because I thought that might make him think I had something to hide; I just said we had only business relations with each other and that I couldn't wish for a straighter man to work for. As for Silver Eagle—I told him that I'd only had the mare a year and that there was nothing wrong with her running; she'd just taken a toss at Shankesbury, as any steeplechaser is liable to do."

Charles Rathlyn was staring in astonishment now.

" What on earth was all that about? " he asked.

"I haven't a clue, Captain. But it seemed that it wasn't this last season he was interested in, but the season before, when she nearly won the Royal. Someone appears to have put it into his head that you had got a mighty lot of money on her in that race and that you got long odds about her because she fell at Hurst Park earlier in the season. Well, why shouldn't she? I asked; if I remember rightly, she was knocked into coming to the last fence. But no, he wouldn't have that; someone—I couldn't get him to tell me who—had said that Dan Maston had deliberately unbalanced her, on your orders."

"That's a bloody lie," exclaimed Charles hotly. "Dan wouldn't do a thing like that, even if I would."

"That's what I said to him, Captain—about Dan, not about you; I sent him off with a flea in his ear, and if it had been the season for horse-flies I'd have put one of them in the other. I thought you ought to know."

Charles thanked him, declaring that he had no idea in the world what it was all about. But as he drove home his troubles settled quickly round him again. Superintendent Hant's enquiries about Silver Eagle were a complete mystery to him, but Casling's story suggested that though the police had ceased to worry him, they had by no means lost their interest in his affairs.

CHAPTER XIV

Fight for Her

DETECTIVE-SUPERINTENDENT HANT had not lost
interest. Far from it. The Coroner's open verdict alone
would have kept it alive, but that was not really needed;
in his bones Hant felt that Mrs. Rathlyn's death had been
no accident, that her husband had either pushed her over
the balustrade when she was sleep-walking or had in some
other way engineered her death to look like an accident.
The Chief Constable, he knew, took a different view, but
Mr. Janson—a sharp fellow that—had encouraged him to
look further, though he had discounted the legacy, large
as it was, as a motive and had not thought that much
importance should be attached to the actual position of
the body on the floor of the hall.

A pity that; Hant had thought that he was on to something there. How could he get proof that this had been
no accident? It would be difficult, unless he could find
someone who had seen or heard something suspicious on
the night of Mrs. Rathlyn's fall. But he had questioned
everybody in the house, and nobody seemed to have seen
or heard anything—except, of course, Captain Rathlyn
himself, who was probably lying. The most likely one
would have been Mr. George Waygold, who alone had
occupied a room in the vicinity of the Rathlyns, but Mr.
Waygold had declared that he had slept like a top and
had even admitted to Hant that he had drunk a good
deal of brandy at and after dinner and that nothing short
of an earthquake would have awakened him—an earthquake or Charles Rathlyn shaking him violently by the
shoulder, which, he declared, was the first he had heard
of the matter.

Surely a scream would have wakened him? Surely, if Captain Rathlyn had flung his wife down into the hall there must have been a struggle, a scream? Even if she had been sleep-walking, that attack would have wakened her and she would have fought and screamed—would she not? But Mr. Waygold had heard no struggle, no scream—damn the drunken fool.

The only other person within possible earshot was Miss Wey, whose bedroom was on the same floor, though at the far end of a wing. And she, too, had declared that she had heard nothing. Hant remembered, though, that after his interview with her on the morning of Mrs. Rathlyn's death he had been left with the impression that she might be concealing something. He remembered, too, that at their next talk, when he was asking her about Mrs. Rathlyn's letter to her solicitor and the possible reason for it, she had seemed to hesitate . . . and then Captain Rathlyn himself had been heard in the hall and she had said: " Better ask him." Was it, he wondered, any good trying her again? He decided to wait until he had got something more definite to go on.

Had Mrs. Rathlyn screamed? Would she not have screamed in any case, even if her fall had been accidental? If she had really been sleep-walking, really had overbalanced, would not that have woken her up—the moment of falling—and would she not have screamed then? If that was so, a scream would be no evidence of murder, even if someone had heard it. It would be as well to find out a bit more about that—from the doctor.

But Dr. Jennerel could not give him much help on that point. He had himself had little experience of sleepwalking, and though he expressed the opinion that a sleep-walker would normally be surefooted, unlikely to overbalance, he was not prepared to be dogmatic about it.

"Why don't you go and see Dr. Sykes?" he asked.

Hant had never heard of Dr. Sykes, but he proved to be the Superintendent in charge of the big mental hospital which served the National Health Service region of which Barryshire was a part. Dr. Sykes was a busy man, with a considerable sense of his own importance, and was not lightly to be interviewed by police-officers, of whatever rank. However, Hant was nothing if not dogged and in due course got his interview. It was worth working and waiting for.

Briefly, Dr. Sykes told Hant that though a sleep-walker might react to shock in many ways, it was perfectly possible that such a one might fall to her death without waking and without crying out.

"What if someone took hold of her and pushed her over?" asked Hant.

"The same applies. She might wake, she might cry out; but it would not be in the least surprising if she never woke. As I say, she might fall to her death, even be thrown to her death, without waking, without being conscious of what was happening to her, and so without screaming or uttering any sound at all."

Hant listened eagerly to this vital information. If that were so, it removed one of the strongest objections to his murder theory that had appeared to him to exist. How, he had wondered, *could* Captain Rathlyn have thrown his wife down into the hall without incurring fearful risk? This was the answer. Then another thought struck him —another objection that had plagued him. Supposing the fall had not killed the woman? After all, a fall of thirty or forty feet was not necessarily fatal. That, again seemed to be a terrible risk for the murderer—that the intended victim might not die, might be able to tell of what had been done to her. Dr. Sykes calmly swept that objection, too, aside.

" Even if she were not injured at all, or if she were injured in any degree, she would probably not have the least idea of what had been done to her."

Quivering with excitement, Hant rose to his feet, eager to tell the Chief Constable what he had learnt.

" You'll be sure not to say a word about this to anyone, doctor," he said. " I don't want it known that we still have our suspicions."

Dr. Sykes froze him with a steely eye.

" All our work is confidential, Superintendent," he said; " it is quite unnecessary for you to give me so elementary a warning."

Hant was much too thrilled to be worried by that rebuke; he felt that he had taken a big step forward in his enquiry. At least, two serious objections had been swept aside. But proof? Proof was still as far to seek as ever.

Feeling in need of a little encouragement, and doubtful of getting it from the Chief Constable, Hant asked for a word with Mr. Janson. The Assistant Chief Constable, as has been said, had had considerable C.I.D. experience with the Metropolitan Police before coming to Barryshire; he was a younger man even than Hant, who himself was young as County Superintendents go, and at first the Barryshire man had been inclined to resent this fact, but he recognised Mr. Janson's ability and had come to respect if not actually to like him.

Janson listened carefully to what the detective had to say and then asked a few questions, to assure himself that Hant had fully interpreted the psychiatrist's opinion.

" That seems to me very useful, Mr. Hant," he said. " If you haven't already done so, I advise you to write down pretty fully what Dr. Sykes said. Then you can put it away in cold storage and produce it if necessary. I still incline myself to the belief that Mrs. Rathlyn's death

was accidental, but you are certainly right to keep on prob-
ing for fresh evidence to the contrary.   Did you look any
further into the question of an alternative motive? Alternative to money, I mean.''

" Woman, sir?   You'll remember that the Chief Constable rather jumped down my throat about that.''

Mr. Janson smiled.

" That was about one particular person, I think.   There
are other women in the world.''

Hant looked enquiringly at his superior officer.

" Anybody particular in mind, sir? ''

Janson shook his head.

" I don't know the cast well enough.   I certainly have
not heard of any lady's name being coupled with Captain
Rathlyn's, apart from what you told us.   But—didn't you
say something about a secretary?   She has gone, I suppose? ''

Superintendent Hant pursed his lips in a silent whistle.

" Miss Wey; I never thought about her in that . . . in
that connection, sir.   She certainly is a good looker, in a
rather hard sort of way.   As you say, I expect she's gone.
I'll make sure about that.   And I'll try and find out
whether there's ever been anything between them.''

" Do it discreetly, Mr. Hant; I needn't tell you that.
We haven't really got anything against Captain Rathlyn,
and it wouldn't be fair to him to stir up a lot of suspicions.''

.   .   .   .   .

It was perhaps fortunate for Charles Rathlyn's peace
of mind that he knew nothing of this conversation.   When
he had slept on the uncomfortable bit of news that Carter
Casling had given him, he was able to persuade himself
that there could not be anything sinister in the enquiries
that the detective had been making into the running of
Silver Eagle.   Probably the man had been just rounding
off his enquiries into Kate's death, in the methodical

routine way that policemen did—especially policemen with not a lot of real work to do—and had picked up one of the dirty little rumours that were always circulating round the race-courses and training stables. In any case, no one was going to bother about such old history—even if there was anything to bother about.

So Charles comforted himself and, still unable to bring himself to face Anne Faery, still longing for a sight of her, decided one non-hunting day in January to take his car round in the direction of the Faery stables in the hope of seeing her, even in the distance, exercising or schooling one of her father's young hunters.

It was a clear, crisp afternoon—too crisp from a hunting point of view, though there was not much 'bone' in the ground. Charles longed to be riding himself, going for a long hack with Anne, talking quietly and happily about trivial or personal things—anything but the grim problem that obsessed him. He had had little chance, in all his life, to talk in a quiet, intimate way with a woman; he had flirted with women, had 'fun' with them, but never treated one of them as a close and equal friend. He had missed a great deal—he realised it now—by not doing so. Even after his marriage, even when he was genuinely fond of Kate, he had never been on terms of close personal trust and friendship with her; he had always been putting on a bit of an act.

Something had made him believe that he could be on just these terms with Anne, even though she was a dozen or more years younger than himself, even though he had never exchanged one intimate word with her. That is a knowledge that comes to a man or a woman without their being able to explain it. So now he drove through country where he thought he might catch a glimpse of her, even though he did not expect or even want to talk to her. He was too ashamed to do that. But when he came to

Captain Faery's farm, which lay back from the road but with the exercising fields and schooling jumps within easy view, there was no sign of Anne. Faery himself was there and a groom, but there was no slim figure in jodhpurs, either mounted or on foot. Charles drove sadly past and, taking a turn to the left, made a detour through the woods that lay behind the farm.

These were coverts of mixed oak and ash, bare now of leaf, but beautiful where the pale sunlight struck upon their stems. Occasional groups of spruce showed that pheasants were encouraged here—the spruce were their roosting places at night. The road ran along a hollow, and it was clear that birds would rise well here as they passed from one wood to the other, away from the tapping sticks of the beaters. Charles's thoughts were on this pleasant, imaginary scene when a rabbit sprang from the hedge on his left and dashed across the road, closely followed by a yapping flash of white—a small, short-haired terrier. They were almost under his wheels when Charles swung the car abruptly to the right; fortunately he had not been going fast and he was able to stop just short of the ditch. Pursuer and pursued passed on, full pelt into the other wood, heedless of the new peril they had so narrowly escaped. Charles followed them with muttered curses and, restarting the engine, which had stalled, backed the car on to the road. As he did so, he saw a girl standing on the bank where the rabbit had come out—a girl in tweeds and jumper, wearing no hat. It was Anne Faery.

Charles stared at her stupidly and she at him. Neither showed a sign of being in the least pleased to see the other. Anne was the first to recover her manners.

" I'm so awfully sorry; I'm afraid Tiger must nearly have upset you."

Charles moved the car to the side of the road, switched

off the engine, and got out. Taking off his cap, he held
out his hand to Anne.

" I'm so glad to see you," he said. " It's been a very
long time."

Nervousness and uncertainty made his voice dry.
There was no smile on his face, and the girl looked at him
with equal uncertainty. In her heart she had wondered
why he had so long neglected her, even though she knew
that there was no reason for him to do anything else.

" I was passing the farm; I thought you might be
schooling."

" No, I'm not riding today. Father is there, though."
Then her eyes went past him into the wood where dog
and rabbit had disappeared. " You know . . . I think
I ought to go after Tiger. He goes down rabbit-holes and
sometimes gets stuck."

Was it a rebuff? Intensely sensitive now, Charles
nearly accepted it as such, and was on the point of saying
good-bye when he realised that to do that would probably
mean the end of their friendship.

" I'll come with you, if I may."

They climbed the bank into the wood and walked
through the trees, Anne whistling and calling. Charles
did not try to distract her with conversation, but watched
the sunlight glinting on her brown hair. Presently they
came to a large rabbit bury; as they did so an extremely
dirty terrier backed himself out of one of the holes, gave
himself a good shake, sneezed two or three times and then,
with tongue hanging out, looked up at his mistress for
approbation.

" Oh, Tiger, you little pig; what a mess you're in."

Anne bent down and brushed some more of the dirt
from the dog's coat; it was little more than a nervous
gesture. Then, standing up, on an impulse that she could
hardly have explained, she said:

"Father's giving up."

Charles stared at her.

"Giving up? You mean—the farm? The business?"

Anne nodded.

"He says the bottom's fallen out of it in this part of the world. He has always gone in for making really high-class, expensive hunters; you know, several hundred guineas. There's no market for them in the provinces now—not enough people who can afford to pay those prices. It's all right in the shires, of course. We could always sell horses of a sort, but he won't do that; it's the making of them that he loves, and that takes time and costs money. So he's going to sell up and . . . he talks of going to Ireland."

Charles felt the blood drain from his heart. To Ireland . . . Anne? It would mean losing her altogether.

"Oh Anne, no. You can't . . . go away like that."

The girl saw the consternation in his face; it told its message more than his halting words could do. She was standing close in front of him; instinctively her hand went up, touched the lapel of his jacket. The next moment she was in his arms and words were pouring from him in wild confusion, like water long pent up by a dam.

"Anne! You mustn't go. Oh, Anne, I love you so. I have loved you from the first moment I saw you. It was hopeless, I knew. . . . And all that horrible trouble . . . the suspicion. . . . Anne, do you care for me a little bit? . . . I have tried to keep away from you. . . . I couldn't bring you into it all. Anne, don't go, don't go."

He was crushing her so closely to him that she could hardly speak, but her quick wit had picked out one coherent sentence from among the jumble.

"Why did you . . . try to keep away from me?"

"I . . . oh, Anne, does that mean you care a little bit? I have never known if you felt anything for me at all."

Anne Faery smiled up at him.

" I could hardly tell you that, could I? But you know now, Charles."

And so they stood, locked together, telling each other of their love. Charles was so wildly happy that the grim shadow had for the nonce fallen from him. Tiger, on the other hand, was bored and began sniffing again at the rabbit holes.

Gradually they came back to the world, to the problems that lay before them, to their plans for the future. Charles recognised the force of Captain Faery's arguments, but how would it be if they joined forces? In Leicestershire, perhaps; why run away to Ireland? There was, of course, a plethora of horse-dealers in Leicestershire and the other shires, but Faery had a reputation and he, Charles, had knowledge and skill, while Anne was the ideal maker, in conjunction with her father, of a woman's hunter. A partnership, the three of them together, Charles married to Anne—it offered a fairy-tale of hope and happiness.

And then Charles hit the ground—as hard a crash as he had hit it when Dashalong jumped into those solid oaken rails. Isabel Wey. Blackmail.

But he had something to fight for now and he was going to fight. Somehow he would get himself out of this mess. Nothing should keep Anne from him now.

" My darling," he said, " this is all going to happen, but I've got a battle to fight first. I'm not going to worry you with it all, but the fact is that the police still suspect that I killed my wife."

Anne stared at him in horror.

" Killed! Oh, how can they? But it was . . . the inquest; they said it was an accident."

Charles smiled.

" Well, not quite, apparently; what they call an open

verdict. But that doesn't stop the police suspecting, and apparently they still do. I'm not going to drag you into that. I'm not even going to ask you to marry me until I'm absolutely in the clear. But I shall be . . . if you give me courage to fight them."

.   .   .   .   .

Charles drove home with happiness and grim determination mingled inextricably in his heart. Whatever happened he was finished with Isabel Wey now. He hated himself for having given in to her, for his weakness and cowardice, his horrible treachery to Anne. But he would be weak no longer. He would challenge her to do her worst; for all he knew her worst might be bluff—she might crumple if he called it. He would call it now, while his blood was up, before he could weaken again.

On second thoughts, better perhaps to wait till the usual time; if there had to be a row, a storm, better that others should not hear it. She almost always came to his study late at night, when Ludd and Philip Monner had gone to bed. She would come tonight.

When she came, looking as she always did now, young and attractive in her soft black frock, Charles was waiting for her in front of the fire, standing with his back to it, facing the big, heavily-curtained window. She came straight to him but instead of kissing her he said:

" Not now, Isabel. I want to tell you that this must stop. I'm not going on with it. If you have anything to tell the police you must tell them."

He spoke quietly and his face showed no anger, but she recognised the tone in his voice. It did not daunt her; she smiled up at him and said, no less quietly:

" I don't think you quite realise. I can *prove* what I say."

" Prove what? It's only your word against mine."

" About the fall, yes—though my unbiased word will

count more than yours. But I can prove that you were making love to Anne Faery and that your wife knew it."

She turned on her heel and walked out of the room. Charles stood, half bewildered, wondering whether she was coming back. She was back within two minutes, standing again in front of him, holding in her two hands a piece of paper for him to read. Instinctively he read it and his heart fell; it was a letter from Kate to Anne; it was not in Kate's handwriting but the words were recognisably hers—not vulgar or offensive, but a little shrill; blunt and perfectly clear—' keep away from my husband '. If there were an original it would be damning evidence of motive. Combined with whatever Isabel might swear she had seen it would almost certainly lead to his arrest, might lead him to the gallows.

Isabel read his thoughts.

" Oh yes, I've got the original all right. I never posted it. And so, you see, I've got you too, my dear man. And I'm not going to let you go."

She came close to him; once again, as on that first night, her arms, white and soft, slipped round his neck. Automatically Charles put his arms round her; he did not pat her shoulder, as he had patted Kate's that night in February, nearly a year ago, but as he looked past her his face, as then, was hard and grim.

CHAPTER XV

Lighted Windows

THE ASSISTANT Chief Constable had warned Superintendent Hant not to stir up suspicions about Captain Rathlyn's possible ' affairs ' with women other than his wife. To be, in fact, discreet. Easier said than done. How could he find out that sort of thing without arousing suspicions? Well, perhaps there was another way; if he could not hear perhaps he could see.

That Miss Faery was the one Hant really had in mind. He had heard a thing or two about the Captain going hunting with her, about her going back to Tandrings in the ambulance with him when he had that fall; that old groom, Penny, had not said much, but Hant had got the impression that Miss Faery had been a good deal more upset than a girl would be about a man who meant nothing to her. Still, he could not find that Rathlyn had been seeing anything of her since then, though that might merely be discretion. In any case, the Chief Constable had whipped him off that line. Hant did not know the expression ' 'ware riot ', but these were hunting people, and there was a freemasonry between them—Colonel Netterly, Captain Faery and his daughter; the two men soldiers as well. Prejudice; influence, thought Hant grimly—a most unjustified and disloyal thought.

However, the Assistant Chief had now laid him on to a fresh line—unconsciously Hant's thoughts were following hunting metaphors. This female secretary, Miss Wey; what about her? A good-looker, right on the spot, wife getting old and fat; what more likely than that the Captain's eyes had wandered to a bit of all right so close at hand. The detective had a rather nastily suspicious mind.

He had said that Miss Wey had probably gone by now, but he soon found out that she had not. The fact at once struck him as suspicious. What would a girl like that—personal, confidential secretary to a lady—want to stay on in the house with the widower for if not for some personal reason? Surely in four months she could have found some suitable fresh employment?

Along these latter lines it might be possible to make some casual enquiries, either from the old housekeeper or from that other secretary, Monner, who also remained; natural enough that he should; no doubt Captain Rathlyn still needed him. Hant had got the impression that Monner was not too fond of Miss Wey—jealous of her, more than likely; jealous of her confidential position with his late employer, whom they had both served while Mrs. Waygold was still a widow. Why she should have needed two secretaries was something Hant could not understand —but, then, presumably rich people had needs, fancied needs, that were beyond his comprehension.

The detective knew that Philip Monner was in the habit of coming into Barryfield at least once a week, to cash a cheque and do any necessary business. He made a point of waylaying him—quite by chance—one day and piloting him into a quiet side-street where he asked casual, friendly questions about how things were going at Tandrings. A sad business all that had been. Would the Captain be staying on there? The secretary thought not. Mr. George Waygold? What about him? He came down every now and then, mostly to talk business with the executors; he was not there now. A glint of a smile crossed the secretary's pale face as he said that he thought Mr. Waygold was a bit disappointed to find just how much—just not *so* much—was coming to him.

" And you yourself, Mr. Monner? You'll be staying with Captain Rathlyn, no doubt."

" For the moment."

The answer was curt.   There was no smile on Monner's face now.

" Well, it's a sad business, breaking up a happy home. That young lady now, Miss Wey; she'll be gone, I suppose? "

" Miss Wey is still at Tandrings."   The voice was flat.

" Ah well, no doubt you all got very fond of each other. Captain Rathlyn wouldn't like to part with you before he must, especially as you had all been in his poor dead wife's employ before he came on the scene.   Mrs. Rathlyn was very fond of Miss Wey, I understand; no doubt the Captain would feel that way too."

But this fly rose no fish, and before long Philip Monner had detached himself, leaving Hant little the wiser.   It seemed unlikely that he would learn anything more definite from either Ludd or Mrs. Tass, and Hant was particularly unwilling to pit his wits against those of the shrewd old housekeeper; if anyone were to get any information out of such a verbal fencing match it would probably be the lady.

So the detective determined to try the alternative mode of ' finding out '—to use his eyes, rather than his ears. Not, perhaps, his own eyes; it is hardly appropriate for a Detective-Superintendent to creep about looking round corners; but here was an admirable opportunity for one of his young detective-constables to prove his worth, and Hant chose the youngest and most active of them for the job—' creeping ' might literally be needed, and even climbing.

Detective-Constable Michael Filblow was twenty-seven years old and had only been in the C.I.D. about eighteen months.   He was of the bare minimum height—five feet eight—and was slim, agile and well-balanced, a first-class footballer and a man with his wits about him.   He had

the additional advantage of boundless ambition and no
marital incubus—it would not worry him if he did have to
be out all night . . . and there would be no one to ask
where he had been or what doing. Hant believed in
taking his subordinates as fully as possible into his confidence, believing that they would always respect it if they
knew that he trusted them, and that a man who knew the
reason why would be able to avoid unconscious blunders.

Filblow listened to the story with eager interest, asked a
few supplementary questions, and having been told that if
he got into trouble the police would disown him—in the
best tradition of the secret service—went off to think out
his plan of action. His terms of reference were: find out
whether Captain Rathlyn has, since his marriage, been
having an affair with any woman other than his wife,
with special reference to the late Mrs. Rathlyn's personal
secretary, Miss Isabel Wey. As he had been told to do it
by observation rather than by questions, Mike Filblow
thought it rather absurd to expect him to find out what
might have happened in the past; he decided to concentrate on the present, which might well be a continuation
of the past, and Isabel Wey in particular.

As it was not to be known that he was a police-officer,
clearly some sort of disguise was necessary—the neat rain-
coat and trilby hat were 'out' for this job. False nose
and moustache find no part in modern disguise; much
more effective it is to let the well-drilled shoulders droop,
the muscled stomach sag. Clothes do the rest—old flannel
bags, pullover and discarded jacket, no hat at all and
unkempt hair; those were the costume for act one—
Stubbins, a gardener out of work. Not that he proposed to
go asking for work—few men need do that nowadays—but
in case he was seen and questioned that would serve. In
the dusk or at night he could be just a poacher, and if he
were nabbed he would 'take it' with a grin and pay his

few bob fine, which is all the modern bench of magistrates deals out to a poacher in the cure-by-kindness state.

At first Filblow tried to keep an eye on both Captain Rathlyn and Miss Wey, but he soon realised that the Captain was too elusive a bird for a detective lacking horse and car. If he could have followed Charles Rathlyn on that drive round Faery's farm his problem would have been quickly solved, but by that time he had switched exclusively to Isabel Wey. He found that she was a young woman of regular habits; she went for a walk each afternoon from two-thirty to four and otherwise did not leave the house, except to go to Barryfield by bus each Thursday afternoon. He watched her on all these occasions and found to his disappointment that she met and talked to nobody. But, after all, if she were having an affair with her employer that could go on quite comfortably indoors —after closing time, so to speak.

That thought encouraged the young detective to use his brains rather more actively than he had so far done. If this affair was going on indoors, when and where would it be happening? That depended partly on how far it had gone. If it were a really nasty bit of work, it would happen in somebody's bedroom and almost certainly with the lights out; there were too many people in the house for any game of that kind without extreme secrecy. But a flirtation, a close and honourable friendship, possibly with marriage in view, might take place with not much more than discretion, in a sitting-room probably, after the normal day's work was done—no interruption likely. If it were anything more open than that Filblow felt that he was bound to have seen them together in daylight.

Very well then, where and when? The detective watched the house as soon as dusk fell and soon got to discover which ground-floor room was which; lights were switched on before curtains were drawn and it was easy to identify pantry, dining-room, study. Philip Monner appearing at the window each evening to draw the curtains showed which was his office, and one day Filblow caught sight of Isabel Wey doing the same thing in a room upstairs. She was not a servant, she would not be doing that in any room but her own. After three nights of watching the detective got the routine pretty clear. Though curtains were drawn at dusk there was usually a band of light to show which room was occupied—and what time it ceased to be. Dining-room, pantry, housekeeper's room, kitchen, each in turn and at regular intervals, subsided into darkness; the study light remained, usually till twelve o'clock or thereabouts. There were lights upstairs till varying hours, but Filblow did not know which room was which, except Miss Wey's, and this in fact was the room she worked in, not her bedroom, so it was normally in darkness fairly early.

From ten o'clock to twelve—those seemed the likely hours for philandering, and the whereabouts?—surely the Captain's study. If only he could look inside! Although on the ground floor it was not possible to look in through the window, even if no curtain were drawn; the ground fell away slightly on this side of the house. What about a ladder? The ground was soft—except when there was a frost; it would not do to give away the fact that there was a snooper about. Then closer inspection showed Filblow that there was a stone string-course— or whatever the correct expression was—running round the house at the level of the ground-floor window-sills; it gave, he found, just a toe-hold, and the friction of hands pressed against the brick wall should keep one upright. At the end of the house it was possible to get on to this course without a ladder; then one would have to edge carefully along it, turn the corner, and edge along again till one got to the study window.

Filblow tried the manœuvre each night, fell off once or twice but too lightly to give himself away, and gradually acquired skill. If only the curtains were not drawn! Even a chink between them might show him what he wanted to see. There was no chink; Filblow cursed the butler as he watched him, evening after evening, drawing the curtains, carefully pulling them together so that they overlapped.

It was useless. Dejectedly Filblow went to his chief and told him that he was learning nothing—told him his ideas and his failure to put them to effective test. Hant smiled at him and said, with no great originality, that patience was a virtue.

The weather turned cold, the ground hard; Filblow toyed with the idea of trying a long ladder to one of the upstairs windows, which he suspected of being the Captain's and where the blinds were not drawn with such meticulous care. But a ladder long enough for that would be heavy, would need two men to manipulate—that could be managed—and would almost certainly make a noise and attract attention. The detective did not want to come up for attempted burglary; on such a charge it would be difficult to keep his real identity secret.

Then, on the second cold night, when he was not looking forward to clinging by his toes and fingers to any wall, Mike Filblow saw what he had been waiting for—a crack, thin as a pencil but definite, between the study curtains. Mounting the ledge at its most easily accessible point, he skilfully worked his way along, turned the corner of the wall and soon reached the window. The walls were thick, so that the curtains did not lie close to the window—his eye was not close enough to the crack to be able to see more than a tiny section of the room. But he could see that clearly enough—just the fireplace opposite him. No chair was visible, nor any human being; presumably there was someone in the room, because the lights were on, but for a long time there was no sign or sound. A clock struck eleven, and almost immediately afterwards a man's figure was visible, moving towards the fire. The man turned round; it was Captain Rathlyn. He appeared to be watching something to one side of the room—possibly the door; there was a look of tense expectancy on his face.

The detective's heart was beating fast now. He felt in his bones that something was going to happen, something that it was vital for him to see. Cold as he was, his fingers and toes stiff and numb, he pressed close to the window, looking, listening. After about five minutes he saw Rathlyn stiffen, his eyes move . . . and then the figure of a woman came between him and the window, a woman in a black dress with short sleeves—unmistakably the secretary, Miss Wey, though her back was to the watcher.

Captain Rathlyn was speaking to her now; Filblow could see his lips moving, hear a faint murmur, but to his bitter disappointment he could distinguish no words. There was little expression on the speaker's face; certainly it did not look like the face of a lover—if anything, it was cold and stern. The detective could see nothing of Isabel Wey's expression, but suddenly she turned on her heel and disappeared, before he could get more than a glance of her face.

Was that all? Filblow's spirits slumped; what a flop! —no kissing and cuddling, not a smile, perhaps no more than orders for tomorrow. Captain Rathlyn was still standing in front of the fire, looking rather puzzled—no doubt he would disappear from view again in a second. The detective began to prepare for his own departure, easing his cramped limbs, flexing the fingers of each hand in turn . . . before he had moved away he saw Rathlyn stiffen again, again that look towards the door, again the back of Isabel Wey. He saw her hold up a piece of paper, which Charles Rathlyn appeared to read—then she moved close to him, her arms went round his neck, his arms round her!

Half an hour later the young detective had retrieved his bicycle from its hiding-place in a shrubbery and was pedalling vigorously back to Barryfield. He was thrilled by what he had seen—lover's meeting beyond a doubt, exactly what Superintendent Hant had put him on to find out about! True, the expression on Captain Rathlyn's face, even with the girl in his arms, had remained stern, even grim, but that might have been a trick of the light . . . or perhaps love took him that way. The embrace had not lasted long, and Miss Wey had evidently left the room, leaving the Captain with his back to the window now, looking down into the fire. Presently he, too, had disappeared from view, and soon the room was in darkness.

Warming up as he pedalled, Filblow planned how he would break the news to his chief. Should he make it as dramatic as possible—write it up, so to speak?—or tell it quietly, as a matter-of-fact, routine report—a masterpiece of understatement? He plumped for the latter, as tending to modesty, which a superior officer generally preferred to swank; that decided him not to wake the Super up at midnight—morning would do.

Morning did very well, and Filblow had no reason to regret his quiet delivery of the news. Superintendent Hant took it calmly enough, but there was a glint in his eyes as he heard of the embrace.

"We'll get him now," he said quietly. "No doubt why he did it, though it'll take some proving. You keep on at it, young fellow; you've done well and you'll do better. Patience . . . you know what I said. Now that I know for a certainty I'll find some way of proving it."

But proof remained as far to seek as ever. Filblow saw no more scenes in the study—the crack in the curtain did not occur again. The days passed and then the weeks, January merging into February with no advance save the snowdrops and a spike or two of early daffodil. Hant discussed the new development with his superiors, who showed interest mingled, on the part of the Chief Constable, with scepticism.

" Kissing a pretty girl doesn't add up to murder," was the way Colonel Netterly put it. Hant remained doggedly determined—and at a loss.

CHAPTER XVI

A Cup of Tea

MRS. TASS leaned back against her propped pillows and sipped the cup of China tea which young Janet Penny, humblest of housemaids, had just brought her. The curtains had not been drawn back because at seven-thirty the light in mid-February was still gloomy at that hour; in the depths of winter Mrs. Tass rose majestically with the sun—round about eight o'clock—and liked to sip and ponder for half an hour ere she rose. Her thoughts now were generally on the approaching change in her mode of life. At sixty plus she could not expect and now, thanks to her dear girl's—her Kate's—generosity, she need not try to find fresh employment. Within a month or two the household would be broken up, Tandrings itself sold, and she herself would move to the comfortable rooms which her sister had found for her at Hove. She would miss the busy life, the pleasant authority of her position as housekeeper in a great house, but that would have had to be faced in any case in a few years, and Amelia Tass had no doubt that she would soon make a new and interesting life for herself, gather round her a fresh circle of friends, in the respectable and sociable surroundings of the Sussex seaside town.

She would be sorry to part from ' her ' staff; the men servants of course—what were left of them—were no business of hers; Mr. Ludd was well enough, he had been trained in good houses, he knew his place and had never attempted to encroach on the housekeeper's domain; she quite liked him, but it would not break her heart to bid him farewell. It was the girls she cared about; Annie—officially Mrs. Meadows—the cook, had been at Tandrings for fifteen years and now, strictly speaking, hardly came within the category of 'girls'. Gwen Tidy, kitchen-cum-scullery, was a clumsy lump and idle, but she was good-natured and not saucy, as some had been; Margaret, head housemaid, was a dour little Scotswoman, not dear to Mrs. Tass's heart, but the sole surviving under-house-maid, Janet Penny, was a dear child, all that could be wished for by her good father, widowed Ben Penny, head groom, and Mrs. Tass would mind parting from those two more than she cared to think.

There remained, of course, Isabel Wey. About her Mrs. Tass had retained an obstinate silence, even to her-self; she had known Isabel from a girl, had encouraged Kate Waygold to take her as her maid, and failed to dis-courage her from turning a respectable, useful maid into a quite unnecessary and soon conceited and impertinent secretary. Isabel, of course, came of superior stock—of some kind; she had been picked from an orphanage by Mrs. Tass herself, who had been struck by her good looks, refined speech and natural good manners. Who her parents had been the Orphanage either did not know or would not say. In her early years of service Isabel had remained a nice, respectable girl, but three years in the A.T.S. had done her no good at all; she had returned too sure of herself, too good-looking, and altogether too clever for either Mrs. Tass or her mistress; almost at once she had slipped into her new position of confidential secretary —or whatever the nonsense was. After her one deter-mined attempt to prevent this had failed, Mrs. Tass had maintained that obstinate silence about the girl, even in her own thoughts, to which reference has already been made.

Mrs. Tass was looking very old at this moment, possibly because she had not yet put her teeth in; while Janet was setting the little tea-tray beside her bed she lay with her back to the girl, merely indicating that she was awake; she would not like the girl to see her without her dentures. They were in a jar beside the bed, and normally she left them there till after she had washed. The effect of their absence was ageing, but as no one saw her now, what did that matter? Perhaps her flickering thoughts, which take long to tell but only seconds to pass through the mind, were ageing too, especially the thought of parting from those she loved—Annie Meadows, Ben Penny and his little daughter; she had even come to find a soft corner in her heart for the good-looking soldier whom her ' baby ', Kate Waygold, had surprisingly taken as a husband. Kate had been happy with him, especially in the early months of their married life, though Mrs. Tass had been distressed by the excessive drinking and fits of temper that had begun to show themselves before the sudden end.

Her thoughts were suddenly interrupted by the sound of hurried footsteps in the passage outside; there was a hurried tap and the door at once opened to disclose Janet, breathless and wide-eyed.

" Oh, Mrs. Tass! Miss Wey! "

Turning her back to the girl, Mrs. Tass reached for the jar, slipped in her dentures and then gave her attention to Janet.

" Yes, Janet; what is it? "

" Oh, Mrs. Tass, she's . . . I think she's dead! "

Tears began to flow down the girl's rosy cheeks; she hiccoughed and choked.

" Shut the door, Janet, and come here. Now tell me, quietly."

Whatever she might feel, Amelia Tass never allowed herself to appear flurried or upset. She did not encourage it in others. Janet obeyed, her tears subsiding.

" I . . . I took her her cup of tea, just after yours, Mrs.

Tass. Well, ten minutes after, I suppose. She says to be called a quarter to eight."

" Much too late," murmured the housekeeper. " Go on."

" I don't switch on the light. She doesn't like it. I just drew back the curtains and then turned to take the cup to her . . . oh! . . ."

The girl's face was screwing up again.

" Now, don't make a fuss, Janet. Just tell me."

" She was . . . she's lying on her back, Mrs. Tass, her face all sort of . . . odd-looking. Her mouth and eyes are open and she's staring . . . oh, horrible! I don't . . . I don't think she's alive."

Action was needed. Orders must be given.

" Does anyone else know? Is Mr. Ludd about yet? "

" I haven't seen him, Mrs. Tass. I haven't told anyone else—I came straight to you."

" Quite right, but go and tell Mr. Ludd now. If he's not about tap at his door; and don't be shy, go right in and tell him, even if he's dressing. Pull yourself together and tell him quietly. Ask him from me to ring Dr. Jennerel at once and ask him to come. I will be down in two minutes."

Mrs. Tass could do that easily. She was always neat and tidy; her scanty grey hair was in two short pigtails— she had only to twist and pin them up. Her long flannel nightgown served as a skirt, her warm dressing-gown was a complete garment in itself and a scarf hid her scraggy neck. Only stockings would be lacking, but her legs would not show. She thrust her small and still well-shaped feet into the padded silk slippers which had been her dear Kate's last incongruous present to her. In less than two minutes she was standing by Isabel Wey's bed, looking down at the dreadful sight that had so distressed poor Janet.

The girl—as Mrs. Tass still thought of her; the woman, as she was—was lying on her back, the upper part of her body uncovered by blankets, as if she had thrust them back. It was covered only—most inadequately covered, as the housekeeper thought—by a very thin peach-coloured nightgown, low cut and sleeveless, a mere wisp of diaphanous nylon. Her beauty should have entranced the eye, even of another woman, but it did not now; the eye could only gaze in horror on the poor dead face, the sagging jaw, half-open eyes, the mottled skin. It was a sight that shocked the nerves even of calm old Amelia Tass.

Quietly she felt for a heart-beat, held a hand-glass before the mouth, then gently covered the dead woman's face with a face-towel. She looked about her and noticed that on the bedside table was a tooth-glass, with a little liquid, possibly water but clouded, at the bottom. Two tablet-bottles lay beside it—apparently empty; on each was the word DORMONAL, with printed directions in smaller lettering. Mrs. Tass did not touch them. She did not even touch the broken cup and saucer which lay on the carpet, stained by the spilt tea, half-way between window and bed, though her fingers itched to remove the disorderly mess before the doctor came. But Mrs. Tass was thriller-trained as well as service-trained; she knew that Isabel Wey had died by poisoning, that the police would come, would want to test all possible 'vehicles' of the poison. Finger-prints, too; no doubt they would be Janet's on this cup; little doubt that the 'poison' was plain overdose of sleeping drug—nasty stuff—taken in the tooth-glass. But better touch nothing.

Dr. Jennerel, when he came, was evidently of the same mind. He touched little more than Mrs. Tass had done, and soon led her from the room and locked the door, pocketing the key, to go down and wait in the hall until

the police came in response to his summons. His face
was grave and lined with anxiety; he spoke very little
to anyone—sure sign of disturbance in so naturally cheerful and garrulous a man.

Charles Rathlyn soon came into the hall and greeted
the doctor quietly. His own face was grave and rather
white; he looked more shaken than he had been even by
his wife's death; that at least had been—or appeared to
be—an accident, but this second death, following so soon
. . . Ludd had told him that it appeared to be due to an
overdose of some sleeping tablets; surely with a young
and healthy woman no accidental overdose could have
caused death in a few hours? Inevitably thoughts must
turn to suicide—if they turned no further.

Quietly the two men discussed the tragedy, each for his
own purpose guarded and restrained. Dr. Jennerel had
been well aware that the police had not been—in the
first place, at any rate—entirely satisfied as to the accidental nature of Mrs. Rathlyn's death. He himself had
doubted that a sleep-walker would lose balance and fall,
but he had little direct experience of the matter. In any
case, the Coroner's finding—'open' as it was—had not
apparently been followed by any further suspicions. But
now . . . another death in the house; another 'accident'. Could there be any connection? It was not his
business to worry about that, but he was going to guard
his tongue. Thank goodness, here was the police car
now, with Superintendent Binnerton and Superintendent
Hant; oh yes, and Dr. Lane-Fallick too—that showed that
they were going to take nothing for granted. Very well,
he, Jennerel, would say as little as possible and get back,
soon as he could, to his own humdrum job of curing
people's ailments.

The police were polite enough to Captain Rathlyn, but,
naturally, they did not ask him to accompany them

when they and the two doctors trooped upstairs. Charles returned to his study, sat down at the writing-table, tried to read his morning mail, but soon gave that up and sat staring in front of him, his fingers—none too steady—playing with a paper-knife. For half an hour he sat there, almost motionless; then the sound of voices in the hall was followed by Ludd coming in to ask if Superintendent Binnerton might come and have a word with him. Soon both the police Superintendents were in the room; evidently the doctors had gone.

" Good morning, sir," said Superintendent Binnerton. " This is a sad affair. Such a fine young lady; a great favourite of the late Mrs. Rathlyn's, I understand."

" My wife was very fond of Miss Wey," said Charles, motioning the two police officers to chairs.

" I have been asking Mrs. Tass about next of kin. She says Miss Wey had no relations, so far as she knows. When she went on holiday she seldom left an address, I understand—just a hotel occasionally. Mrs. Tass tells me that Miss Wey came to Mrs. Waygold when she was still a young girl—Miss Wey was, I mean; she came from an Orphanage, of which I have the name. They may be able to tell me something, sir—possibly Mrs. Rathlyn may have told you something."

Charles shook his head.

" I'm afraid I have no idea; we never talked about Miss Wey in any personal way."

" Well, that's a pity, but we'll do our best. Now I'm bound to ask you, sir, about these sleeping tablets. It seems likely, the doctors tell me, that the poor young woman took a very large overdose, that caused her death. Did you know she was in the habit of taking such things, sir? "

Charles frowned.

" I don't . . . wait a minute, though; now you ask

me, I remember that when I had rather a bad fall last season my wife gave me some tablets to help me sleep. She told me afterwards that she had borrowed them from Miss Wey. But Dr. Jennerel was here; he could tell you all about that."

" Dr. Jennerel did tell me about that incident, sir. He was not himself Miss Wey's doctor and did not prescribe the tablets, but he knew she had them. I just wondered whether it was a frequent practice with Miss Wey—taking these tablets."

" I shouldn't think so. She seemed healthy enough; surely a frequent use of such things would show up, one way or another. But I wouldn't know; again, why not ask Dr. Jennerel? "

Binnerton nodded, as if grateful for a helpful suggestion.

" I will, sir; I will. Now just one other thing; about last night—did you see Miss Wey at all? Did she seem in any way unusual? Depressed, or anything like that? "

Superintendent Hant, keeping his mouth shut but using his eyes, saw that dead-pan look come over Captain Rathlyn's face.

" I saw her for a few minutes after dinner. She came to ask about a situation she was thinking of applying for. She seemed perfectly normal and cheerful."

" That's very interesting, sir. Seems unlikely she would consult you on such a point if she was thinking of taking her own life."

" Did she often do that, sir? Come to talk to you in the evening? In your study, would that be? "

It was Hant speaking now. Charles Rathlyn turned to look at him.

" In my study, yes. No, not often; sometimes she did."

" Not every night? "

" Oh, no."

" Was she normally cheerful? Good company? "

" Miss Wey was a secretary, Superintendent, an employee," said Rathlyn quietly. " It would not be a question of ' good company '. She was normally cheerful, or at any rate not gloomy. Rather quiet, I should say."

Once again Superintendent Hant was finding it hard to know just how far to push his questioning. After all, at the moment this was Superintendent Binnerton's job; it had not yet been handed to him, Hant, as a C.I.D. matter by the Chief Constable, though he had little doubt that it would be. Still, Hant believed firmly in the motto: strike while the iron's hot—especially where anyone may have a tender conscience, or who might like to have more time in which to think out his answers.

" About this situation of Miss Wey's, sir—the one you say she was asking you about last night, can you tell us any more about that? Who it was to be with, or anything of that kind? "

Again that steady, searching look from the old soldier.

" I don't quite see how that can help you in whatever you may be enquiring into, Superintendent, but as a matter of fact I can't. It was the type of employment she was asking my advice about—a secretarial job with a very big firm of turf accountants; she didn't tell me the name of the firm. Perhaps I should say that she always struck me as being a rather secretive type of girl—not for any particular reason, but just a natural habit—to give nothing away unless necessary. I told her that my advice, for what it was worth, was that she should stick to private employment, even though the pay would be less good. Miss Wey was a good-looking girl, Superintendent; it may be within your experience that some types of employers can make life rather difficult for their secretaries and typists. In any case, Miss Wey is not really a trained secretary; if you can't offer words per minute you won't get a well-paid job in commercial life . . . unless you are prepared to offer something else. In private employment that is not nearly so much the case; as in the case of my wife, what she wanted was a nice girl whom she felt she could trust. It should not have been difficult for her to find such a job again."

Charles Rathlyn's face broke into one of its rare smiles.

"Forgive me for lecturing you on something you probably know more about than I do," he said.

"It sounds very good sense, sir," said Binnerton, looking enquiringly at his colleague. But Hant had not finished.

"That's one of the points I have been wondering about, sir. It shouldn't have been difficult for her to find such a job again . . . and yet here she is, four, nearly five months since Mrs. Rathlyn's death. How would one account for that?"

Again Charles Rathlyn smiled.

"I couldn't hope to say what was in any woman's mind, but may she not just have been reluctant to leave a home in which she had been happy before she must? We have all got to leave soon; the household is being broken up next month, but up to now we have all remained."

Once more Hant hesitated; once more his eagerness drove him on.

"There would be no more . . . personal reason than that, sir?"

Charles looked at him steadily.

"Not that I know of."

"Nothing personal to yourself?"

"What exactly do you mean by that?"

"There was no intimate or affectionate relationship between you and Miss Wey?"

Charles Rathlyn's steady grey eyes seemed to bore through the detective but he answered quietly enough.

" I hope you are not intending to be offensive, Superintendent. There has been no intimate relationship between Miss Wey and myself."

CHAPTER XVII

The Colonel's Turn

ISABEL WEY'S death occurred, or had been discovered, on the morning of Tuesday, 15th February. On the evening of the following day Colonel Netterly called a conference—the usual party plus Dr. Lane-Fallick, who was at once asked to present his report.

"You won't want technical terms, Colonel, though they are all down here in writing. Death was due to a gross overdose of an hypnotic drug, known as Dormonal. It is one of the derivatives of barbituric acid; it is an American product and came on to the market during the war. It is an exceptionally powerful preparation and the more dangerous in consequence. As I said, I am speaking in lay rather than in medical terms."

"That any child can understand," muttered the Chief Constable.

"Exactly." Lane-Fallick's lean face broke into a quick smile. "I shall have to be more professional at the inquest —and probably much less comprehensible. A safe dosage of this drug is one tablet, containing twenty grains, or at the most two tablets; anything more than that would be liable to have a harmful effect and, with certain subjects, would be dangerous, though one would not expect so quick a death from anything less than two hundred grains —ten tablets, probably more. Each of these bottles contains eighteen tablets."

"That seems pretty stupid," said Colonel Netterly.

Dr. Lane-Fallick shrugged his shoulders.

"The whole question of hypnotic drugs is riddled with stupidity . . . and danger," he said.

"And can you go into a chemist's and buy half a dozen

bottles?" asked the Chief Constable. He knew the answer quite well, but it was a subject on which he felt bitterly.

" Oh no, these hypnotics are only supplied on a doctor's prescription, and the chemist retains the prescription and will not repeat unless the doctor has said so, or unless he gives a fresh prescription. I am speaking, of course, of a reputable chemist; unfortunately there are plenty of the other kind about, though not, I am sure, in Barryfield."

Colonel Netterly nodded.

" This is not a case of signing a poison book, I believe? "

" No, not that. Just the limitations I have described."

" Right. Well, go ahead, doctor; what had this girl got inside her? "

" I have the analyst's report here. He estimates two hundred and fifty to three hundred grains."

Colonel Netterly whistled.

" Nearly a whole bottle-full. No likelihood of accident there."

" None at all, I should say. You know, I am sure, that there were two bottles beside the bed."

" Yes, I knew that. Nothing to tell if they had both been full, of course. Where were they bought, Mr. Hant? "

" No chemist's name on the bottle, sir. Just the proprietary label. One appeared to be considerably older than the other. Dr. Jennerel had not prescribed them; she was not his patient; her panel doctor was Dr. Lews, and he had not prescribed them for her either. I have not been able to trace the purchase from any chemist in Barryfield, nor in Bascot, nor Hale."

" Odd. Well, we shall have to trace it, somehow. Where did she spend her holidays? "

" That's the odd thing, sir; nobody seems to know. I have one or two addresses of hotels, one at Bournemouth, one at Clacton; I will try there, of course. We have not been able to trace any next of kin; the housekeeper gave me the name of an Orphanage that the girl came from originally, but that closed down soon after the war and nobody seems to have kept their old records."

Colonel Netterly looked thoughtfully at the detective.

" All that seems rather peculiar," he said. " You searched her room, of course? "

" Yes, sir. I could find no address, no letters, nothing to indicate any private life outside her work."

The Chief Constable turned abruptly to Dr. Lane-Fallick.

"We mustn't keep you any longer, doctor; you're a busy man, I know. If you'll leave your report and the analysis we shall no doubt have to ask you some more questions later."

As soon as the surgeon had gone, courteously ushered out by Colonel Netterly, the latter returned to his chair.

" Pretty obvious suicide," he said; " but why? Love affair? Well, I know what you reported, Mr. Hant, but I find that difficult to swallow—as a cause for suicide. Of course, we must probe it; we'll discuss that later. But there seems to be some mystery about this girl's life; nobody knows anything about her—except the house-keeper, apparently, and she hasn't said much. Anyone got any ideas? Mr. Janson? "

" Has Miss Wey a bank account? " asked the Assistant Chief Constable.

" I have not enquired about that, sir," said Hant.

" Better find out; the manager might know something. That your idea, I suppose, Mr. Janson? Local clergy-man? Doctor? Lews, did you say his name was? "

" He knows nothing personal about her, sir. I didn't think of the clergyman."

" Worth trying. And what about that other secretary

—Monner, isn't it? Could there have been any affair with him, do you think, Mr. Hant? "

Hant shook his head.

" Rather the reverse, I should say, sir; didn't like each other, as far as I can make out. In any case, he's no lady-killer, I'm sure—in either sense of the word. A dull, prudish young man, I should say—well, not so young; getting on for forty, I suppose—and certainly hasn't got the guts to kill anyone; bit of forgery, perhaps, or fraud, or dirty sex business, but not murder."

" I wasn't suggesting murder," said the Chief Constable dryly. " I was looking for an explanation of suicide."

Hant was looking for something quite different, but he did not propose to argue the point now.

" Well, if no one's got anything else to suggest, I propose to go out to Tandrings with you tomorrow, Mr. Hant, and have another word with the housekeeper. If anyone knows anything interesting about the poor girl it will be she."

So the following morning, soon after eleven o'clock, Colonel Netterly rang the front-door bell at Tandrings and, learning that Captain Rathlyn was out, asked if he might have a word with Mrs. Tass. At the last minute he had decided to come alone. Superintendent Hant had clearly not been pleased by this decision, but it had occurred to Netterly that his rather brusque C.I.D. chief might have treated the old housekeeper with inadequate respect and tact; he might have dried up this promising source of information. Nor did Colonel Netterly ' send for ' Mrs. Tass; he asked Ludd whether the housekeeper would receive him in her room, knowing from the experience of his earlier, more spacious days that that sanctum was where the good lady would feel at ease—that she would appreciate his asking to be allowed to call on her there.

He found exactly what he expected to find: a neat and cosy room, with a neat and cosy coal fire in the hearth, a room crowded with bric-à-brac, the memories of former days, with many photographs of long-departed relatives and friends. Mrs. Tass herself, whom he had not previously met, was the housekeeper of tradition—like her room, cosy and neat, but with a definite air of dignity and authority . . . combined in this instance with respect for a gentleman and a Colonel. Netterly could well believe that Hant might have failed to appreciate the tactful handling that was needed here.

He began by offering his sympathy to Mrs. Tass for the second tragedy that had fallen upon Tandrings. Gently he led her to talk about the dead girl, but to his disappointment he learnt little more than Hant had done. Certainly Mrs. Tass painted a fuller picture of Isabel Wey's character, standing against a very hazy background of early history, but this did not really clarify the portrait that had already formed in his own mind. Mrs. Tass knew nothing of Isabel's origin or of her early family life; Colonel Netterly was satisfied that she was concealing nothing from him.

Approaching the more delicate ground, he told the housekeeper that the police were bound to investigate the possibilities of suicide and that meant looking for the reason. Money, for a girl in her comparatively sheltered position, seemed an unlikely cause; could there be some more personal, more intimate reason? Did Mrs. Tass know of any affair of the heart that might have gone wrong? No, Mrs. Tass had never heard of anything of the kind; it was true that Isabel was of a secretive nature, not likely to tell others her innermost thoughts, but Mrs. Tass did not herself believe that Isabel's heart had been in any way troubled. A tentative word about her fellow-secretary only brought a shake of the head; the two had not liked each other, she was sure; each had been jealous of the other's position with their mistress. In any case, Mr. Monner was a quiet, rather dull man, who could surely not have raised a spark of excitement in the girl's breast, let alone caused her to do away with herself by reason of a broken heart.

Colonel Netterly drew in his breath and ventured delicately on to the really dangerous patch of ice.

" Now, Mrs. Tass, I must ask you one more question that may seem to you very impertinent, even improper, but I have my duty to do, and you are a woman who has seen much of life and its tragedies. Is there any possibility at all that there has been any intimate relationship between Miss Wey and Captain Rathlyn? I would not ask this if I had not some ground for fearing that this might be the case."

The housekeeper's small body seemed to tighten, her lips pursed; Netterly feared that she was about to freeze him with her angry scorn. But she did not; she spoke quite quietly, even gently.

" No, sir; I am quite sure that is not so. I was not happy when my . . . when Mrs. Waygold married again, but I have come to respect Captain Rathlyn and to trust him. He is a gentleman. He would not do anything wrong—like what you suggest—and I am sure that nothing of that kind could happen in this house without my knowing of it."

Alas, thought Netterly, for infallibility; in view of what Hant had told him, he feared that he must discount the value of Mrs. Tass's assurance. Well, he had learnt nothing . . . except that his own exquisite tact had proved no more effective a weapon than his detective's thrusting forcefulness. But Mrs. Tass was speaking again.

" No, sir, if there was anything of that kind in Isabel's

life it didn't come from this house; more likely, if at all, it happened when she was in the Army."

" The Army? " Netterly sat up abruptly.

" She was in the Army for three years in the war, sir. I never thought her quite the same girl after."

Mrs. Tass told him what little she knew of this period in the dead woman's life, which really amounted to nothing, but the Chief Constable had now got a real piece of information, from which more might flow. Gently he detached himself, thanking the housekeeper for her help and apologising for any distress he might have caused her.

In the hall he found Ludd, correctly waiting to see him off the premises. It occurred to him that Hant had told him nothing of the butler's views, so, learning that Captain Rathlyn was still out, he jockeyed the man into the dining-room and questioned him, using a slightly different technique—officer to trusted servant. In sum, Ludd's views coincided with those of Mrs. Tass; he did not believe the young person had been in love with anyone except herself. He could think of no reason for suicide, but he knew that she did suffer from insomnia, and he had heard Mrs. Rathlyn talk to her about taking tablets to help her sleep; she was certainly ' edgy ' at times, and perhaps the thought of having to find a new situation—after all, she had no real qualifications as a secretary—might have worried and depressed her.

Netterly got the clear view that the butler, as other members of the household, did not much like Miss Wey.

" About the night of her death, did you see her at all? "

" Yes, sir, I did. You may not know that Miss Wey and Mr. Monner take their meals together in his office. It is not an arrangement I have been accustomed to in any other situation in which I have been, but it was so here. Normally the meal was taken in by the footman, but as the household is breaking up and there is now no

footman, at Captain Rathlyn's request I have consented
to oblige . . . for the short time left. I took in the meals
myself."

There was an infinity of disapproval in the butler's
voice, but his manner was correct.

"Mrs. Rathlyn was a very kind-hearted lady, sir; it
was her wish that everyone should be comfortable and well
looked-after. She liked Mr. Monner and Miss Wey to
have wine twice a week; sometimes oftener, but normally
a bottle of claret or burgundy—of a kind—was served to
them on Mondays and Fridays. There was a bottle of
St. Emilion this last Monday, and I noticed that Miss
Wey seemed more talkative and in more cheerful spirits
than usual when I cleared away. Nothing to suggest
intended self-destruction, sir. Unless . . ."

"I know; 'let us eat and drink for tomorrow we die '',"
muttered the Chief Constable. "Go on, Ludd."

"Nothing more, sir. I did not see her again, alive."

"No other drink? Brandy? Liqueur?"

"Oh no, sir. Mr. Monner had a decanter of whisky
and a syphon in his cupboard and occasionally had a
night-cap, but not as a regular thing."

"Not that night?"

"I think not, sir; the housemaid would have brought
the glass to the pantry next morning to be washed; I do
not remember it being there."

"Just clear up the point and let me know—or Mr.
Hant next time he is here, will you? He may have to
come again."

Quietly warning the butler to keep their conversation
to himself, Colonel Netterly took his leave, returned to
headquarters and, sending for Hant, told him what he had
learnt.

"Doesn't amount to much, I'm afraid," he said.
"You didn't tell me Miss Wey had been an AT."

"Nobody had told me, sir," said Hant shortly, displeased at having been caught napping.

"Well, that'll probably give you the answer to one question. There'll be a 'next of kin' somewhere on her papers. Better get along to A.T.S. Records, Winchester, and find out."

CHAPTER XVIII

A Great Name

FROM BARRYFIELD to Winchester is a straightforward train journey, and there seemed no point in Superintendent Hant taking one of the force's none too numerous cars for this job. He had a quick lunch before starting and was in Winchester by three o'clock. The A.T.S. being now disbanded—or converted into the new W.R.A.C., whichever is the correct interpretation of the event—their record office is no longer the hive of ordered industry that it was in the late war; none the less, it is still a live affair and able to produce information accurately and efficiently. As soon as Detective Superintendent Hant had established his *bona fides* he learnt what he wanted to know; the next of kin of WEY, ISABEL was given as HONORIA CHASTERTON, relationship: mother; address: 26 Corran Road, Bournemouth.

Mother! Then why had the girl been found in an orphanage? And why 'Wey'? Well, that could easily be discovered now, assuming Mrs. Chasterton to be still alive, and even if she were dead surely she at least would have traceable relatives. To Bournemouth then, another simple train journey. Hant rang up his headquarters to say where he was going and that he would probably be away for the night; he asked that Mrs. Hant should be told.

The detective's first move on reaching Bournemouth was to pay a call at the Police headquarters. He found that the Superintendent in charge of the Division was a man he had met on a course not many years previously, so relations were at once easy and there was no necessity for any formalities to be followed.

"You've got a big job here, Willan," Hant said. "I

don't know what the population of Bournemouth is, but I doubt if you know the name of every one of them. Fortunately I've got that; I'm looking for the next of kin of a young woman who's just committed suicide or been murdered in our parish. Name of Chasterton, the mother is."

Superintendent Willan stared at him.

" Chasterton? That's not a common name, but it can't be her."

" Honoria Chasterton is the full name."

" My word, it is then. But good lord alive, man, she can't be the mother; she's ' Miss '."

Curiouser and curiouser. Still, thought Hant, she wouldn't be the first ' Miss ' who had had a baby and tucked it away in a home. Anyway, it didn't matter; he was not interested in the mother, only in what she could tell him about her daughter.

"What sort of a person is she, this Miss Chasterton? How do you come to know of her so pat? Is she a local celebrity or something?"

" You mean to say you've never heard of her! Man, where's your culture in Barryshire? Honoria Chasterton is well known all over England, I should have thought, and outside it—or was till she fell sick. A great musician; concert pianist, don't they call it?"

Utterly unmusical himself, Hant was dimly aware now that he had years ago seen the name somewhere on a bill —stuck up, perhaps, outside the Albert Hall or the Queen's Hall or such place. It had meant exactly nothing to him.

" Crippled by arthritis these last ten years; a proper tragedy," Willan was saying. " Of course, it matters to us here; she's a Bournemouth woman, and used to play here a lot. But a child—I never heard of one. Don't know that I believe it now, saving your presence."

Hant explained how he had got the information, and as it was now past six o'clock he thought he had better pay his call without further delay.

" I'd offer to come with you," said Willan, " but if you are going to talk about an illegit. daughter it would add to the poor lady's embarrassment to have a local man know about it."

Good sense, thought Hant; tactful, too—he preferred to work alone. Within ten minutes he was in Corron Road, a short, winding street of neat little houses, not very close to the sea-front. Ringing the bell of No. 26, he sent in his personal card by the rather youthful maid who opened the door and asked if Miss Chasterton would see him for a few minutes. A moment later he was in the sitting-room, introducing himself to its striking occupant.

Miss Chasterton was now some sixty-five years old, grey-haired, white and thin of face, but beautiful in a cold, classical way and sitting bolt upright in a wheeled chair. A pair of steel-blue eyes searched her visitor's face.

" Who are you, Mr. Hant? Ought I to know you? " she asked, as soon as the door had closed behind the maid.

" No, madam, you won't know me."

Hant held out his warrant-card for her to see, and immediately her mouth tightened, the knotted hands on her lap closed on one another. She knew, thought Hant, what he had come about.

" A young lady in our county—a Miss Isabel Wey—has just died under circumstances that have to be enquired into. We could not at first find out who her relatives were, but A.T.S. records have just shown us, madam, that she gave your name as her mother."

Not a trace of emotion appeared on the pale, calm face. Just that tightening of the lips, an ' awareness ' in the blue eyes. Miss Chasterton did not speak and, rather embarrassed, Hant continued.

" May I ask, madam, if that is correct? "

Still silence for a while and then:

" What does it matter, if she is dead, who her mother was? "

" The Coroner will want to know that, madam, and if there remains a doubt as to how she met her death, we shall have to enquire closely into her private life. Her mother should be able to help us. Perhaps you read of the . . . the happening in the papers? "

Miss Chasterton inclined her head as if in assent, but she did not speak. A minute passed, two minutes; she was thinking . . . God knew, she needed to think. Hant realised full well what that word ' Coroner ' must have meant to her, what he had intended it to mean. It meant publicity.

At last Miss Chasterton straightened her back—if it were possible further to straighten it.

" Is it absolutely necessary, Superintendent, for this to become known? This . . . relationship? I am a well-known woman; I have done much, played much for charitable and religious institutions. My name means something, and if it is smirched, harm will be done to others besides myself. I was never married. No one, I believe, knows that I have a daughter—that I had one. Must it be known now? "

Hant hesitated. He had no authority to pledge anyone to silence; still . . . he saw the point.

" That is something I can't answer myself, madam. The Coroner must know, and of course the Chief Constable. It is possible that, if you help us in the way we want, they may find it not necessary to publish the name."

This combination of bribery and threat did not appear to shock Miss Chasterton. She recognised it for what it was worth and took her decision. All this time Hant had been standing; she waved him now to a chair.

" I will tell you my story, Superintendent, and I trust you to do your utmost to keep it secret if that is at all possible. I think you will see that, since her birth, I have really played no part in my daughter's life and can tell you nothing that will account for her death."

Hant bowed and felt that it would be unseemly to scribble in his notebook. He must trust to his excellent memory.

" As a girl I had no interest in young men. I was wholly devoted to music; I thought and dreamed of nothing else—lived for it wholly. I was well-trained and soon made a name for myself. Even the war—the Great War—did not hinder my career; young as I then was, I played—I am a pianist, you know—in concerts all over the country and even in France. I was a good-looking girl and the troops liked to see as well as hear me. But that meant nothing to me—it was only music that mattered, and I found that they would listen with complete enjoyment to great music—Bach, Beethoven, Mozart, Brahms."

Miss Chasterton was leaning back now, her eyes almost closed. It was as if she had forgotten the detective.

" After the war it was the same—my music, nothing else. Until suddenly, as sometimes happens in life, I met somebody and fell helplessly in love with him—the more utterly and helplessly because of my previous inexperience. He was a Russian, a musician, too, though not of my calibre; we had a short romantic interlude and then parted as suddenly as we had come together. I returned to my career, and then one day discovered to my horror that I was about to become a mother."

A quiver of horror, as if the very memory could arouse it, passed over the white, beautiful face.

" I need not tell you of all that. A friend of mine, a dear friend of my youth, though older than me, came to my rescue. She was then the matron of an orphanage, run by private charitable funds. She took my baby and promised that no one should ever know. She knew what my music meant to the world and what a disaster it would be if scandal touched my name. I trusted her, and my secret remained a secret . . . until she suddenly died. Even then it remained a secret for a long time, but Isabel, my daughter, when she grew up, somehow learnt from the new matron the name of her mother. I suppose it had had to be recorded for some official purpose—the Home Office, perhaps.

" During this last war Isabel, who had been in domestic service, joined some military corps—I think you mentioned its name."

" The A.T.S., madam," murmured Hant.

" With cruel lack of discretion she gave my name as her next of kin. It must have been seen by many eyes, but nothing became public; perhaps in the pressure of war no one had time to spread such a story, or perhaps women who join such a service are of a type to whom a great name in music means nothing."

Hant blushed hotly at the thought of his own ignorance.

" I had by that time begun to suffer from the rheumatism that has since completely crippled me. But I still worked for music. I organised concerts, for the Red Cross, for the great charities, for the Church. My name still carried great respect. And then, suddenly, Isabel appeared here. She was on holiday, she said, and she came to see me. Oh, she was discreet; she told no one else. She wanted to stay with me, but I told her that that was impossible, that I never had anyone to stay with me and that people would at once ask questions. She stayed, instead, at a small, pleasant hotel of which I knew."

Hant remembered that one of the ' holiday addresses '

he had been given was of a hotel in Bournemouth. He
had it tucked away somewhere in his note-book.

" She is a strange girl. Perhaps I am not qualified to
understand her. She is very good-looking . . . I suppose
I must say ' was '. But utterly cold, it seemed to me;
utterly self-centred, with a queer, bitter sense of humour.
She told me nothing of her life—nothing at all. She
spoke only of people she was meeting on her holiday. I
never heard her mention a man as if she cared for him."

Hardly surprising, thought Hart, with such a mother—
but was it true . . . that she did not care for men? At
least it was something that he had come to find out about.
That, at any rate, was answered. Miss Chasterton seemed
to have finished her story, and Hant ventured on a question.

" Did you know that your daughter was in the habit of
taking drugs to make her sleep, madam? "

" Drugs? What sort of drugs? "

" Well, sleeping tablets, really; but containing an
hypnotic drug."

Miss Chasterton shuddered slightly as if in disgust.

" I know nothing about that," she said.

" How often did she come here? "

" Three times; twice in August and once at Christmas.
The third time—it was in August about eighteen months
ago—she . . . I told her not to come again."

Miss Chasterton looked towards the fire, back to the
detective, hesitated . . . and spoke again.

" I think perhaps I must tell you this, though it is very
dreadful. She tried to make me give her money. I have
very little money now—I no longer earn. Just enough
saved to live here very quietly, I hope till I die. She
asked me for . . . a lot of money—five hundred pounds.
I thought at first she was joking, but it seemed she was
serious. I told her I had none to give her, and she

declared she did not believe me. She . . . she said that what she could tell about me was enough to ruin my name. She did not seem to mind about that at all—not at all. She laughed when I spoke of what my name meant in the world of music."

For the first time Hant saw emotion in the calm face. A glint in the blue eyes—a glint of tears. Miss Chasterton drew herself together again.

" I told her to do what she liked," she said firmly. " I told her that I would give her nothing and that I would not see her again. I have never seen her again."

' Publish and be damned ', thought the detective as he walked away from the house. ' Good for the old girl; she's got courage, cold and selfish as she may be.'

And then a thought struck Hant, and he came to a dead stop. Isabel Wey had tried to squeeze money out of her own mother. Blackmail! Was that the answer to the whole puzzle? Did that, rather than intrigue, explain what Filblow had seen? Had she been blackmailing Charles Rathlyn, and was the answer not suicide, but murder?

CHAPTER XIX

A Visit to the Bank

IT WAS too late that evening to do anything more in Bournemouth, but there was something Hant wanted to do next morning—two things, in fact. So he booked a room in a modest hotel, had some supper and went off to see a ' flick ', hoping to distract his mind for a time.

First thing next morning he presented himself again in Willan's office and asked for the names and addresses of all banks in the town. A large order, it appeared; there seemed to be plenty of banking business to be done in Bournemouth. Hant explained that an idea had occurred to him; Miss Wey had no established home, but she had been to Bournemouth for three of her holidays, at least; he had not been able to discover that she kept a bank account in Barryfield; was it possible that she had one here?

" No bank statements among her effects? You looked, I suppose."

" I looked," said Hant, nettled at the suggestion that he might neglect so obvious a step.

" Probably didn't use a bank, then. But no harm in finding out. I can help you there; the banks are on very good terms with us and will tell us what they might not tell a stranger. I'll arrange with Betteridge for two of his detective-constables to go round to each branch and find out in the first place if there is such an account. Then if there is, you can go straight to the spot. Save you hours."

That was a truly noble offer, and Hant accepted it gratefully. While Willan's detectives were doing the preliminary work he could do his second job—visit the hotel at which Isabel Wey had stayed on her holidays in Bournemouth.

The Casterbridge Hotel was, as Isabel's mother had said, a small, pleasant hotel, evidently intended for those of modest but not straitened means. The manageress— or more probably proprietress—was a comfortable body, not grim of mouth, as so many are who have to make their livelihood from seasonal visitors. Taking Hant into her own sitting-room, she insisted on giving him a glass of sherry and took one herself. She remembered Miss Wey, of course, and had been shocked to read in the paper of her death. Not that she had exactly *liked* her—the girl was too remote and uncongenial for that—but she had admired her looks and liked to have good-looking people in her hotel, so long as they behaved themselves, as Miss Wey certainly did.

Hant quickly cleared up that point; no love-affair in Bournemouth. Indeed, it hardly interested him now; he was convinced that he had the answer to the riddle of Isabel's death. He knew why she had died; all he had to do was to prove it. Well, that was going a bit too fast, perhaps, but he did feel sure that blackmail, not amorous intrigue, was the answer. Blackmail for what? That he would find out in due course. Meantime he would clear up the point that he had really come about—and clear it up he did. The proprietress, Mrs. Dolling, remembered that Miss Wey had complained of insomnia, had said that she had left her bottle of Dormonal at home; Mrs. Dolling had taken her round to her own doctor—Dr. Wisselton— such a go-ahead young man—who had given her a prescription for a fresh supply.

It did not take Hant long to find Dr. Wisselton, who was still in his surgery; his records showed the name, the date —December 1952—the quantity—one bottle only, no re- petition order. The chemist would probably have been

Mewton and Jade, to whom he usually sent his patients.
It was Mewton and Jade; they looked up the prescription;
there had been, so far as they were concerned, no repeat.
Well, that accounted for both bottles of tablets; the girl
had had one (Hant did not know where she had obtained
it), and, having left it behind, had obtained another here
in Bournemouth. As easy as all that. The date—December 1952—suggested two things: that she was not a frequent user of the drug and that suicide had not been in
her mind when she bought this bottle, more than two years
ago. But in Hant's present theory, suicide was out.
Murder was in his mind. But how the something did one
get a girl to swallow twenty or thirty tablets of sleeping
drug? That would take some answering.

Returning to police headquarters, Hant learnt that the
Union Street branch of the Provincial and South Coast
Bank had owned to an account in the name of Miss Isabel
Wey. The manager, Mr. Jolliphant, would be glad to
see Superintendent Hant.

"Like me to come too?" asked Willan. "Might be a
help if you want to rob him of anything. Not like the old
lady's good name."

Hant saw the force of that. He did not want to get
entangled in red tape; the local Superintendent might be
able to cut his way through it.

Mr. Jolliphant proved to be a pleasant, middle-aged
man, by no means overburdened with a sense of his own
importance. The Bournemouth detective had told him
that a Barryshire Superintendent was investigating a case
of suspected suicide, and though the bank manager had
not heard of Miss Wey's death—the name, indeed, meant
little to him—he had got out the ledger containing her
account and was prepared to give such information as he
thought proper.

Miss Wey, it appeared, had opened her account with the

bank as long ago as August 1950. She had then paid in
seventy pounds; one of the cashiers remembered the occasion and said that she had paid in five-pound notes. Since
that date sums of ten pounds and twenty pounds had been
paid in at fairly regular intervals of a month; in the last
two years the amounts had tended to increase, and there
had also been a sum of two hundred pounds in November
of 1954 and a further two hundred pounds on 15th January
in the present year, 1955.

Hant's heart quickened its beat as he listened. Here
was almost certain proof that his suspicions were correct;
not proof as yet to satisfy a jury, but proof enough for
himself. A large payment within two months of Mrs.
Rathlyn's death, another last month . . . and now
Isabel Wey was dead herself!

" Paid in here, sir? By cheque? "

Not, of course, Rathlyn's cheque; that would be too
much to expect.

" In cash each time, sent by registered post with a short
covering letter—so I am told," said the manager. " Miss
Wey has, so far as we are aware, not personally visited the
bank since August 1950, and she has drawn none of it
out. Her instructions were that it should be placed upon
deposit. The total amount on deposit now, including
accumulated interest is thirteen hundred and seventy-five
pounds odd."

Hant whistled. A tidy sum, it seemed to him. Then a
thought struck him. Those smallish sums, ten and twenty
pounds a month, would they be her salary? If so, what
had she done with it before opening this account. It was
a point he would have to enquire into. He did not know
what her salary had been, what it was likely to have been,
what a young woman secretary may expect to earn in
addition to her keep.

He studied the ledger carefully, and soon realised that

if there was any significance in these figures, apart from the two sums of two hundred each, he would have to have a copy of the whole account at his disposal for reference. He asked the manager, as a great favour, if one could be got out for him.

Mr. Jolliphant hesitated, looked at Superintendent Willan, and apparently obtained encouragement there.

" I think that may be possible, Superintendent," he said, " but I shall have to obtain confirmation from my head office."

Hant wanted no doubt about it and no delay. After a moment's thought he leant forward and said in a lower voice:

" I think I had better tell you, sir, that the case I am investigating may turn out to have been murder, not accident or even suicide. I have had my suspicions of that strengthened even since I came to Bournemouth yesterday. It is of the first importance that you should give me all the information you can and with the least possible delay."

Superintendent Willan was looking startled; Hant had said nothing to him about murder. Mr. Jolliphant, too, was startled. He, too, thought for a minute.

" In that case, Superintendent, I think I must tell you something more," he said. " Miss Wey has, I am told, from time to time sent to us sealed envelopes for safe keeping. I do not, of course, know what is in them; they remain sealed. But they may contain something of significance to your enquiry."

Naturally Superintendent Hant was not going to decline this offer. Mr. Jolliphant disappeared, taking the ledger with him, and after a rather long delay returned with a handful of fat yellow envelopes of the size—9 in. by 4 in.— in which folded foolscap sheets are conveniently enclosed. He also brought a typewritten sheet bearing the figures copied from Isabel Wey's ledger account.

" I have had a word with my head office," said the manager, " and they feel that under the circumstances they must release these documents for inspection by the police. I imagine that you will want to take them away with you. If you give me a receipt, that will be in order."

Hant suppressed a sigh of relief; that was something he had wanted but had not expected so easily to get. There were six of the envelopes, each merely displaying the typed name: ISABEL WEY; there was a dab of sealing-wax on the flap of each. No doubt they had come in larger envelopes, with some letter of instructions, but these Mr. Jolliphant had not produced. Calmly Hant wrote out a receipt on an official form, locked the envelopes away in his attaché case and rose to his feet.

" I can't thank you enough for your help, sir," he said. " My Chief will be most grateful and, of course, if these documents are not needed they will be returned to you."

Outside in the street he expressed even warmer thanks to his Bournemouth colleague.

" Without your being with me I doubt if he'd have parted so readily. I'm more grateful than I can say."

" More than welcome," said Willan. " Like to come along to my office and look through them? Then a bite of lunch."

Hant glanced at his wrist watch.

" Thanks," he said, " but there's a train at 12.37 that will get me back. Besides, my Chief will want to open these himself."

That was pure invention, but Hant wanted no other nose in this pie. He held out his hand and shaking Willan's, walked briskly off in the direction of the station. The Bournemouth man watched him with a rueful twist of his mouth; he had been itching to see inside those envelopes.

" Of all the ungrateful so-and-sos," he muttered.

Then, with a smile, " Oh well; perhaps I'd have done the same."

.   .   .   .   .

Hant reached Barryfield soon after three o'clock, and finding to his delight that both the Chief Constable and Mr. Janson were out, retired to his own small office to examine his treasure trove. Slitting open the first of the envelopes, he drew out a bundle of sheets, not of foolscap but of octavo size. On each was typed a list of dates, each with a sum of money entered against it, generally £10 or £20, but occasionally a larger figure, up to £50. The figures were totalled up, usually to amounts varying between £100 and £200 per month. At the head of each sheet was the month and year—1952. Included in the envelope with these monthly sheets of figures was another sheet containing a series of dates only, this time in pencil—not typewritten; there were only about thirty of these dates, covering the whole year. The dates on this sheet appeared to bear no relation to the dates on the sheets showing sums of money.

Hant found it difficult to decide what the significance of these dates and figures might be. The monthly totals were considerably higher than the amounts which Mr. Jolliphant had said that Miss Wey sent to the bank each month. A glance at the copy of Miss Wey's account showed Hant that this was so; apart from the £70 paid in in August 1950, when the account was opened, there had been no sum larger than £30 paid in until the figure of £200 in November 1954 and £200 in January 1955. In the year 1952, to which the dates and figures in this envelope were confined, the largest sum paid into Miss Wey's account was £20, which occurred in July, with further sums of £20 in October and December; all the other amounts paid in had been for £10.

For the moment it was difficult to see the connection.

Hant shrugged his shoulders, pushed the bundle of sheets on one side and slit open the next envelope. The contents were of a similar nature, but bearing the date 1950. There was, however, one difference which might prove to have some significance: the lists of dates and figures dealt only with the months April to December and the hand-written list of dates began in May 1950. Bearing in mind that Miss Wey had opened her account in Bourne-mouth in August 1950, it did seem possible that there might be some connection, though what it was was not at all clear.

The amounts paid into the Bournemouth bank might, of course, represent her salary, or such of it as she did not spend. But what had she been doing with it before August 1950? The figures shown on these dated sheets clearly could not be salary; Hant did not know what a secretary, living in, would receive, but it certainly would not be £100 to £200 a month, in varying amounts.

Opening another envelope, Hant found the same thing —for the year 1954. It was most disappointing; evidently each envelope contained the same—lists of dates and payments, but for different years. Closer examina-tion might, of course, reveal something significant, but it seemed very doubtful. They went back too far. Mrs. Rathlyn had died in September 1954; she had married Captain Rathlyn in . . . when was it? Somewhere in 1953, Hant thought. How could these dates in '50, '51, '52 and so on affect this enquiry? The only two items that mattered, Hant felt sure, were the sums of £200 paid in by Miss Wey in November 1954 and January 1955; they were, indeed, of supreme significance, and would have to be probed to the utmost.

An examination of the 1954 lists did, however, produce evidence of importance. The dates and the payments ceased in September of that year; clearly both lists had some connection with Mrs. Rathlyn herself. Probably they were some accounts of hers, and so could surely be explained, either by Captain Rathlyn or by the other secretary, Monner, or by the auditors—if it proved that Mrs. Rathlyn's accounts were audited. Since she had been a very rich woman, it was not at all improbable that they had been. It should be easy to clear up this point— disappointingly easy, Hant felt; there was not likely to be any mystery about them. He would have to consult the Chief Constable on the point; Captain Rathlyn, of course, was a suspect—at any rate in his, Hant's, mind; it might be unwise to question him and put him on his guard.

That brought the detective back to his own definite view of the case; he was pretty sure now that Isabel Wey had been blackmailing Charles Rathlyn. What about, he did not know; possibly she knew something about the death of Mrs. Rathlyn, something she had seen or heard that might point the finger of suspicion at him. If that were so, it seemed but a step to the suggestion that not only had the Captain murdered his wife but that, being blackmailed, he had murdered Isabel Wey too, to silence her. A very neat theory, thought Detective-Superintendent Hant; all right, now go ahead and prove it.

There remained three envelopes, one much slimmer than the others. Slitting it open, Hant found that it contained only another envelope of correspondence size. One glance at this, however, set the detective's heart pounding in his breast. The envelope was of good quality, bearing a postage stamp but no postmark; it was addressed in what was evidently a woman's hand to Miss Anne Faery, Noolands Farm, Little Lawton, Barryshire. Handling it with great care, because it might yet disclose finger-prints, Hant drew out the letter which it contained. As he read the brief contents of the letter the detective's eyes sparkled with excitement.

CHAPTER XX

Two Missions

COLONEL NETTERLY looked in at headquarters that evening to see whether Superintendent Hant had returned. He found his C.I.D. chief eagerly awaiting him.

"I've made quite a bit of progress, sir," said Hant, as soon as he was seated in the Chief Constable's office.

"Half a moment." Colonel Netterly flicked a switch on his house-telephone. "You there, Janson? Come in, will you?"

When the Assistant Chief Constable also was seated Hant took up his tale, beginning correctly at the beginning —Winchester—and working steadily through to the end —the letter to Miss Faery. His superior officers listened without interruption—admirable trait in a well-trained force.

"The letter is signed 'Katherine Rathlyn', sir, as you will see. I have seen a specimen of her handwriting, and I have no doubt that this is hers, but of course I will check up on that."

He handed the letter to Colonel Netterly, who read it and passed it to Mr. Janson.

"Not much doubt what was in her mind, I'm afraid. But from the envelope—the unfranked postage stamp—it does not appear to have reached Miss Faery."

"No, sir. My guess is that Mrs. Rathlyn gave it to Miss Wey to post and she didn't post it. Guessed what might be in it, opened it, and used it to blackmail Captain Rathlyn. If he was having an affair with Miss Faery, that would be a motive for his killing his wife, sir."

"I imagined that that would be your idea," said Colonel Netterly dryly. "But this letter is no proof of an 'affair';

it merely tells Miss Faery, rather crudely, to keep away from Captain Rathlyn. You yourself jumped to the conclusion that there was such an affair because Miss Faery stopped to help Captain Rathlyn when he had a bad fall and went back in the ambulance to Tandrings with him. To my mind the mere act of any decent woman in the hunting-field, but I can quite see that a wife of jealous temperament might well have given it a more personal interpretation. That fall occurred—I remember it well; I was there myself, you know—in January last year; this letter is dated the 18th of February—a few weeks later. The connection is obvious. Unless you have some further grounds, some confirmation of your suspicions, I don't see that this letter takes us much further."

All that was dogged and determined in Detective-Superintendent Hant appeared in his jutting chin. This, he told himself, was the drawback of these gentlemen Chief Constables; they stick to their class—and this was a hunting class to stiffen the connection; Captain Rathlyn, Miss Faery, Colonel Netterly, all hunting folk who had a sort of freemasonry that beat the Freemasons themselves. This feeling was a gross libel on the Colonel Netterlys of our police forces, but Superintendent Hant sincerely believed it.

" I propose with your permission, sir, to question Miss Faery," he said

Colonel Netterly's hand gently tapped the blotting-pad in front of him.

" I agree that she should be questioned," he said quietly, " but I will question her myself—in the first place, at any rate."

Hant recognised the look on his chief's face; with difficulty, but success, he restrained himself.

" Very well, sir. And these other papers that Miss Wey had sent to the bank; will you wish to look through them yourself? As far as I can make out, they are some accounts of Mrs. Rathlyn's—possibly some cash accounts. They cover the last five years. I daresay Mr. Monner could explain them."

" I'm sure he could. Ask him. If he can't, then ask Captain Rathlyn."

" You think that wise, sir . . . under the circumstances? "

" He already knows he's under suspicion, if that's what you are afraid of, Mr. Hant. He is no fool. If he is a guilty man you may be able to startle him into some unwise answer."

" There is that, sir," Hant agreed. " Shall I leave Miss Wey's bank statement too, sir? The two significant entries are the figures of two hundred pounds in November last and January this year. The rest are comparatively trifling sums that may just be Miss Wey's unexpended salary."

" I doubt that," said the Chief Constable. " If that were so, what was she doing with it—with the money she did not spend—before January 1950? "

" That did occur to me, sir, and it is a puzzle. The trouble is that I have not been able to trace any local bank account of hers."

" Have you thought of the Post Office? " asked Mr. Janson quietly.

Hant looked at the Assistant Chief Constable in something like consternation.

" I never thought of that, sir," he said. " The P.O. Savings Bank."

" Check up on it, please," said Colonel Netterly.

. . . . .

Colonel Netterly felt extreme reluctance in carrying out his self-imposed task. It was most unpleasant to have to question a decent girl about her relations with a married man, particularly as the questioning must suggest some connection with the death of that man's wife. However gentle, however tactful he was, there would obviously be no police questioning at all if there were no suspicion. The Chief Constable realised that there was ground for suspicion; apart from their own doubts, the ' open ' character of the Coroner's finding showed that accident could not be unreservedly accepted as the explanation of Mrs. Rathlyn's death. A scintilla of doubt must remain, and that scintilla hovered—if such things do—over Charles Rathlyn; with Superintendent Hant it was a very lively spark.

But Netterly was not going to leave this very delicate questioning in the hands of his forceful Detective-Superintendent. Hant was an able officer, but some of his methods were crude, and in this case his victim would be a young girl of decent family and upbringing, against whom he had never heard one word of unkind criticism. It would be brutal to have her feelings lacerated by rough handling. Colonel Netterly, himself childless and unmarried, was perhaps a little old-fashioned in his ideas as to what the modern young woman can ' take '; he was also, perhaps, a little out as to Anne Faery's age—she was twenty-eight, though she did not look it. In any case, his sentiments did him credit, and he was entirely within his rights in deciding to do this questioning himself.

It was not easy to settle on the right time and place. He did not want to question her in front of her father; after all, if there had been anything between the girl and Charles Rathlyn it was entirely her own affair, and it would not be right to expose her to parental criticism. The next morning, Saturday, was a hunting day, and at an early hour he put a call through to Noolands Farm, being lucky enough to be answered by Anne herself.

" Miss Faery? This is Colonel Netterly speaking—you

know. Look; I want to have a word with you, if I may. Are you hunting? "

" I am, yes. It's Lazard's Copse; are you going to be out? "

" No—not hunting. I don't want to stop you, but could you possibly get back home a bit early? I'd like a word with you alone."

There was a pause, and Netterly thought he detected a note of nervousness in the girl's voice when she spoke again.

" I will be back here by two, if that's all right. Father won't be back till late; he's taking two horses, and I know he means to give each of them a good go."

So it was that at a little after 2 p.m. the Chief Constable drove into the yard of Noolands Farm and soon found himself in the snug sitting-room with Anne Faery. The girl was still in her hunting kit, though she had removed her velvet cap. She offered him a drink, which he declined. Then a thought struck him.

" Have you had your lunch? " he asked.

Anne shook her head.

" Not want," she said. " Please go on."

That, to Netterly, was a sure sign of nervousness, but he took no notice of it.

" Well, it's just this," he said. " You know we have still not quite cleared up the problem of Mrs. Rathlyn's death, and now there's this about her secretary, Miss Wey. You must wonder why I bother you, but the fact is that we have come across a letter that concerns you and that . . . that might possibly throw some light on Mrs. Rathlyn's death. It is a most unpleasant thing to do, but I am bound in duty to ask you about it."

He took from his pocket-book the letter addressed to Miss Faery by Katherine Rathlyn, and handed it to her. As she read it he saw her face flush and then turn white.

" I never had this," she said, a quaver in her voice.
" What is it? Why . . .? Why should she think . . .?
I only met Captain Rathlyn out hunting—that was all.
Oh . . . oh yes, and I did go to a play with him in
London once. He was there on business, and I was
staying with my aunt. We went to a play and then had
supper and danced at the Berkeley. That was all. There
was nothing, nothing at all."

The brown eyes looking up so frankly into his carried
complete conviction to Colonel John Netterly. Still, he
must make absolutely certain. His voice was rather gruff
and curt with embarrassment as he asked :

" You give me your assurance that there was nothing
between you and Captain Rathlyn that would justify any
jealousy . . . any anxiety on the part of his wife."

" Nothing. No, nothing. I promise you absolutely."
Netterly's face relaxed.

" I'm so glad," he said, in a different voice. " I am so
sorry to have had to ask you. Please forgive me . . .
and thank you."

Anne did not leave the room with him, but stood in the
window watching him drive away. Her face was still
white and there was now a glitter of tears in her eyes. She
had told the truth. An honest girl can tell the truth, tell
nothing but the truth . . . and yet not tell the whole
truth—up to date. It was not till long after Mrs.
Rathlyn's death that she and Charles had told each other
of their love.

.   .   .   .   .

While Colonel Netterly was carrving out his delicate
mission Detective-Superintendent Hant was doing his
own job at Tandrings. In fact, he had got it done before
the Chief Constable started. He was not in a good temper,
and nobody could expect to be the better for that fact.
Without any tactful asking of permission from Captain

Rathlyn, the detective told Ludd that he had come to see Mr. Monner and was at once taken to the latter's office. His appearance was therefore unexpected and Hant thought that the secretary seemed startled and by no means pleased to see him. However, he put a chair for his visitor and himself sat down again at his desk, waiting for Hant to state his business.

The detective put his attaché case on his knee and unlocked it.

" Still here? " he asked.

" Still here, but not for much longer."

" Got a new job? "

Monner did not like the police officer's tone, but he was not going to show that. His pale face remained calm, his hands were clasped on the table in front of him.

" I am glad to say that I now have a situation to go to. I leave on the third of next month."

" Same sort of thing? "

" Not quite. An office job, in London. In what way can I help you, Superintendent? "

Hant opened his case and taking out one of the sets—the 1952 set—of dated and figured sheets that Miss Wey had sent to her bank laid it before the secretary.

" What's all that about? "

Monner slowly turned over the sheets, astonishment showing in his face.

" Where did these come from? " he asked.

" It's I who am asking the questions, Mr. Monner. What are they? "

The secretary frowned.

" I asked you a perfectly reasonable question," he said. " These pencilled dates are something of Miss Wey's; they are in her handwriting. I have no idea what they mean. The others seem to be . . ."

He rose from his chair and walking to a tall filing

cabinet took out a folder and returned to his seat. Taking some sheets from the folder he compared them with those which Hant had given him.

" Yes, these are Mrs. Rathlyn's cash accounts, though I don't know where you got them from."

Philip Monner held out to the detective a set of similar sheets, set out rather differently and evidently done with a different typewriter, for the year 1952. At the bottom of each sheet was a bold signature—K. Waygold. Monner explained to the detective, as he had done to Charles Rathlyn soon after his marriage, how Mrs. Rathlyn's—previously Mrs. Waygold's—cash requirements, extremely erratic and sometimes large, were provided for; how he cashed a substantial cheque once a month or oftener, keeping the money in his safe and handing it out to her as she required it; how at the end of each month he submitted to her an account of what she had had, and how she signed it—two copies, one which she kept herself and one which he filed. He explained that the auditors had suggested that it would be better if Mrs. Waygold signed for each amount doled out to her but that she had declined to be bothered to that extent—once a month was bad enough. This copy, which he held, was what she had had in the month shown.

" And are these things that I have got the other copies —the copy you gave her? I thought you said she signed them too."

" She did. These are not the ones. I don't know what they are. I still don't know where you got hold of them."

Hant hesitated, then said that they had been found among Miss Wey's papers. Why, he asked, should Miss Wey have copies of these accounts?

" I have not the least idea, Superintendent," said Monner. " Accounts were in no way the concern of Miss Wey. Unless . . ."

He hesitated, biting his lip and tapping the table with his long, sensitive fingers.

"Miss Wey was jealous of my position as Mrs. Waygold's—Mrs. Rathlyn's accountant. She was also an extremely inquisitive and ambitious young woman. It would not surprise me if she had had some idea of supplanting me in this, as in other secretarial duties."

His voice was trembling; Hant sensed the bitter dislike which the man felt, in common with other members of the household, he thought, for this pushing and egotistical young woman.

"That may be the answer. And you don't know what these other dates of hers mean?"

"I have no idea at all."

"Would Captain Rathlyn be likely to know?"

"He might. I really can't say."

Nothing more to be got here, thought Hant. He went along to the hall and rang the front-door bell.

"Your master in?" he asked when Ludd appeared.

"Captain Rathlyn is somewhere in the precincts, I believe," said the butler coldly.

"Tell him I . . . oh, there he is."

Captain Rathlyn, in riding breeches and jack-boots, was coming across the gravel sweep in front of the house. As he came in at the front door, opened to him by Ludd, he looked enquiringly at the detective.

"Do you want me, Mr. Hant?"

"Just a word, sir, if I may."

Charles led the way into his study and shut the door.

"Been hunting, sir?"

"Not hunting; just riding. I haven't hunted for a long time now," said Charles quietly.

Hant felt somehow as if that was supposed to be his fault. Opening his attaché case he took out the papers he had shown to Monner and handed them to Captain Rathlyn.

" I understand that those typewritten sheets refer to Mrs.
Rathlyn's cash accounts, sir, but I have not been able to
make out what the pencilled dates are. Mr. Monner
thinks they are in Miss Wey's handwriting."

Charles looked at them.

" But these are 1952. I wouldn't know anything about
them. I wasn't on the scenes then," he added with a
smile.

Hant took them back, frowning at his own lack of
thought; in their place he handed over the sheets dealing
with 1954—the dates that stopped in September 1954.
Looking at them Charles Rathlyn's face grew grave.
Going to his writing-table he took a Badminton diary
from a drawer—his old 1954 diary. Carefully he compared the pencilled dates with his diary.

" It isn't very easy to say what they are. I find that in
one or two cases they correspond with dates when my
wife and I were away from Tandrings—look, the first
Newmarket summer meeting; we stayed up there with
friends. And Ascot—two days away then. And, of
course, there was that fortnight when we were in the
south of France, back in February. I'm afraid I didn't
make a note of our day-to-day movements, but if we were
staying away for a race meeting or something like that—
well, I did have a note of that. These other dates—quite
a lot of them, aren't there?—I don't know what they are."

Nor did it seem to Hant to matter. What he was
itching to do was to question Charles Rathlyn about the
two £200 entries in Isabel Wey's bank account. But he
had not yet got the Chief Constable's leave to do that, and
in any case he wanted to think over very carefully how he
was going to approach the matter. But he was going to
do it. Oh, yes, this was the real line, and he was on it;
he was not going to be whipped off by anyone—not even
by the Chief Constable.

CHAPTER XXI

Direct Attack

AFTER HIS talk with Anne Faery, Colonel Netterly went straight home. A week-end was a week-end, and he had already given up most of Saturday afternoon to duty. But, in any case, he did not want to see Superintendent Hant again just yet. He was not feeling any too happy about this case and realised that he was at cross-purposes with the head of his C.I.D. Hant was a shrewd man, but the Chief Constable doubted whether his obvious suspicions about Captain Rathlyn were justified. He wanted time to think over the matter more thoroughly before discussing it again.

As far as Anne Faery was concerned he was now quite satisfied. He would have backed to the utmost his belief that she had not been lying to him. It was just as well, though, that she had told him quite frankly about that evening in London; if she had not done so, and if Hant had found out about it—as he well might—it might have been difficult to give it an innocent explanation. Even as it was it did suggest that there had been *some* feeling, rather stronger than casual friendship, between the two; a married man did not normally ask an unmarried girl, ten or fifteen years younger than himself, to spend an evening in London with him unless she interested him more than a little. Natural enough that she should; he had often seen them together out hunting, and her care for Rathlyn when he was hurt did show something of the same kind—whatever he himself might have said to Hant on the subject. Probably there had been just enough to make Mrs. Rathlyn jealous, though not enough to justify that extremely unpleasant letter. Of that he felt quite sure, after hearing Anne's firm denial, after seeing the frankness and honesty in her eyes.

But about Rathlyn himself he could not feel so happy. That ugly story of what Detective-Constable Filblow had seen through the curtains of the study window stuck in his gizzard. 'Kissing a pretty girl is not murder,' he had said to Hant; no, it is not, but could he be sure that that had not been going on during Kate Rathlyn's lifetime? Even if it had, though, that would have been no reason for him to kill his wife; it was not to be supposed for a moment that such a man as Rathlyn would want his freedom in order to marry a girl like Isabel Wey. No, it was not that, but the incident gave him an uneasy feeling about Charles Rathlyn, whom previously he had been inclined to like.

Hant, of course, had clearly now gone further than the mere idea of an 'affair'. The entries in Wey's bank account—the two entries of two hundred pounds—suggested to him that she had been blackmailing Rathlyn and that Rathlyn might even have murdered her to stop that horrible game. If that had been what she had been doing, Netterly could almost have sympathised with the man who so dealt with her. But blackmail on the strength of that letter of Mrs. Rathlyn's to Anne Faery was altogether too thin. Netterly simply did not believe in it.

The other papers which Hant had brought back from Bournemouth so far meant nothing to the Chief Constable. He had taken them home with him on Friday evening, looked through them, made nothing of them, and returned them to Hant on Saturday morning. None the less, they interested him. There must be a reason for Isabel Wey having deposited these papers in her bank; they were apparently so innocuous, so devoid of interest; why should she want to store them so securely, so secretly, away from where she lived and worked?

Could it be that the girl had been engaged in some fraud? Apparently she had been completely in her employer's confidence, probably handled her money. Rich women were often careless of money, over-trustful where their affections were concerned—and Kate Waygold had evidently felt considerable affection for Isabel Wey. There was some mystery about the girl. None of the staff seemed to like her; her background, her aloofness, her favoured position—all those might account for the dislike. But had she been really an honest girl? Had she perhaps been defrauding her employer? Could it be that someone—perhaps the other secretary, Monner—had found that out and threatened to expose her? Could that account for her suicide?

Most of these thoughts passed through Colonel Netterly's mind as he drove home from Little Lawton. As he garaged his car he determined to have another look through those papers on Monday. Meantime, clear it all out of one's head—a rubber of bridge tonight, a game of golf tomorrow; re-creation of mental and bodily vigour.

. . . . .

As in the case of Mrs. Rathlyn, the Coroner had adjourned the inquest in order to allow the police time to pursue their enquiries—but this time only for a week. To Mr. Purde this was clearly a case of suicide; it was proper for the police to try and find out the reason for it— if there ever is an adequate reason for self-destruction— but it was not a matter, he felt, that should take up too much time and money; finding the reason would not bring the poor girl back to life again, and it seldom resulted in blame for a third party, though shame there might be. So, at least, thought this particular Coroner— a man not devoid of individuality.

The police, therefore, felt constrained to push ahead with their enquiries, and on Monday morning Super-

intendent Hant once more asked for an interview with the
Chief Constable. He began by telling Colonel Netterly
what he had learnt on Saturday from Philip Monner and
Captain Rathlyn—little enough, so far as the sheets of
dates and figures were concerned. He then said that he
wanted authority to question Captain Rathlyn about the
entries of £200 in Miss Wey's bank account. At this
point Colonel Netterly interposed to tell him of the
interview he had had with Miss Faery on Saturday
afternoon, ending by an assertion that he was entirely
satisfied that, in denying any affectionate association
between herself and Captain Rathlyn—anything to
justify jealousy on the part of Mrs. Rathlyn—the girl had
been telling him the truth. Superintendent Hant
listened in silence, and his next words showed that, so
far as he was concerned, the matter was by no means
cleared up.

" I should wish to question Captain Rathlyn about that
letter, sir, as well as about the entries in Miss Wey's
account."

Colonel Netterly looked at him thoughtfully.

" You are pressing him very hard, Mr. Hant," he said.

" Yes, sir. I think he killed his wife."

" I doubt it, you know. He was much better off with
her alive."

" That may be so, sir, but money isn't the only motive.
My belief is that he wanted to be free to marry again."

" You heard what I said about Miss Faery, Mr. Hant.
I have a good deal of experience, and I believe I know
when someone is lying to me. I am quite sure that Miss
Faery was telling me the truth."

" That may be so, sir, and yet he may have wanted to
marry her—even without her knowing it."

Colonel Netterly shrugged his shoulders.

" I suppose that that is possible, if not very likely.

You are quite right to make sure. Tell me, what exactly is it that makes you suspect Captain Rathlyn of murder? "

Hant pulled himself together. This would not be too easy; he was conscious that his suspicions, strong as they were, were not of a very concrete nature—they were inclined to dart about from one point to another, some of the points being contradictory to one another.

" In the first place, that fall, sir. The doctors say that it is most unusual for a sleep-walker to lose balance; they are normally very sure-footed. In any case, the body was not directly under the point at which he says he saw her leaning over the balustrade; if she merely toppled over, she would have fallen straight down, but her body was lying some three feet farther out into the hall, as if she had been pushed or thrown outwards from the gallery where she stood. Dr. Sykes said that that could be done without her waking or screaming."

" A big risk," muttered the Chief Constable. " She was a fairly big and strong woman."

" Yes, sir. Alternatively he may have struck her a heavy blow with some weapon before throwing her over. Remember, a broken neck was the cause of death, but there was a severe fracture of the skull on the right-hand side as well."

" In that case, if he struck her on the right side of the head and if she had fallen on the left side she would have had a fracture on each side—a bit awkward to explain away."

" Yes, sir, a risk, of course; a fifty-fifty chance. Personally I think he just gave her a shove."

The words of the old music-hall gag came floating back out of the past, not for the first time, into Colonel Netterly's mind:

" *Did she fall or was she pushed?* "

Its vulgar jocularity was so tragically apt.

" And why? "

" Several alternative motives, sir. Money, in the first place. As you say, sir, he was better off with her alive, but was he going to stay better off? What if she was going to divorce him? You'll not have forgotten, sir, that she had sent for her solicitor. He says he doesn't know what she wanted him for, and probably now nobody knows—except, perhaps, Captain Rathlyn. What if she was going to speak about a divorce—and Captain Rathlyn knew it? What if she was going to instruct him to alter her will—and Captain Rathlyn knew it? "

Hant paused, to let these ideas sink in. He thought a lot of them, and he could see that the Chief Constable was impressed.

" I hadn't thought of that. Go on, Mr. Hant."

" Then, sir, there are the other alternatives, partly overlapping, partly contradictory, that you know of. That he wanted to be free to marry Miss Faery, or to marry or carry on an intrigue with Miss Wey. And that brings one to the second case—Miss Wey's death. May she not have been blackmailing him? And if so, isn't it likely that he put her out of the way? "

The Chief Constable sat for a minute in silence, frowning at his own lean hands.

" I follow your chain of thought," he said at last. " It is logical, and I am sure that you are right to test it as fully as you possibly can. Even if you are right, it will be extremely difficult to prove either case—without an eye-witness. The second case particularly; how on earth could he have persuaded Miss Wey to take twenty tablets of Dormonal? Still, I agree that you must go on trying. You want to go out and question him now, I gather? Very well, I agree. If anything more is to be done, it is time for a direct attack."

" Thank you, sir." Hant rose to go.

" Before you go, just leave me those sheets of dates and figures you got from the girl's bank. I didn't really examine them very closely. I take it you won't want them when you talk to Captain Rathlyn, though you may want her bank statement."

" I have had copies made of that, sir. I will bring you one, together with the other papers."

. . . . .

A drizzle of fine February rain was falling as Hant drove out to Tandrings. It was a depressing scene, to a casual eye, but to a countryman who knew where to look there were already signs that the year was turning; winter was still here, but spring not far behind. Little specks of green showed here and there on hedge and bush; in sheltered woods a few shy primroses and wild violets had begun to thrust their heads through the fallen leaves, snowdrops, too, and even a precocious crocus or two gave their beauty to humble gardens, and the tall spikes of daffodils threatened to burst into yellow bloom. Even in the fields the swollen bodies of ewes gave rich promise of the coming spring.

Detective-Superintendent Hant was blind to these sights. He was not using his eyes at all now, except subconsciously; his whole being was concentrated in his mind. Subconsciously he parked his car at the side of the carriage sweep, walked across to the front door and rang the bell. A minute later he was in the study facing its occupant, who, in a tweed suit, stood with his back to the fire. A glance at the detective's face told Charles Rathlyn that the attack was coming; he remained standing and did not offer his visitor a seat.

Hant took from his pocket-book the letter which Colonel Netterly had returned to him that morning.

" I must ask you to look at that, sir."

The tone of voice was curt and formal; no easy tact, no light-handed fencing would be used today.

Rathlyn's face stiffened as he saw his wife's handwriting —the name and address on the envelope. He knew what this would prove to be. There had been just a chance that Isabel had been bluffing when she said she had the original, just a chance that she had merely copied it, after perhaps steaming open the envelope and later closing and posting it. In that case, though, Anne would almost certainly have told him when they had opened their hearts to each other in the Lawton woods.

Trying to keep his fingers steady, he drew out the letter and read it. Then he looked up at the detective.

"Where on earth did you get this from?"

For a moment that need not be answered.

"Can you explain it, please?"

Charles Rathlyn's eyebrows rose in well-simulated disdain.

"Does it need explaining . . . to you?"

"Yes, sir, it does, and I won't beat about the bush. I am not satisfied—the Chief Constable is not satisfied— that Mrs. Rathlyn's death was accidental. It must have been clear to you that the Coroner was not satisfied either, and it is my duty now to ask you a number of direct questions. They may sound very offensive, but I have to ask them, and I want straight answers. In the first place, how do you explain this letter?"

Charles Rathlyn put the letter back into its envelope and returned it to Hant.

"Very well, Superintendent. My wife got it into her head that I had been paying too much attention to Miss Faery. She was quite mistaken. Apart from meeting her out hunting and apart from her staying to help me when I had a bad fall, I saw no more of Miss Faery than of any other casual acquaintance, except that on one occasion we went to a play together in London. Actually my wife did not know of that, and I did not tell her because she had already shown signs of being jealous of Miss Faery. As it turns out it was stupid of me to take Miss Faery to a play, but there was really nothing in it at all—nothing serious. These things do happen, you know, Superintendent. I can only assure you that my wife had no ground for jealousy at all . . . and that I did not kill her, as you seem to be suggesting."

As had been the case with Anne Faery and Colonel Netterly, Charles Rathlyn's frankness in telling of that London evening had its effect upon Hant; it took one puff of wind out of his sails. But it did not deflect him from his voyage.

" The fact remains that Mrs. Rathlyn was jealous; this letter proves it."

" But what is this letter? Where did you get it? It does not seem to have been delivered."

" No, sir; I will come to that later. Mrs. Rathlyn was jealous, and within a short time Mrs. Rathlyn was writing to her lawyer asking him to call on her urgently the next morning. On that very night, the night of writing the letter, the night before the lawyer was to call, she fell to her death."

Rathlyn's face was an expressionless mask as he looked at the detective, but his eyes did not waver.

" Well? " he asked quietly.

" I suggest that you knew of that letter, sir, and that it was your wife's intention—or that you feared that it might be her intention—to alter her will or possibly even to consult her lawyer on grounds for divorce."

What seemed to be genuine astonishment showed on the soldier's face.

" Good lord," he said; " you've got a lively imagination, Mr. Hant. That one about divorce, I mean. As a matter of fact I did not know about the letter, but it didn't surprise me."

"It didn't?" exclaimed Hant eagerly.

"Superintendent, you asked me about this before. Don't you remember? I told you then that although I knew nothing about the summons to Mr. Lorriner, my wife had told me that her brother-in-law, Mr. George Waygold, had come down to get some money out of her to pay his gambling debts. I suggested to you that that might have been what she wanted to see Mr. Lorriner about—to raise that money for George Waygold; or possibly . . ." for the first time a smile lightened Charles Rathlyn's face ". . . if you are so eager to change my wife's will, might she not have wanted to cut poor old George Waygold out of it?"

Hant was taken aback. He remembered now the suggested explanation which Captain Rathlyn had given, though not the last part of it. *Was* that the explanation? It seemed possible. Another puff of wind left the sails. Doggedly Hant drove on.

"Now I come to the death of Miss Wey, sir."

Watching carefully, he saw the dead-pan look return to Rathlyn's face; the smile had gone and it was not to return that day.

"You told Superintendent Binnerton the next morning that you had seen Miss Wey after dinner the night before she died. You remember that, sir?"

"I remember very well."

"You said that she seemed in good spirits, I think."

"In her normal spirits. She was normally a quiet, reserved girl and she was that evening."

"She did not appear depressed—as she might appear if she were about to take her own life?"

"No, she did not."

"Why did she take her own life, Captain Rathlyn?"

Charles looked steadily at the detective.

" I have no idea," he said.

" You believe she did? "

" What else can one believe? "

" You do not think she might have been murdered? "

The steady stare of the grey eyes did not waver.

" That seems to me most unlikely."

" Very well. Now, sir; you told us that Miss Wey came to you that evening to ask your advice about taking a situation with a firm of turf accountants."

" Yes."

" Would she be interested in a situation if she was about to take her life? "

With a thrill of excitement Hant saw that little beads of sweat were forming on Rathlyn's forehead. His voice was calm enough as he answered.

" I don't know the answer to that. It certainly seems unlikely."

" This was a real situation she was asking about? "

" So I gathered."

" She told you the name of the firm? "

Rathlyn shook his head.

" I think I may have already told you this. Miss Wey was a most secretive girl. She gave nothing away unless she had to. It was entirely in character for her to ask me for advice about such a situation and not tell me the name of the actual firm."

" You believe it was a genuine enquiry? "

" I do."

" Then how do you account for this? We have thoroughly searched Miss Wey's papers, both in her room and in another place, and there is no sign of any letter from a firm of turf accountants, or from an agency; no newspaper cutting, nothing to suggest that she was looking for a situation."

There was silence for nearly a minute as the two men looked into each other's eyes. Then Rathlyn said:

" I am sure the answer to that must suggest itself to you as well as to me; if she was indeed not looking for a situation, then perhaps it was because she *had* decided, for some unknown reason, to take her own life."

Again that flap of the sails; Hant swung the tiller to bring his boat into the remaining wind.

" Or is it, sir, that what you have told me is untrue? That she was not looking for a situation because she was counting on you to keep her? "

Charles Rathlyn drew himself sharply up.

" That is a gross suggestion," he said. " I shall not answer it."

For a moment Hant hesitated, wondering whether to use his knowledge of what Filblow had seen through the curtains of this very room. He decided to keep that card up his sleeve a little longer.

" Very well, sir. Now I come to another matter. Miss Wey . . . by the way, sir, can you tell me what her salary was? "

" Not off-hand. Monner will know that; he pays the salaries and wages."

" I see, sir. Miss Wey, I find, paid certain small sums into a Post Office Savings Bank account from time to time, but she also had an account with the Provincial and South Coast Bank in Bournemouth. She paid comparatively small sums into that also, from time to time, but within the last few months—since Mrs. Rathlyn's death in fact— two large amounts, of two hundred pounds each, were paid into her account. I have to ask you whether you know anything about those two payments."

For the first time the detective saw signs of weakening in the man opposite him. A hand went up to his mouth . . . and was taken quickly away.

" How on earth should I know about them? I know absolutely nothing of Miss Wey's bank account."

" May I ask you, sir, to give me access to your own bank account, to instruct your Bank Manager to . . ."

" No, I will not! " Rathlyn's voice was angry . . . and it was shaking. " I will not give you access to my bank account or anything else, unless you produce a warrant. And I have had enough of your damned insinuations. Will you please take yourself off! "

Hant turned on his heel and walked out of the room and out of the house, the tail of his eye catching the figure of Ludd as he hurried to answer the ringing of the study bell. On the detective's face was a look of grim satisfaction.

CHAPTER XXII

A Lot of Dates

AS SOON as Superintendent Hant had left, Colonel
Netterly cleared off the most urgent of his routine work
and then settled down to examine the papers which had
come from Isabel Wey's Bournemouth bank. The one
most likely to prove important was the bank statement
itself—the copy of actual entries in her ledger account.
These began in August 1950 with the deposit of £70 and
were followed at fairly regular monthly intervals by sums
of £10, £20, and occasionally £25 and £30, these larger
sums appearing in 1953 and 1954. Interspersed with
these entries were the periodical entries of sums repre-
senting deposit interest. Finally there were the two
entries which had excited Superintendent Hant's interest—
£200 on 20th November 1954, and £200 on 15th January
1955.

Well, Hant was enquiring about those now, and it was
not worth speculating about them until he reported what
he had discovered or failed to discover. Netterly turned
to the discarded sheets of dates and money entries. So
far as the sheets of mere dates were concerned, these—as
has been said—were written in pencil in Isabel Wey's
hand, according to Monner. They looked as if they had
not been written at the same time; it seemed to the Chief
Constable that each date had been scribbled down as it
occurred, rather than that a list of dates had been written
down, one below the other, at the same time. There
might perhaps be some significance in that.

The other lists, of dates and figures, gave a different
impression. They were typewritten and the spacing of
lines was exact; the sheet could not have been taken out

and put back again as each entry occurred. The whole sheet was clearly done at once.

Colonel Netterly thought that if anything was to be made of them it would be better to concentrate on one year. He chose 1954, as being the latest and also because Charles Rathlyn had made a suggestion about one or two of the dates in the pencilled list for that year. Taking, then, the typewritten sheet for January 1954 he examined it carefully. It took the following form:

Jan. 4th	.	.	.	.	£20
Jan. 8th	.	.	.	.	£15
Jan. 11th	.	.	.	.	£50
Jan. 13th	.	.	.	.	£20
Jan. 16th	.	.	.	.	£10
Jan. 22nd	.	.	.	.	£30
Jan. 27th	.	.	.	.	£20
Jan. 30th	.	.	.	.	£10

Looking at the pencilled list of dates for 1954 Netterly saw that the only ones noted for January were:

9th January
10th January
12th January
25th January

These did not correspond with any of the typewritten dates.

Turning to February, Netterly found much the same thing; the dates on typewritten and pencilled sheets did not correspond with one another. There was one large gap in this month; no cash amounts were shown for the period 10th–25th February, but there was a cash entry for £200 on 9th February; on the pencilled sheet there appeared only one entry, so shown: 10th–24th February. That, Netterly believed, was the period when Charles

Rathlyn had said that he and his wife had been in the
south of France.

Well, that was what was to be expected. Monner had
told Hant that the typewritten sheets showed the amounts
of cash which he had doled out to Mrs. Rathlyn. If she
was away in France, naturally he would not have doled
out any cash to her. What was all the mystery about?
Why should he think there was a mystery? Only because
Isabel Wey had taken the trouble to send all these sheets
of dates and figures to her bank for safe keeping. Why had
she?

Methodically the Chief Constable plodded through the
rest of the year, up to September, when both lists ceased—
clearly, at the death of Mrs. Rathlyn. He found the same
sort of thing throughout: payments amounting to between
£100 and £200 each month, on dates corresponding in
no case with the dates on the pencilled sheet. There
must be some explanation for that, and the simple one was
the one suggested by Charles Rathlyn—that those
pencilled dates were ones on which he and his wife—or
his wife alone—were away from home. Simple enough?
But why had Isabel Wey bothered to keep them?

The Chief Constable was on the point of pushing the
whole subject on one side—after all, this was a C.I.D. job,
not the Chief Constable's—when a surge of obstinacy
drove him back to the task. Somehow he and Detective-
Superintendent Hant had got across one another; he did
not agree with Hant's suspicions, and knew that Hant was
annoyed by the disagreement. Hant had discarded this
set of papers, as of no interest; what a score it would be—
Colonel Netterly was not above that schoolboyish senti-
ment—if he should find gold where his expert had recorded
dross!

Gradually the Chief Constable worked backwards,
through 1953, 1952, 1951. It was quite a surprise when,

in June 1951, he found a date on the typewritten sheet
which corresponded with a pencilled date. A slip of the
pen, perhaps.

1950. Here the first month on the typewritten sheet
was April; on the pencilled list there was no date before
8th May. Turning, then, to the May sheet of typewritten
entries Colonel Netterly found the following set out:

May 2nd	.	.	.	.	£10
May 5th	.	.	.	.	£20
May 8th	.	.	.	.	£20
May 10th	.	.	.	.	£10
May 13th	.	.	.	.	£30
May 17th	.	.	.	.	£20
May 21st	.	.	.	.	£20
May 26th	.	.	.	.	£10
May 31st	.	.	.	.	£20

But he had already noticed the date 8th May on the
pencilled list of dates. Looking at this again, he saw that
17th May also appeared on this list. Also slips of the pen?
Or was his theory not correct?

Turning to June, he found much the same thing; three
of the pencilled dates, which he had assumed to be days
when Mrs. Rathlyn—then Mrs. Waygold—was away
were dates on which the typewritten list showed that payments were made to her. One of these days was 15th
June, and Netterly, hunting through his old Badminton
diaries, found—as he expected—that it was in Ascot
week; Ladies' Day, in fact.

Much the same thing occurred in July—two pencilled
dates coincided with two typewritten dates, but in August
this coincidence ceased, and it did not recur in September,
October, November or December. And August 1950
was the month in which Isabel Wey had opened her bank
account in Bournemouth.

Like an old foxhound Colonel Netterly felt his hackles rising as he owned to the faint scent. Surely, surely there was a fox somewhere in this covert? Was it strong enough? Was he sure enough to give tongue?

A thought occurred to him; these typewritten lists were not originals, they were apparently—Monner had told Hant—copies made by Isabel Wey. They might not be correct; they might be cooked in places where cooking mattered. Monner had the originals; should he ring and ask him to bring them or send them over by Hant? Then another idea struck him; there had been, he understood, another copy of each monthly statement kept by Mrs. Rathlyn herself. Where would they be now? Reaching for the telephone, he dialled a number.

" Mr. Lorriner in? Put me through, please; Colonel Netterly . . . That you, Lorriner? Netterly here. Look; am I right in thinking that you are one of Mrs. Rathlyn's executors? I thought so. Well, did you impound all her business papers, accounts and so on? There's something I'd like to have a look at . . ."

The Chief Constable explained what he wanted; Mr. Lorriner had the accounts referred to and truth to tell had thought they might well go for salvage. He would just get formal consent over the telephone from his co-trustee, and would then send them round. They arrived within half an hour.

Before they did so Superintendent Hant had returned. Obtaining permission to report, he came eagerly into the Chief Constable's office to find ' the old buzzard ', as he disrespectfully thought of him at that moment, poring over those dreary sheets of dates and figures. Colonel Netterly looked up.

" Ah, Mr. Hant; how did you get on? "

" On the right line all right, sir. I'm pretty sure he killed them both, and I *know* she was blackmailing him."

" Has he confessed? "

" Confessed? Oh, no, sir. I wouldn't expect that."

" A confession is what is needed, I fancy," said the Chief
Constable quietly.

" I'll get him all right, sir, now I know."

Colonel Netterly smiled. " Nothing like confidence,"
he said. " Mr. Hant, have you looked carefully through
these lists of dates and payments? "

" I've looked through them, sir. Not to say carefully,
perhaps. No significance, I fancy, sir; just a lot of dates.
The bank statement is what matters—those two two-
hundred-pound entries."

" Yes, the bank statement certainly is significant. So
I fancy, are these others. I should like to ask that
secretary chap, however, one or two questions about
them." Colonel Netterly glanced at his watch. " Get
yourself a bit of lunch and then slip back in the car and
ask him to come over."

Hant stared in astonishment.

" Don't you want to hear my report, sir—about
Captain Rathlyn? "

The Chief Constable pulled himself together.

" Yes, of course. Let's have Mr. Janson in."

When they were all seated Superintendent Hant told
his story, beginning in a minor key and gradually working
up to the *molto agitato* of Rathlyn's refusal to give Hant
access to his bank account.

" What do you propose to do about it? " asked Colonel
Netterly.

" Well, if necessary, sir, we might get an order of the
Court—for access to his bank account, I mean."

" We might. What do you think, Janson? "

" The Court would want some good grounds before they
made such an order, sir. What exactly has Mr. Hant got
against Captain Rathlyn? "

" Ah, I forgot; you aren't quite up do date.   Well, we shall have to go into all that.   But not just now; get your lunch, Mr. Hant, and then go off and do as I asked, will you, like a good chap? "

.   .   .   .   .

It was half-past two by the time Superintendent Hant returned with Philip Monner. The lanky secretary looked nervous, as anyone might paying his first visit to police headquarters in company with a Detective-Superintendent. Hant himself saw with astonishment that in one corner of the Chief Constable's room a uniformed officer, one of the headquarters clerks, was seated at a small table quietly scribbling away on some sheets of foolscap; his presence, of course, meant nothing to the layman, Monner.

The Chief Constable greeted Monner quietly and motioned him to a chair on the opposite side of his writing-table. On the table were the little piles of paper which Colonel Netterly had been examining during the morning.

" I just wanted to ask for your help with some of these accounts that are puzzling us a bit.   I believe Mr. Hant has already asked you about some of them."

The rather prominent Adam's apple worked up and down in Monner's throat.

" Yes, sir."

" I understand that these typewritten ones are copies of some cash accounts that you kept for Mrs. Rathlyn—notes of payments of cash made to her by you from time to time, as she required them."

" That is so, sir."

" She wrote a cheque from time to time, you cashed it and kept the cash in your safe—that right? "

" Quite right, sir."

" And each month you gave her a statement of what she

had had—one of these dated sheets, in fact—and she signed it. That was by way of check, of course, and for the benefit of the auditors."

"Exactly, sir. Those sheets you have, though, are not the statements I made out; they appear to be copies, made possibly by Miss Wey, though of that I am not sure. I made out two copies each month and Mrs. Rathlyn signed them both; I kept one, she kept the other. If I had known what you wanted, sir, I would have brought my original copies."

"No matter," said Colonel Netterly quietly; "I have Mrs. Rathlyn's copies here." He tapped a pile of paper beside him. The answer seemed to add to Monner's nervousness; Hant himself was rather taken aback.

"We had better deal with these originals, I think. Will you have a look at this sheet, showing the cash payments for January 1954?" Colonel Netterly handed the sheet across the table to Monner, who bent over it.

"Eight payments during the month, totalling one hundred and seventy-five pounds. Would that be a normal amount?"

"Rather above the average, I should say, sir."

"Mrs. Rathlyn used a lot of cash, I take it. What sort of things would that be for?"

A pale smile flickered across the secretary's face.

"Betting, I think, sir. Mrs. Rathlyn did not bet in large amounts, either before or after her second marriage, but she enjoyed putting the money on herself with different bookmakers. She did not keep an account with any one bookmaker. She once told me that she found it more exciting to handle the actual cash—took her back to the days of her youth, she said."

"Not very successful, it would appear, as she needed so much, so often."

"Not very, sir; but she had other uses for cash. She

was very generous, and would often give a five-pound note, or even more, to someone whom she thought in trouble."

" I always heard she was a generous woman," said the Chief Constable. " A generous employer, too, I believe. Eh, Mr. Monner? "

Somehow this question seemed to upset the secretary. He flushed hotly, the colour contrasting oddly with his normal pallor.

" Very generous indeed, sir."

" Right; then January 1954 was a slightly above average amount. You have the dates of those payments in front of you; now would you compare them with the dates on the pencilled sheets—made, I understand you to have said, by Miss Wey. The dates do not appear to correspond at all, do they? "

Again Monner bent over the sheets of paper. Superintendent Hant stared at his chief; what on earth was all this about?

" No, sir; they don't correspond."

" Any idea what those pencilled dates mean? "

" I have no idea whatever, sir."

" Captain Rathlyn has himself suggested that they might be dates on which Mrs. Rathlyn was away from home. In certain cases—these dates in February, for instance, and in June—they were, he told Mr. Hant, definitely dates on which he and Mrs. Rathlyn were away from home. That being so, of course, they could not correspond with the days on which you gave out cash to Mrs. Rathlyn."

" No, sir."

Monner's voice was little more than a whisper. Hant saw that his hand, holding the sheet of paper, was trembling violently. The Chief Constable did not appear to notice.

" Well, that explains that, then," he said easily.

" Though it does not explain why Miss Wey had made a note of these dates and kept them locked away in her bank. Does it, Mr. Monner? "

The secretary did not answer. He was staring at Colonel Netterly as a rabbit stares, fascinated, at a stoat. Foxhound and stoat! Two similes applied to himself by Netterly that day.

" A little difficult to understand what she wanted them for, isn't it? Well, now let us look at a different year. 1950. Here I notice that the copies which she made of your cash statements only begin in April and the pencilled dates only begin in May. Some reason for that, no doubt. But here we come on something different. In May two of the pencilled dates—dates which appeared to mean that Mrs. Rathlyn . . . Mrs. Waygold, I should say . . . was away appear also in your statement as days on which you paid out cash to her. How would you account for that, Mr. Monner? "

White in the face, Monner swallowed twice before replying.

" A slip, perhaps, sir. Or . . . I don't know what these pencilled dates mean. They may mean . . . they may not mean that she was away."

" I fancy that that was what Miss Wey thought they meant," said the Chief Constable quietly. " The same in June—three corresponding dates, in July—two corresponding dates, but not in August and never again in four years, except once—a slip perhaps, eh, Mr. Monner? "

White, shaking, Philip Monner stared at the stoat. Inexorably the quiet voice of the Chief Constable went on. Superintendent Hant listened in awestruck astonishment.

" And August was the month—August 1950—when Miss Wey began to pay into her bank regular sums of ten pounds or twenty pounds a month, right up to the date of her death. Can you account for those, Mr. Monner? "

Slowly Philip Monner started to rise from his seat.

" I . . . I don't feel well," he said.   " A little air . . ."

" A little drink, perhaps," said Colonel Netterly. " Jennings, some whisky."

The uniformed constable bent down and drew up from beneath his table a bottle of whisky and a glass.   Like a rabbit from a hat, thought the astonished Hant. Jennings poured some whisky into the glass and walked across towards Monner with it, holding it out to him. Monner stared at it, held out his trembling hand.

" You do drink whisky, don't you, Mr. Monner?   In the evenings, sometimes.   Did Miss Wey drink whisky? "

Philip Monner swayed for a moment, then crashed forward in a dead faint.

CHAPTER XXIII

A Sorry Tale

SUPERINTENDENT HANT knelt down beside the fallen man.

" Give me a hand, Jennings," he said sharply. " We'll get him out of here."

" No, no; leave him where he is," said Colonel Netterly. " He'll be round in a minute. Then we may get something."

Hant looked at his Chief in shocked admiration. Had he planned all this—deliberately?

" There, he's beginning to come to. Give the whisky to Mr. Hant, Jennings, and then get back to your seat and carry on as I told you. Feeling better, Monner? Give him a sip of that whisky, Mr. Hant; he'll soon be all right."

In another minute Philip Monner was back on his chair, elbows on knees, head on hands. For a minute he sat like that, two minutes, three minutes, while the others remained silent. Then he looked up.

" I'll tell you," he said hoarsely.

" Better not say any more, Monner," said the Chief Constable quietly. " There is no need for you to make any statement, but if you do I must caution you that it will be taken down in writing and may be used in evidence."

The words rang with deadly implication in Philip Monner's aching head. How often he had read them, or something like them, in novels of crime, or murder; now they were being said to him.

" I can't stand any more of it," he muttered. " I'd rather tell you straight away."

" Better see a solicitor first."

" It's no good. You know all about it. I'll tell you."

Colonel Netterly sat more upright in his chair; he nodded imperceptibly to Jennings, who poised his Biro pen over a clean sheet of foolscap.

" Very well; go ahead."

Suddenly Monner sat upright, a flash of anger in his dark eyes. His voice was clear and strong now.

" I'm glad I killed her! " he exclaimed. " She was a devil—a bad woman. She was blackmailing me and at the same time making me . . . making me make love to her. I . . . I did love her. And I hated her and feared her. She found out that I'd been . . ."

The voice trailed off, and again Monner sank his face into his hands.

" I meant to go straight. I did really, but there's rotten blood in my veins . . ."

" Oh lord, the fellow's going to whine," thought Netterly.

" My father defrauded his employer—I expect you know all about that. I swore that I would go straight and I did until . . . I heard them all talking about a horse of Mrs. Waygold's that was sure to win. My mother was ill and couldn't go out to work; my pay wasn't enough to keep us both. I wanted money—for her, not for myself; I put some money on the horse and it won. It was too easy. I did it again, a little more money. I lost. I lost again and . . . then I began."

The old, sorry tale. So hackneyed, so tragic.

" You know about those cash payments to Mrs. Waygold, sir. She was criminally careless; I don't think she ever counted what I gave her, nor looked at the monthly statements which she signed. The auditors quite rightly wanted to tighten up those cash accounts, but she wouldn't be bothered. It was all too easy. I began by putting down a little more than I had actually given her—

fifteen pounds instead of ten, thirty pounds instead of twenty-five. She didn't notice. Then I began to put in dates and payments when actually she had had nothing. Still she didn't notice. But Isabel Wey did."

There was a bitter note in the man's voice now.

" I think the first time was when I had given Mrs. Waygold fifteen pounds and she had put them down somewhere and sent Isabel to look for them. She counted them—fifteen pounds. She must already have known about the monthly statements, and of course she could easily get access to any paper of Mrs. Waygold's. She remembered the date and the amount, and at the end of the month, when I handed in my statement to Mrs. Waygold, Isabel Wey saw that I had put down twenty pounds for that day.

" I think that was in March or April 1950. She didn't do anything about it at once—she wasn't going to scare me until she had got proof—she told me that. She soon spotted the fictitious dates, when I had given Mrs. Way-gold no cash but entered it in the statement—money I kept myself. Then she began to copy the statements and to keep a note of the days when Mrs. Waygold was away from home, and so *couldn't* have received cash from me. That would give her proof, she said.

" For three months she kept those notes and watched the discrepancies—May, June, July 1950; you've got them there in front of you, sir. You spotted them at once."

Hant was uncomfortably conscious that *he* had not spotted them.

" Then she told me what she had found and calmly asked for what she called a ' rake-off '. She demanded fifty pounds, and I gave it her, because I knew she could ruin me. I swore that I would stop, but she just laughed at me and told me to go ahead; all she wanted was ten pounds a month—or a bit more if she needed it. I could easily squeeze a bit more, she said."

Monner paused, reached out his hand to the glass of whisky and drank it off, neat as it was. He shuddered, but spoke more firmly.

" That went on for three more years, almost without incident; it became a normal thing, but of course I didn't make any more slips about entering payments on days when she was away."

Except once, thought Netterly; one slip of the pen in June 1951.

" It was a queer association, that of ours. Living so close together, having our meals together, even sitting together sometimes after dinner. And all the time she was blackmailing me. And more than that. I . . . don't know how to describe it—she fascinated me; she was very beautiful when she took that cold, hard expression off her face, and sometimes I suppose it amused her to tease me, to excite me, to lead me on to make love to her—or try to. Sometimes it was almost more than I could bear, but she knew exactly how far she could go. She once said that she was my partner in crime, but not a . . . not a sleeping partner."

Astonishingly, the man was blushing.

" Then Mrs. Waygold married Captain Rathlyn, and I thought we should have to stop—faking the cash payments, I mean. But he didn't interfere in Mrs. Rathlyn's private affairs; he did once ask me about these payments, and I could see he thought it a slipshod arrangement, but he didn't interfere. I wanted to stop, but Isabel drove me on. I ought to have defied her, but I knew she could ruin me; an accountant who has been dishonest can never get another job—especially if he has had a dishonest father."

Again the whining note jarred on Colonel Netterly.

" She began to put on the screw; she wanted more and more, and I had to give her more, even though it meant keeping nothing for myself. I was almost mad, too, with . . . with wanting her. She was driving me mad—she was a devil, a fiend. I had to . . . I had to . . ."

His voice, which had risen almost to a scream, dropped almost to a whisper.

" I realised that it had got to stop . . . that there was only one way to stop it. Otherwise, she would be a mill-stone round my neck all my life. Once I had decided I became quite calm. I began to plan; something that happened when Captain Rathlyn had a bad hunting fall put the idea into my head. She told me, rather con-temptuously, that Mrs. Rathlyn hadn't even got an aspirin in the house—she, Isabel, had lent her some of her Dormonal tablets, which were much stronger. I asked her about those, what she had them for, that sort of thing, quite casually. I began to look up hypnotic drugs in the forensic medicine books in the public library. I learnt how much was likely to be a fatal dose."

Monner took out his handkerchief and began to rub the palms of his hands.

" Mrs. Rathlyn's death, terrible as it was, made little difference to us. At first I thought I might get away from it all, but she soon let me know that she would never let go, wherever I went. I had got so far with my plans; I could see how to do it here—at Tandrings; I might never have such a chance again."

He looked at the Chief Constable, almost with admira-tion.

" I don't know how you knew about the whisky, sir; but of course that was it. We often had some wine for dinner, but that wouldn't do; it was too early, even if it would conceal the taste of the tablets. But whisky would do—last thing at night. I began to encourage her to have a glass of whisky last thing; she seemed to be excited about something after Mrs. Rathlyn's death, and she often sat up late and liked the whisky. I encouraged her to take it in ginger-ale—to help conceal the taste. She liked that, too. Not every night; sometimes she would go off soon after dinner and not come back, but sometimes she did come back and we . . . and we drank whisky and enjoyed ourselves. My God, enjoyed ourselves!"

What a mockery of enjoyment that had been.

"It was the tablets themselves that were the main difficulty. I soon found that they could not be got without a prescription, and I dared not ask for that, even at home when I was on holiday. If there was any suspicion it would be too dangerous. I took to going up to London on my days off and hunting round for the dishonest chemists that I knew must exist. I found them all right, and got two bottles of Dormonal—at a price. I'll give you the name of that chemist if you like."

Yes, that would be needed, but no questions must be asked from a suspect once he had been cautioned.

"I experimented a bit on myself with the tablets from one bottle. I knew that I must have them ready dissolved, ready for the opportunity when it came. No good dissolving in whisky and keeping it, because the whisky would evaporate—lose its potency. I dissolved three tablets in water and kept it three days, then added a little whisky and ginger ale and drank it. There was no peculiar taste, and within three hours I was asleep and didn't feel too good when I woke up. Then I managed to get hold of an extra whisky tumbler from the pantry and locked it up—not where I normally keep the whisky. When no hue and cry was raised over the glass I decided that the time had come. I dissolved fifteen tablets in water in that goblet and locked it up. That very night Isabel had gone away for an hour after dinner, but came back; she seemed excited, almost angry, and said she wanted a drink.''

Suddenly Monner slumped in his chair, as if exhausted. Hant looked enquiringly at the empty whisky glass, but the Chief Constable shook his head. One thing to give whisky to a fainting man, another to prime a confession.

"What happened after that was a nightmare," said Monner at last. "There was no difficulty in preparing the drink without her noticing what I was doing—adding whisky and then ginger ale. She drank it off and asked for more, but I didn't want to give her more; I knew there would be an autopsy, and I wasn't sure how long whisky would be traceable—whether it would evaporate in the time. I knelt down by her chair and put my arms round her and . . . and made love to her, hoping she would begin to get drowsy and go up to bed. I knew that she did not lock the door of her bedroom and that I should be able to go up later and do what was necessary.''

A cool, calculating murderer, whatever his justification, thought Netterly.

"But she didn't; she was gay for a time and then suddenly became somnolent. I could see that there was no chance of her going up under her own steam. I should have to carry her. It was late now and everyone would be in bed, except perhaps Captain Rathlyn, and he never came our way at night. I could carry her up the back stairs. I took off my shoes; it was a risk, in case I did meet anyone, but I had to be silent in everything that remained to be done now. She was not terribly heavy and I got her up all right and into her bedroom. I . . . I undressed her and got her into bed.''

Again that astonishing blush, red-hot now.

"I folded her clothes, as I thought she would fold them, though probably a woman would have noticed something wrong.''

Mrs. Tass had not noticed, thought Hant bitterly. But, then, why should she? Wiser to take a policewoman, another time, perhaps.

"Then I hunted round and found her own Dormonal tablets; in fact there were two bottles, with a few in each. I emptied them and put those into her toothglass and dissolved them in a little water—left just enough to look like the dregs of a full glass and poured the rest away. I thought it safer to leave her bottles than mine, and of course I wiped off my prints and pressed her fingers round the bottles before putting them on the table beside the bed."

All the tricks that one learns from reading detective stories, thought the Chief Constable.

"She was completely asleep by this •time," went on Monner, "her face flushed and blotchy, her breathing very heavy; rather a horrible sight—I tried not to look at her. I hunted everywhere, both in her bedroom and in her little office next door, trying to find the papers that I was sure she had got; I didn't quite know what, but some sort of proof which I knew she had. I couldn't find anything except some bank statements from a bank in Bournemouth and her Post Office Savings Book. I took those, because they might have suggested something to anyone investigating her death. I took some letters too, that I had not time to read then. There might have been something that pointed to me. Of course I dared not put them back later. I burned them."

Hant itched to ask about the two entries of £200, but the no-question rule must be obeyed.

"I could see that most of what I had given her must have been paid into the Bournemouth bank, but there was more besides. Of course, I had been getting nothing except my salary since Mrs. Rathlyn's death and I had had to pay Isabel by drawing on my little bit of capital; I had

been able to accumulate a bit during the first three years.
How you have found it all out I don't know; I thought I
had quite satisfied Superintendent Hant when he
questioned me."

Hant flushed, feeling that he had been fooled all along
the line. The whole story was incredible to him, but it
must be true. He had been so sure that Rathlyn had
killed her—he had shut his eyes to any other possibility—
a fatal mistake.

Philip Monner had stopped speaking. His eyes were
dull and lifeless as he slumped back in his chair. He
looked utterly exhausted.

" Is that all you want to say, Monner? " asked the Chief
Constable quietly.

The man shrugged his shoulders, but said no more.

" Very well. Jennings will have to transcribe that into
long-hand and then you will be asked to read it through
and sign it. You will be charged and brought before a
magistrate tomorrow, and there will probably be a remand
in custody. Have you a solicitor? "

Monner shook his head.

" I will find one for you, if you like. Not Mr. Lorriner,
perhaps. Mr. Hant, take Monner along to your room,
will you, please, and get one of your people to stay with
him while the transcribing is being done. Then come
back here yourself."

Hant touched Philip Monner on the arm, and he rose
and accompanied the detective out of the door, not
looking back at the Chief Constable. Colonel Netterly
turned to the clerk.

" Got that all right, Jennings? "

" Yes, sir, I think so."

" Well done! Get it transcribed quick as you can and
take it along to Mr. Monner. Mr. Hant will be back there
by the time you have finished."

Left alone, Colonel Netterly leant back in his chair and passed his hand over his forehead. He was feeling exhausted. It had been a strain, the whole thing—not work he was accustomed to, or trained for. Not a Chief Constable's job. But Superintendent Hant had been on the wrong line; he had felt that instinctively all along, and that had made him hunt his own line . . . and kill his fox. Life in the old dog yet, he thought with a grim smile.

Presently Superintendent Hant came back and stood respectfully before him.

" Well, Mr. Hant? "

" Sir, may I be permitted to congratulate you? I was all wrong and you were right, though how you knew I just can't make out."

Colonel Netterly smiled.

" Well, of course I didn't know. I just felt that there *must* be a reason for the Wey woman storing all those sheets of dates and figures. There had to be. I just plodded my slow way through them until I saw daylight. Monner did the rest."

" But, sir, how did you know he would . . . would talk? You had Jennings here all ready to take it down."

" I thought he might if I could startle him, and I didn't want to check him by having to wait while a shorthand writer was sent for. Not quite orthodox, perhaps; but not, I think, improper. I certainly was not in a position then to charge him, so there was no need to caution him."

Sly old fox, thought Hant—attributing to his Chief yet a third animal simile.

" It was the whisky that really did the trick, sir. How on earth did you know that Monner had given it her in whisky? "

The Chief Constable smiled.

" When I was over at Tandrings on Thursday, Ludd told me something about the meals that Miss Wey and Monner had together; Ludd thought it all a most questionable arrangement, especially as he was having to serve them himself now that they have no footman. He told me that they had wine twice a week, and he happened to mention that Mr. Monner also had a decanter of whisky and a syphon in his cupboard. I thought nothing of it at the time, but this morning, when I was trying to work out whether Monner might have killed Miss Wey, it suddenly occurred to me that that was how it might be done. It was a long shot, I suppose, but it came off."

" It certainly did, sir; it made him talk all right. And yet, when he wanted to talk you tried to stop him. Why was that, sir? "

The Chief Constable shook his head.

" It was my duty to caution him, to give him every opportunity to hold his tongue. But I felt sure he would talk; that sort, once they break down, like to get things off their chests."

Superintendent Hant's new-found respect for his Chief was, if anything, enhanced.

" That was a nasty piece of work, that young woman, sir. Leading him on to make love to her while she was blackmailing him. And what about what Constable Filblow saw? "

" Yes, a strange type. Some sort of suppressed nymphomaniac, I should say."

That was a bit over Hant's head.

" Blackmailing right and left. Her own mother, this chap Monner, Captain Rathlyn."

Colonel Netterly smiled.

" You still think that, Hant? "

" Why . . . why . . . you don't mean to say, sir, that Monner killed Mrs. Rathlyn too? "

The Chief Constable shook his head.

" Oh no, of course not.   I never believed that anyone killed her.   I am quite sure—I always have been—that the death of Mrs. Rathlyn was a pure accident."

CHAPTER XXIV

All Shake Hands

AS SOON as he heard of Philip Monner's arrest the Coroner adjourned his inquest *sine die*, and that allowed the police to concentrate their attention upon their case for presentation to the magisterial bench and subsequent Assizes. A confession is, of course, a great help, but it carries with it a certain danger to the prosecution of over-confidence; a confession may be repudiated, and it has even been known for defence counsel to suggest that senior police officers have fabricated vital parts of a prisoner's statement, even though given by him after due caution and signed by him in the presence of those officers. Whether such a suggestion by counsel helps the defence is another matter, but it is certainly a disagreeable one from the point of view of the officers concerned.

The Barryshire police decided to rely as little as possible upon Monner's signed statement and did their utmost to build a case without it—not at all an easy matter. Fortunately he had, while waiting in Superintendent Hant's office, volunteered to him the name and address of the London chemist from whom—' at a price '—he had obtained the two bottles of Dormonal. Superintendent Hant was able to scare this ignoble member of a fine profession into remembering the details of the sale and the appearance of the purchaser; this invaluable evidence, given on behalf of the Queen, would save the chemist from immediate peril of prosecution himself, but he would have to watch his step very carefully in future if he did not want to see the inside of Wormwood Scrubs.

Ludd, the Tandrings butler, reported that he had indeed missed a whisky tumbler but, as the household was breaking up, had not bothered about it. What had surprised him was that in counting these glasses a week later the tally had been correct. More important, however, was the discovery in the waste pipe of Miss Wey's lavatory basin of traces of the drug Dormonal; this appeared to confirm Monner's own statement that he had dissolved extra tablets in the girl's toothglass, left some dregs and 'poured the rest away'. Another useful discovery in his own room was his bank statement for the last quarter of 1954, as well as previous statements, which showed that whereas he had been paying in regularly up to mid-September 1954, no further payments in were made after that date, and in November and December he had actually drawn from his deposit balance.

In the event it proved that Monner had no intention of repudiating his own statement. He wished, in fact, to plead guilty, but this he was not allowed to do. With great generosity Mr. George Waygold had joined Captain Rathlyn in financing a proper defence for the accused man, and that distinguished silk, Mr. Luton Howe, was briefed to lead. Having read his client's statement and learnt the general structure of the Crown case as outlined at the hearing before the bench of magistrates, Mr. Howe decided that the only hope was a plea of insanity. With great assiduity and fed by an excellent young solicitor, not to mention his own junior, Mr. Howe unearthed and laid before the jury an early history of epileptic fits, which, he declared, might be taken as presumptive evidence of mental instability. Added to this, he put into the witness box a fashionable psychiatrist who discoursed upon the subject of 'split mind' and having, he said, examined the accused 'at least twice', was satisfied that he might well not have appreciated the seriousness of any action he might have taken in the throes of erotic emotion.

Mr. Howe had decided not to put his client into the

witness box, which was a great disappointment to Superintendent Hant, who had counted on prosecuting counsel —prompted thereto by himself—extracting from Monner some statement or some opinion about the two entries in Miss Wey's bank account of two hundred pounds each, which were still nagging at his imagination. Mr. Jolliphant, manager of the Bournemouth bank, had merely said that he had no knowledge of where any of these payments in originated, other than the fact that they were sent to him in cash by Miss Wey herself.

It did not appear that Mr. Howe's plea of insanity, or his principal witness in support thereof, made any deep impression on the judge, but they may have had some effect upon the jury, who, finding Philip Monner guilty after a brief retirement, recommended him to mercy. The judge said that that recommendation would be forwarded to the proper quarter, and sentenced him to death. Monner, who had spoken only three or four necessary words throughout the trial, bowed, gave one quick look round the court, and disappeared from view.

. . . .

Until after the execution—or the possible reprieve— Superintendent Hant proposed to hold his tongue. After that he was going to have one more crack at the Chief Constable, because he could not rest happy while there remained unexplained those two large entries in Isabel Wey's account, and that apparently amorous scene which Detective-Constable Filblow had witnessed through the curtains of the study window. If the Chief Constable chose to ignore them and to instruct the head of his C.I.D. to do so, Hant would have to accept that decision. But he could not let the matter go by default.

Nor was he going to lose sight of Captain Charles Rathlyn. The household of Tandrings was by now dispersed, the house itself in the market; Captain Rathlyn

—Hant knew—had taken a room in a farmhouse half-way between Tandrings and Little Lawton—a significant direction in the detective's suspicious eyes.

Charles had, in fact, done more than this; he had asked Anne Faery to marry him as soon as this unhappy case was all over, and Anne, after some hesitation, had consented. In the meantime, the executors had kindly allowed him to keep two horses, Dashalong and Primrose, in the Tandrings stables, and old Ben Penny had happily consented to look after them. Charles did not feel that it would be decent for him to start hunting again while the Tandrings tragedy was still in the air, but he rode regularly and from time to time was lucky enough to meet a horse— and rider—exercising from the direction of Nooland's Farm.

It was an intense relief to both Charles and Anne when, a fortnight after the trial, the Home Secretary recommended Her Majesty to commute the death sentence on Philip Monner to one of imprisonment for life. Home Secretaries are not called upon to give reasons for the dreadful decisions they have to make; in this case it may have been that the jury's recommendation or the medical evidence weighed with him . . . or could it be that he felt that he who eliminates a blackmailer is deserving of that mercy which the Sovereign alone is empowered to exercise?

Two days after this decision became known Superintendent Hant discovered to his fury that Captain Charles Rathlyn had disappeared. Unwilling to admit that he had been caught napping, he did not at once report the fact to the Chief Constable, but made far-reaching enquiries about the absentee. It took him nearly forty-eight hours to discover the truth, and then he appeared before Colonel Netterly with an expression of grim determination, almost of accusation, on his face.

" Are you aware, sir," he asked, " that Captain Rathlyn has married Miss Faery? "

Colonel Netterly looked at him in mild surprise.

" No, has he? " he asked. " Good for him." Then, reading his subordinate's mind, he broke into a laugh. " Do you still think he killed Miss Wey? "

" No, sir, of course not. I was wrong there. But I think . . . I'm not sure . . . I want an explanation of those two entries in Miss Wey's account."

" You asked him about those, didn't you? "

" Yes, sir, I did. He put me off. And he refused to give me access to his own bank account."

" Which he had a perfect right to do," said the Chief Constable dryly. " Well, Mr. Hant, I take it you want to ask him again. Is that so? "

Hant's bulldog chin stuck out a mile.

" Yes, sir, I do."

Rather to his surprise, the Chief Constable replied quite mildly :

" Very well, Mr. Hant, I don't want to prevent you doing what you believe to be your duty. But if you don't mind, I should like to come with you this time. Where is he now? "

" I understand somewhere in Leicestershire, sir. He and Miss . . . Mrs. Rathlyn are expected back at Nooland's Farm some time next week."

" Think you can wait till then? "

Hant hesitated.

" Yes, sir. I suppose I must. Thank you, sir."

" Good; now about this man Pettigrew . . ."

The Chief Constable slid off into another subject. He was just the least little bit in the world bored with Mr. Hant and his anti-Rathlyn obsession.

In the meantime Charles and Anne Rathlyn were in that seventh heaven that is reserved for lovers from whose

path insuperable obstacles have suddenly melted away.
Neither had been really in love before, each was con-
vinced that the other was the ideal mate. Further than
that, the nebulous plans that they had discussed on that
afternoon when they had met in the woods and realised
their mutual love had now developed into firm intention.
Anne's father, yielding to pressure, had given up his plan
of 'running away' to Ireland and had agreed to join
forces with Charles in a bold bid to set up a 'horse-
coping' business in the cream of England's hunting
country. An old brother officer of his, well established
near Melton Mowbray, had had a bad fall the previous
month and was looking for the right man to go into
partnership with him or to buy him out. Captain Faery
was up at Melton now, going into figures on the basis of
the latter proposition.

That tactful expedition allowed Charles and Anne to
have Nooland's Farm to themselves for a week or ten
days, but they had invited Gerry Fanthony to come down
and spend the week-end with them. Gerry had not seen
a great deal of his friend since Kate Rathlyn's death, and
he had been worried at not being asked to share whatever
trouble Charles might be in; that there was trouble of
some kind the shrewd ex-cavalry man had been quite
certain. But now clouds seemed to have rolled away, and
the invitation from Charles and Anne—whom he had only
met for a short half-hour at a registrar's office—had been
so warm that he had cut an existing engagement in order
to accept this one. The week-end had begun on a
Friday evening, and Gerry had hoped for a real long
gossip after dinner, but for some reason Charles had not
seemed to want to linger over his nightcap whisky, and
'lights out' were blown a good deal earlier than Gerry
was accustomed to.

On Saturday morning, however, the weather was so

wet and blustery that a projected ride was cancelled, and as Anne said she had work to do in the harness-room, the two men settled down in front of the sitting-room fire with their pipes. Gerry at once suggested that his host should ' come clean ', and as this was something that the friends had been accustomed to do with one another all their soldiering life, Charles Rathlyn did not hesitate long before complying. He began by telling of the occasion when he had found Kate sleep-walking, how she had begged him to tell no one else, so that when she fell to her death from the landing outside her bedroom the police had been sceptical as to whether she had really been walking in her sleep.

" Not even her doctor knew, old boy, so it was all a bit awkward for me, especially as she had left me a thumping fat legacy. They practically suggested that I had pushed her over."

" Good God! "

The shocked surprise on his friend's face made Charles Rathlyn smile.

" They have to earn their money, you know—must look at the worst side of everything before accepting the simple truth. The Chief Constable was all right—a very decent chap; a Gunner—but there was a Detective-Superintendent who had it in for me good and hearty. Not only about Kate; he even practically accused me of murdering . . . ."

Charles stopped abruptly. There was the sound of a car outside and presently a ring at the bell.

" Better answer it. Don't think there's anyone else in."

Glancing through the window on his way to the door he checked abruptly, then, turning to Gerry, said quietly:

" Stay with me, will you, Gerry? Don't try and do a tactful fade-out."

Gerry Fanthony saw that his friend's face had set into the old, hard, expressionless mask that he knew so well—that he had seen a hundred times when there was ' a spot of bother ' to be circumvented. Never, even with a shattered leg on the quay at Dunkirk, had he known Charles fail to circumvent it. A moment later his host returned, accompanied by a thin, pleasant-looking man wearing a tweed suit and another, younger, stockier and much less agreeable of expression, wearing a dark blue suit and a macintosh.

" Gerry, this is Colonel Netterly, our Chief Constable, and this is Detective-Superintendent Hant. This is Gerald Fanthony, Colonel—an old brother officer of mine. May I offer you a drink? "

Colonel Netterly shook hands with Fanthony and Superintendent Hant rather reluctantly did the same.

" Thank you very much, Rathlyn, but I've really come over to see you on a private matter—or rather, an official matter."

He glanced at Captain Fanthony, but Charles Rathlyn smiled.

" I hoped you had come to congratulate me on my marriage," he said.

" Oh, I do indeed, with all my heart," said the Chief Constable, looking rather uncomfortable.

" Thank you very much. You can talk freely in front of Fanthony. As I say, we were boys together and know all each other's sins."

" I really think it would be better . . . we shall not keep you very long."

But Charles shook his head.

" Better play a foursome," he said. " I never liked a three-ball match, and I shouldn't have a chance against your and Mr. Hant's best ball."

Colonel Netterly shrugged his shoulders.

" As you like," he said. " Mr. Hant wants to ask you a question or two. I am only a spectator."

Again Charles Rathlyn smiled.

" A single, then—though I'm no golfer. Fire ahead, Superintendent."

Hant had had some difficulty in following all this back-chat about balls and golf; it appeared to be some sort of joke, and he was in no mood for that.

" I want to ask you again, sir, whether you can account for the two entries of two hundred pounds in Miss Wey's bank account? "

Charles looked at him steadily.

" Still thinking it was I who killed her? " he asked.

Out of the corner of his eye he saw Gerry's shocked expression. Poor old boy, it was a bit rough on him, being dragged into this, but Charles wanted a friend by him now.

" No, sir, but I think you can account for those entries," said Hant doggedly.

" What makes you think that? "

" Will you answer my question, please, sir? "

Charles shook his head.

" I have already told you that I know nothing about Miss Wey's bank account. How could I? "

" I suggest that you knew a great deal about Miss Wey, sir—that you were on intimate terms with her."

Charles saw that Gerry Fanthony's lean, strong hands were clenched in two very tight fists.

" Steady, old man," he said. " You and the Colonel are keeping the ring. This is a shock to you, but I was beginning to tell you about it when these gentlemen appeared. Now, Superintendent, tell me just exactly what you mean by that."

Superintendent Hant's temper was not standing up too well under this cool treatment. He was going, now, to use the trump card that he had previously withheld—and in his view it was a smasher.

" If you were not on intimate terms with her, how does it come that one of my men saw you holding her in your arms in your study at eleven o'clock one night a week or two before she died? "

The card—the blow, a better metaphor—had got home. There was no doubt of that. All three men saw Charles Rathlyn draw himself together as if he had been struck, saw the colour drain from his face. He stood, white and silent, staring straight in front of him. He stood so for a minute, two minutes—it seemed an age. Then suddenly he relaxed and answered in a quiet, firm voice.

" As you know that," he said, " I had better tell you everything." He turned to Gerald Fanthony. " Old boy, will you scout outside and keep Anne occupied for five or ten minutes? I don't think it need be longer . . . but of course I don't know."

He glanced at the Chief Constable, and when the door had closed he said :

" As a matter of fact, what I am going to tell you now I have already told my wife, but it would be awkward for her to come in while I tell it to you. You know now that I am married to Miss Faery and you, Colonel, have a pretty shrewd idea when I began to fall in love with her. It was only a beginning, and except for one incident— which you both know about—we saw nothing of each other except in the hunting-field, in public, and we said no word to each other of affection of any kind, until some time after my wife's death. I had not the least idea that Miss Faery cared for me at all. But I did know that I cared for her, even that I was beginning to fall in love with her. I tell you that quite frankly."

Colonel Netterly was watching closely, and he felt

convinced, as he had felt when Anne Faery had talked to him, that he was hearing the truth.

"But my wife suddenly became jealous, suddenly suspected—or made out that she suspected—some sort of intrigue between us. What flared it up, Colonel, was one day last February—I forget whether you were out—when my wife suddenly decided to hunt after not being out at all that season. It was a poor day and her back hurt her and she wanted to go home, but my horse was mad fresh, and when hounds found—at the very moment she said that—I couldn't hold him and I saw the hunt out. She thought I had done it deliberately, and when I got home she rated me at the top of her voice, accusing me of staying out with Anne—Miss Faery. Isabel Wey heard her, and next day, or whenever it was, when my wife gave her a letter addressed to Miss Faery to post, she didn't post it. She kept it, and you have got it now, Colonel—or you, Mr. Hant."

Superintendent Hant nodded, instinctively patting his breast pocket.

"She kept it to blackmail me with, though at that time she didn't know what a weapon it was going to be. She just thought that she could play me up with it, I suppose. She was a born blackmailer, as appears from what she did to poor Monner."

Again Hant nodded, knowing even more about that than Captain Rathlyn did.

"Then came my wife's death—that fall when she was sleep-walking. You were not satisfied that she *was* sleep-walking, Mr. Hant; you thought that in some way I killed her. I don't know what you thought, Colonel?"

That was an embarrassing question. Netterly had never believed any such thing, but he could not appear to let his Superintendent down. He brushed it aside with a gesture.

" That was where Miss Wey saw her chance.   She knew that motive might prove a crucial point; the general idea, I believe, was that I killed my wife to get eighty thousand pounds—regardless of the fact that I lost not only my wife but my very comfortable home and a standard of living far higher than I shall ever know again. But here, thought Isabel Wey, is where I come in. I produce evidence of the real motive—or rather I threaten to. Rather than let that happen, this sap Rathlyn will stump up."

Once again Superintendent Hant saw that beads of sweat had formed on Rathlyn's forehead.   What was he going to say next?

" That was just what that sap Rathlyn did. If it had been just the danger of being run in for murder, I think I should have faced it without hesitation, but it was the horrible threat of dragging Anne Faery into the case, as a motive for murder, that cracked me.   I gave in, or at any rate I gave in to a limited extent.   She wanted money; I told her that I would give her five hundred pounds, two hundred the following month—November, two hundred in February, and the final hundred when the household broke up in March and when she would hand me that letter of my wife's.   I made it quite clear that that was my limit, that if she tried to raise me I should call her to show her hand—and that I should charge her with blackmailing me.   That price—five hundred—I was prepared to pay to keep Anne out of it, but I was not prepared to face a lifetime of blackmail."

Against his will Superintendent Hant was gradually coming to believe Rathlyn's story.   Its devastating frankness was undoubtedly convincing.

" She accepted that," said Charles Rathlyn, " with one astonishing variation.   She wanted me to be what she called ' a little nice to her '.   I suppose she was a bit starved in that way, but anyway that was what she wanted. I don't mind telling you that it stuck in my gizzard much more than the five hundred pounds; you will understand that, bearing in mind what my feelings for Miss Faery were at the time. I was so astounded that I actually put my arms round her when she said it; partly to give myself time to think, partly, I suppose, because she had put her arms round my neck and my action was almost automatic."

He turned towards Hant.

" I don't know whether that was what your man saw, Superintendent, or some other occasion like it. That, of course, was back in October, but it happened more than once."

Hant was on the point of saying : 'No, January', when he realised that he was being led. He merely shook his head.

" Oh well," said Charles, " that was part of the price, and I hated paying it, but it was for Anne's sake. The worst part was telling her about it, but I did tell her— before asking her to marry me. I have told her the whole thing and, bless her, she took it in her stride. It's an odd thing, you know, Colonel, but girls seem to take that sort of fence better than men do."

There was silence in the cosy sitting-room when Charles Rathlyn finished speaking. Colonel Netterly looked at his subordinate, but Superintendent Hant avoided his eye. The Chief Constable rose to his feet and walking across to Charles Rathlyn held out his hand.

" Thank you for being so frank," he said. " It can't have been easy for you."

Charles Rathlyn's face cleared.

" Thank you for believing me," he said. Then, turning to Superintendent Hant, who had also risen, he held out his hand to him.

" You too, I hope, Mr. Hant."

The detective looked him steadily in the eye, then slowly raised his hand and took Charles's. He did not speak.

"We'll be off now," said Colonel Netterly cheerfully. "Taken up too much of your time already. Please give my regards to Mrs. Rathlyn; I hope we may all meet again in the hunting-field next season."

Charles Rathlyn saw them to their car, and when they had disappeared down the road, returned to the sitting-room. He stumbled slightly as he crossed the threshold, but reached his chair and sank back in it, his face white and drawn.

.   .   .   .   .

That evening there was a celebration dinner at Nooland's Farm, small but select—Charles Rathlyn, his wife, and Gerry Fanthony, his friend. Captain Faery, before going up to Melton, had given them the run of the cellar, small as it was.

"If we're going to move, we'll move soon," he said. "Better drink that stuff up."

So two bottles of Bollinger '45 went the right way that evening and none of the three was the worse for it. Gerry Fanthony, indeed—notoriously light of head—was distinctly 'the better'. When in that condition his discretion—and indeed his tact—had always been noticeable for its absence. Raising his glass—the seventh or eighth —he toasted Anne and told Charles Rathlyn what a lucky man he was.

"You know, old man," he said, "if you had given poor Kate a push it would have been well worth it!"

"Oh Gerry," exclaimed Anne, "how can you be so horrible!"

Charles Rathlyn said nothing, but, looking at his charming young wife, he assured himself that it had indeed been well worth it.

THE END

If you enjoyed this book you'll want to know about THE PERENNIAL LIBRARY MYSTERY SERIES

Nicholas Blake

☐	P 456	THE BEAST MUST DIE	$1.95
☐	P 427	THE CORPSE IN THE SNOWMAN	$1.95
☐	P 493	THE DREADFUL HOLLOW	$1.95
☐	P 397	END OF CHAPTER	$1.95
☐	P 398	HEAD OF A TRAVELER	$2.25
☐	P 419	MINUTE FOR MURDER	$1.95
☐	P 520	THE MORNING AFTER DEATH	$1.95
☐	P 521	A PENKNIFE IN MY HEART	$2.25
☐	P 531	THE PRIVATE WOUND	$2.25
☐	P 494	A QUESTION OF PROOF	$1.95
☐	P 495	THE SAD VARIETY	$2.25
☐	P 428	THOU SHELL OF DEATH	$1.95
☐	P 418	THE WHISPER IN THE GLOOM	$1.95
☐	P 399	THE WIDOW'S CRUISE	$1.95
☐	P 400	THE WORM OF DEATH	$2.25

E. C. Bentley

☐	P 440	TRENT'S LAST CASE	$2.50
☐	P 516	TRENT'S OWN CASE	$2.25

Buy them at your local bookstore or use this coupon for ordering:

HARPER & ROW, Mail Order Dept. #PMS, 10 East 53rd St., New York, N.Y. 10022.

Please send me the books I have checked above. I am enclosing $ _____ which includes a postage and handling charge of $1.00 for the first book and 25¢ for each additional book. Send check or money order. No cash or C.O.D.'s please.

Name _____

Address _____

City _____ State _____ Zip _____

Please allow 4 weeks for delivery. USA and Canada only. This offer expires 5/1/82. Please add applicable sales tax.

Gavin Black

☐ P 473 A DRAGON FOR CHRISTMAS $1.95
☐ P 485 THE EYES AROUND ME $1.95
☐ P 472 YOU WANT TO DIE, JOHNNY? $1.95

George Harmon Coxe

☐ P 527 MURDER WITH PICTURES $2.25

Edmund Crispin

☐ P 506 BURIED FOR PLEASURE $1.95

Kenneth Fearing

☐ P 500 THE BIG CLOCK $1.95

Andrew Garve

☐ P 430 THE ASHES OF LODA $1.50
☐ P 451 THE CUCKOO LINE AFFAIR $1.95
☐ P 429 A HERO FOR LEANDA $1.50
☐ P 449 MURDER THROUGH THE LOOKING
　　　　　GLASS $1.95
☐ P 441 NO TEARS FOR HILDA $1.95
☐ P 450 THE RIDDLE OF SAMSON $1.95

Buy them at your local bookstore or use this coupon for ordering:

HARPER & ROW, Mail Order Dept. #PMS, 10 East 53rd St., New York, N.Y. 10022.

Please send me the books I have checked above. I am enclosing $ _____ which includes a postage and handling charge of $1.00 for the first book and 25¢ for each additional book. Send check or money order. No cash or C.O.D.'s please.

Name _____

Address _____

City _____ State _____ Zip _____

Please allow 4 weeks for delivery. USA and Canada only. This offer expires 5/1/82. Please add applicable sales tax.

Michael Gilbert

☐	P 446	BLOOD AND JUDGMENT	$1.95
☐	P 459	THE BODY OF A GIRL	$1.95
☐	P 448	THE DANGER WITHIN	$1.95
☐	P 447	DEATH HAS DEEP ROOTS	$1.95
☐	P 458	FEAR TO TREAD	$1.95

C. W. Grafton

☐	P 519	BEYOND A REASONABLE DOUBT	$1.95

Edward Grierson

☐	P 528	THE SECOND MAN	$2.25

Cyril Hare

☐	P 455	AN ENGLISH MURDER	$1.95
☐	P 522	TRAGEDY AT LAW	$2.25
☐	P 514	UNTIMELY DEATH	$2.25
☐	P 523	WITH A BARE BODKIN	$2.25

Robert Harling

☐	P 545	THE ENORMOUS SHADOW *(available 8/81)*	$2.25

Buy them at your local bookstore or use this coupon for ordering:

HARPER & ROW, Mail Order Dept. #PMS, 10 East 53rd St., New York, N.Y. 10022.
Please send me the books I have checked above. I am enclosing $ _____ which includes a postage and handling charge of $1.00 for the first book and 25¢ for each additional book. Send check or money order. No cash or C.O.D.'s please.

Name _____

Address _____

City _____ State _____ Zip _____
Please allow 4 weeks for delivery. USA and Canada only. This offer expires 5/1/82. Please add applicable sales tax.

Matthew Head

| ☐ | P 541 | THE CABINDA AFFAIR | $2.25 |
| ☐ | P 542 | MURDER AT THE FLEA CLUB | $2.25 |

M. V. Heberden

| ☐ | P 533 | ENGAGED TO MURDER | $2.25 |

James Hilton

| ☐ | P 501 | WAS IT MURDER? | $1.95 |

Elspeth Huxley

| ☐ | P 540 | THE AFRICAN POISON MURDERS | $2.25 |

Frances Iles

| ☐ | P 517 | BEFORE THE FACT | $1.95 |
| ☐ | P 532 | MALICE AFORETHOUGHT | $1.95 |

Lange Lewis

| ☐ | P 518 | THE BIRTHDAY MURDER | $1.95 |

Arthur Maling

☐	P 482	LUCKY DEVIL	$1.95
☐	P 483	RIPOFF	$1.95
☐	P 484	SCHROEDER'S GAME	$1.95

Buy them at your local bookstore or use this coupon for ordering:

HARPER & ROW, Mail Order Dept. #PMS, 10 East 53rd St., New York, N.Y. 10022.

Please send me the books I have checked above. I am enclosing $ _____ which includes a postage and handling charge of $1.00 for the first book and 25¢ for each additional book. Send check or money order. No cash or C.O.D.'s please.

Name _____

Address _____

City _____ State _____ Zip _____

Please allow 4 weeks for delivery. USA and Canada only. This offer expires 5/1/82. Please add applicable sales tax.

Austin Ripley

☐ P 387   MINUTE MYSTERIES $1.95

Thomas Sterling

☐ P 529   THE EVIL OF THE DAY $2.25

Julian Symons

☐ P 468   THE BELTING INHERITANCE $1.95
☐ P 469   BLAND BEGINNING $1.95
☐ P 481   BOGUE'S FORTUNE $1.95
☐ P 480   THE BROKEN PENNY $1.95
☐ P 461   THE COLOR OF MURDER $1.95
☐ P 460   THE 31ST OF FEBRUARY $1.95

Dorothy Stockbridge Tillet
(John Stephen Strange)

☐ P 536   THE MAN WHO KILLED FORTESCUE $2.25

Henry Wade

☐ P 543   A DYING FALL $2.25
☐ P 548   THE HANGING CAPTAIN *(available 8/81)* $2.25

Buy them at your local bookstore or use this coupon for ordering:

HARPER & ROW, Mail Order Dept. #PMS, 10 East 53rd St., New York, N.Y. 10022.
Please send me the books I have checked above. I am enclosing $ _____ which includes a postage and handling charge of $1.00 for the first book and 25¢ for each additional book. Send check or money order. No cash or C.O.D.'s please.

Name _____

Address _____

City _____ State _____ Zip _____

Please allow 4 weeks for delivery. USA and Canada only. This offer expires 5/1/82. Please add applicable sales tax.

Buy them at your local bookstore or use this coupon for ordering:

HARPER & ROW, Mail Order Dept. #PMS, 10 East 53rd St., New York, N.Y. 10022.
Please send me the books I have checked above. I am enclosing $ _____ which includes a postage and handling charge of $1.00 for the first book and 25¢ for each additional book. Send check or money order. No cash or C.O.D.'s please.

Name _____

Address _____

City _____ State _____ Zip _____
Please allow 4 weeks for delivery. USA and Canada only. This offer expires 5/1/82 . Please add applicable sales tax.